The Origin Point's Renaissance

Michelle Rivera

This one, once again, goes out to the OGs on Wattpad.
To my most beloved friends who have supported my writing, even when it hasn't been their forte.
To the people who have heard me say I've written books, and responded "oh, that's so cool;" even the ones who don't read.
And to the weird kids out there, the ones who search for their found family within fictional media, and especially for the ones who may become enthralled with characters of mine; pleased to meet you all, and I can only hope I do right by you all.
Remember that there is always more ahead.

Copyright © 2023 by Michelle Rivera

All rights reserved.

No part of this publication may be reproduced, distributed, or transmitted in any form or by any means, including photocopying, recording, or other electronic or mechanical methods, without the prior written permission of the publisher, except as permitted by U.S. copyright law. For permission requests, contact the author at iridescentlyraynu@ou tlook.com.

The story, all names, characters, and incidents portrayed in this production are fictitious. No identification with actual persons (living or deceased), places, buildings, and products is intended or should be inferred.

Book Cover and Illustrations by Michelle Rivera.

Contents

Prologue

Progress. Development. Innovation.

If one were to ask a resident of Compositora to describe the transition of their small city, it would be impossible to listen to the explanation without coming across at least one of those three words. However, none of them were unwarranted. Compositora had gone through a fair deal of all of those, through the dedication and hard work– and, of course, magic– of its people. The age of industry had made it to the city, and bringing it into its new, more modern era took a lot of time and effort.

Almost immediately after it was safe to do so, most of the city's residents had risen with the sun to begin the complete overhaul of the town, in a multitude of different ways depending on the manner in which they intended to improve their home. The first city-wide improvement that was to be done was restoring the old streets of the city; there had been a time, long ago now, that there had been proper streets and sidewalks, paved in brick and stone. Proper neighborhoods and districts, marked by the distinct layouts of the buildings within them. If Compositora were to become the city of legend that it once was, it would need those streets back; and so, the streets were paved first, giving everyone a general idea as to where everything would go.

The large-scale building projects, such as those dedicated to homes, storefronts, schools, and the like were next. The people responsible for building these large buildings were also the first to spring into action, laying foundations and paths for others to follow and build upon.

After that came the agricultural revitalization project, dedicated to breathing new life into the area's native plants and animals; and striving to make it a beautiful place again, in the process. This was a collaborative effort with other cities and towns in this part of the world, one which was happily agreed upon. To restore a city–especially one with so much historical significance– was to restore the true beauty of the desert lands, which was a goal no one in the area could say no to.

There was a lot of debate around what to do with the city's former palace; the first idea contributed was to demolish it, which made sense given how much it had fallen into disrepair. With the newly cleared land, there would be room for another large project. Perhaps some kind of farm? However, this did not come to pass mainly because, with the scarcity of rain within the city limits, a farm didn't seem viable. This caused some assessment to be done on the palace, which led to the ruling that restoring the building wouldn't be terribly difficult. This led to discussion regarding what to do with the building once it was restored. With this, it was almost unanimously decided that it was past time for Compositora to have its first place of advanced scholarship in decades; and so, the palace was transformed into a university.

Having a university brought about even more opportunities for growth. Dormitories for the students to live in. Inns and hotels, if their families came to visit them. Restaurants, so that all of these people could eat and relax. This would likely be the biggest pull for people from other areas to relocate here; if not to study, to work, or to marvel at the repurposed palace. After all, it was historically significant, even if said history wasn't good.

The laying of train tracks meant that Compositora was connected to its nearby towns for the first time in decades. With this came that boom in both population and industry; whether it be for a change in scenery or for its cultural significance, people began to flock to the town.

But this did not mean that everything was perfect. The world was changing in more ways than the industrial improvements of Compositora. As the days passed, it became more and more obvious.

No one knew when it had started, but there had been a point where strange, spherical objects began to float in the air, and then disappear at random. That unusual objects began to appear in places they shouldn't be. That the earth itself would sometimes be torn into by defiances of the natural order of things. The first few times this happened, it was so rare and fleeting that it wasn't thought to be an issue. But as the frequency and length of these occurrences increased, so too did the people's worry, and so, research began. It was determined shortly after that these strange occurrences were fissures– but through what, and caused by what, remained a mystery. So far, though, they didn't seem to be directly harmful to the populace apart from invoking fatigue and vague unwellness from people that happened to be around them. Within hours, the local Resistance had notified the entire city to be wary of the fissures, and these instances had drastically declined since then. Everyone was thankful for the Resistance's continued efforts to keep everyone safe and continue developing the town.

Well, perhaps "everyone" would be a tad generous.

Although most of Compositora's citizens would sing the praises of the Resistance if asked, there were those few that did not share the belief that they were a benevolent organization. And, lately, those types were beginning to become more plentiful– or, at least, more loud about their contrary nature. No longer did they keep to the shadows of the town; they were becoming more comfortable with voicing their dissent in public spaces.

"Well, well. It certainly shows that the Resistance thinks of themselves as some kind of provisional government, especially recently." The group's leader spoke, his black robe with ornate patterns concealing most of his body aside from a few pieces of long, wavy white hair poking out from the hood. He paced along the scaffolding he stood upon, overlooking a crowd of about twenty people, all dressed in similar attire. "But we must keep in mind that no one asked them to do this. In such a short time after we've overthrown our last dictator, why should we be in favor of another group taking this city and bending it to their will?"

"We're not!" a voice called from the crowd, with several voices joining in, in agreement.

"We are not!" the leader agreed, pointing in the general direction of where the first voice had come from. "You are correct! And that's why it's high time we started doing something about it. We have to retain our autonomy, and that means opposing anyone who would impose their own agenda on us– even if it means going against the very organization that liberated us. Are you all with me?!"

Shouts of assent echoed from the crowd below.

"Then let us prepare to fight. For liberation, once more!"

Large-Scale Operations

In February, the climate in Compositora was cooler than in the summer and autumn seasons; it wasn't uncommon to need a light jacket when going about one's daily errands. Today was a sunny day, like many others before it, and there appeared to be no problems as the Resistance gathered within their headquarters. It wasn't used very often anymore; ever since real houses had begun to be built in the town, most of the remaining personnel decided they'd rather live above ground, in places that had windows, and where a nice summer's breeze could be felt when the season was appropriate. This was also, undoubtedly, why the Resistance's numbers were the lowest they had been since its inception. Still, the last few members made sure to keep everything as neat and organized as possible inside headquarters– which was useful whenever it was time to hold a meeting, like today.

"Are we ready to commence our meeting?"

At the edge of the table stood the Resistance's head strategist, Hunter; his bright red hair brushed back into a sleek statement of style, as he waited for everyone's word on whether or not it was okay to begin the presentation. His pale hands held a stack of pristine white index cards, each containing a summary of the topics he'd prepared for today's discussion. It was the first meeting to be held in a few months— these meetings had been delayed for various reasons, but today seemed to be the day that everyone's schedules had lined up.

Sitting at the seat to the right of him, the Resistance's captain Thunder surveyed the area, his long dark brown locs looking a lot more gray these days, even if his umber skin hadn't yet begun to show too many signs of aging. The man had been under a lot of stress as the leader of the Resistance, especially where land distribution came into play, but not so much that he'd lost (too much) sleep. He could only hope things would continue this way.

Also at the table, there was Phoenix, the Resistance's head of communications and the second-most senior member now— colloquially the vice-captain, although this had not been officially stated– seated across from Thunder, as she frequently did; her dark, curly hair pulled up into a high ponytail, dressed for comfort as always, in a bright yellow long-sleeved sundress. When Thunder thought about it, the young woman hadn't often left his side in the almost ten years that she'd been a part of the Resistance. He'd have been more surprised if she *wasn't* present.

If it were any other day, he'd have been equally surprised that her younger brother wasn't currently in the room– but today, that was expected. He was busier than usual these days.

"Oh, that's right. Logan isn't here yet," Hunter noticed then. "Were we including him as a part of this meeting?"

"We are." Thunder nodded. "He has a few prior obligations, which I'm sure you're both aware of. But he should be arriving soon, so don't worry about him."

The final person at the table was a young man named Handel, one of the Resistance's engineers and one of the few people that still lived at headquarters. Months ago, when the organization was facing off against a relentless bunch of magical zombies called holzomen, the usually quiet man had shown that he could be a leader, and so, he was voted to be the head of the household by everyone still living at HQ. He was not always present for meetings, but one of today's notes on the itinerary had to do with the headquarters building, so it made sense for him to be there. He was clearly nervous about it, as one of his hands continued to grab a different curl to spin around his fingers.

"We're waiting, then?" he asked. "For Logan, I mean."

Hunter's response was to look at the index cards he held. "Let's see. We have... hm, one, two... it appears that almost all of our bulletins are ones that we cannot discuss without him, so it's probably in our best interest to wait. Please help yourself to some water if you're nervous, Handel."

"Right." He nodded, grabbing one of the empty cups. "I'll do that."

***

The missing member of the Resistance's meeting was the organization's combat trainer, Logan; the youngest on the panel, he often was the person to bring in new, innovative ideas, and did so with the peppy personality of a golden retriever. In addition to his knowledge of combat, he was also incredibly book-smart, and was able to approach things in a scholarly way that the other members often wouldn't– or couldn't– consider.

The sun was beginning its descent as he started his walk to headquarters, the wind gently blowing in his newly cut hair, brushed to the side and flipped at the ends. With becoming one of the first attendees of Compositora's university came a strong urge to revitalize his appearance into that of a more professional man, which was why he'd traded his parachute pants for more fitted slacks, and had greatly improved his collection of shirts and vests. No one in the Resistance could tell if he'd arrived at this desire himself, or if he'd been mortified walking into his first class and being the only person in sandals and with his shirt open, but the new haircut and wardrobe did suit him very well, and he seemed to like it. There was no room for complaints, really.

When Logan had first begun this academic journey, the walks home gave him an indescribable feeling; having to leave the building where the former dictator once resided, and weaving through the crowds to pass unfamiliar buildings... all of the developments in

Compositora were exciting, but there was also that foreign feeling. He felt like a stranger here in some ways, much like he had felt when he'd first moved here from the City of Garnet, which had been such an alienating experience that he'd second-guessed his living situation almost every day. He thought to himself, more than once, that perhaps this was yet another way that he could relate to his current companion.

At the end of the onslaught of holzomen, Thunder had reached out to one of his old friends: Herman Navarrete, an influential man in the city of Trelana, the nearest city to Compositora. He'd asked for his guidance in making Compositora a thriving city again, one like it had been around the time when it was first established. The two men hadn't spoken in years, but that had apparently meant little to Herman. He'd happily agreed to help as much as he humanly could under one condition: that Thunder house– and take under his wing– his son, who was set to attend Compositora's new university.

Herman, as far as Thunder remembered, had been a huge man, in both height and weight; he'd often been described as a grizzly bear (with the personality of a teddy bear). He'd had to have a specially tailored formal suit. He often had to duck under doorways. Basically, Thunder had been expecting someone like this to show up at the train station. There were no words to describe his confusion at seeing the young man that had actually arrived. The only thing he had in common with his father was his brown hair; he was short, thin, and had a pair of blue eyes that were as captivating as the night sky. He was also much more fair than Herman was, so it took a few minutes of convincing to be sure this was the person Thunder had been expecting. But after a few minutes of conversation, as well as reading the letter of introduction he'd been given, there was no doubt: this was Arrigan, Herman's only child, and so, he was brought to Thunder's house to live while he attended the university.

It wasn't that Arrigan didn't fit in with the Resistance, but it became evident within the first few hours of him living with them that he would benefit from being around his contemporaries, and so, Thunder all but assigned him to Logan since they'd be attending university together. And– minor disagreements notwithstanding– it had worked. The boys were getting along so well that they were already almost like brothers. Logan may have lost most of his hair, but he'd gained a shadow; and at this point, he wouldn't have it any other way.

"Oh, can we stop here?" Arrigan asked, timidly pointing to a food stand. The chef seemed to be pan-frying something in a skillet, and Logan had to admit that the aroma was enticing him, enveloping him in a comfortable blanket of hunger. But he remembered then that the Resistance meeting would be starting soon...

"I don't know if we'll have time," was his reply.

Arrigan nodded, and it was easy to pick up on his sullen mood from being turned down. "Right. I forgot about our prior commitments."

"But..." Logan said, sighing softly. "The line isn't long, so it shouldn't add too much time onto our commute. Let's hurry over there before more people decide they want whatever's in that skillet."

The two hustled over, and once they were in line, Logan then asked, "What *is* in that skillet, by the way? You stopped with such purpose that it implies you may have recognized what the chef is cooking."

The two watched as one of the chefs cut round shapes into the dough they'd rolled out onto the table, and then scooped a mixture of meat and potatoes into the center before pinching them closed. From here, they were placed into a pot of boiling water, before being finished in the skillet they'd both seen when they approached the stall. "Oh. Yeah, I do," replied Arrigan. "My mother makes these at home, so I hope you don't mind a little bit of homesickness being my motivation for stopping us."

"Far be it for me to do that." Logan gave him a reassuring smile. "It would make me a hypocrite of the highest caliber. When I first moved here and got homesick, I was at least fortunate to have my older sister around. The situation is much different for you."

After all, Arrigan was an only child. One could argue that this was part of why his social skills were as stunted as they were. Logan had the advantage of growing up with his sister; the two often arguing, but also having each others' backs when needed.

"Witamy! What can I get you boys?" The girl running the order stand said as Logan and Arrigan reached the front of the line. She seemed to be around the same age as the both of them, her dark blonde hair pulled into twintails.

"Oh, um, dzień dobry," Arrigan replied with the most timid of hand waves.

As Arrigan and the clerk spoke to each other in a language that Logan couldn't understand, his eyes began to wander. Compositora looked a lot different these days, but not in a way that caused him to feel any negative emotion about it. In fact, he quite liked the diversity in cultures settling into the city. He'd read that this was what the city had been like many years ago, before its decline. It felt wonderful to be this close to what such an important city had historically been. His inner history nerd was delighted in the way things were changing.

Logan's eyes, then, caught that strange occurrence again: the cluster of small glowing orbs with rings around them, slightly warping the view of the area around them just enough that it felt uncomfortable to look at. Just as he felt Arrigan nudge his arm, though– enough to make him look away for just a second– the strange occurrence had disappeared.

"Everything okay?" Arrigan asked, handing a small plate of the pan-fried dumplings to Logan.

"What? Uh... yeah, yeah, sorry about that. And thanks," Logan replied, taking a bite from one of the dumplings. "I saw one of those weird fissures again. Every time I see them, it feels so unnerving, you know? It's as if my very soul is being unraveled."

"I don't disagree," Arrigan said in reply. "The first time I saw one of those was the day before I was set to leave Trelana. I remember it affecting my mom so badly that she had to lie in bed for the rest of the day. I have no idea what's causing those to happen, but I really hope someone finds out soon– and that the solution is easily doable."

"Yeah." Logan nodded, eating another dumpling. "These are really good, by the way. I can see why you wanted us to stop."

Arrigan smiled. "Yeah. Yeah, they are, aren't they?"

Logan nodded again. "Now come on, we should be hurrying back home so everybody doesn't start worrying about us."

***

A few minutes later, Logan arrived at headquarters, with Arrigan trailing not far behind him. As if it were clockwork, the two took their seats at the table, ready to start the meeting.

"You two finally decided to show up," Thunder teased lightly. "Go on, have a seat and we can get started."

"Sorry about the delay, everyone," Logan apologized as he sat. "While we were on our way here, I caught a whiff of some of the most delicious-smelling food I've ever experienced in my life! And the two of us were on the same wavelength, because Arrigan was the one that stopped us so we could buy some, uh..."

"Pierogi," Arrigan finished helpfully. "I bought a whole box of them so that we could have them for dinner later; I put it in the fridge, since I didn't know how long this meeting would run."

Hunter smiled at this, because it meant he no longer was on cooking duty. "That is much appreciated, Arrigan, and Logan as well. I hope you both had a fortuitous day of class."

"I can tell you all about it later," Logan replied.

"Delightful." With a tap of the cards onto the table to straighten them, Hunter was now ready to commence the meeting. "Now that everyone has arrived, we may now officially begin."

"We have four issues to discuss today," Hunter started. "I ordered them based on the order they came in and not urgency, so make sure you'll be able to be completely alert for the duration of this meeting, to give each missive the appropriate level of care. Now, let us begin with our first order of business: maintenance on the fountain in the square. Phoenix, I do recall that you were the person looking into this?"

"You recall correctly." She nodded, opening her own notebook. "The fountain, as we all–" she paused– "*most of* us know, has been inactive for quite some time. Admittedly, most of the work here has been done by the Compositora Regeneration Effort. They've even gone to the effort of surveying the townspeople, and the only real concern is that we're absolutely sure restoring the fountain won't lead to another flood, like... you know."

The aforementioned flood, which had transpired eight months ago, had caused casualties for both the Resistance and the town's civilians; it had been a horrid day. No one present liked to think of it, least of all Thunder, who still felt some form of responsibility for the lives lost.

"As it happens, we've got a damn good engineer that helped us stop that disaster right here." Thunder turned to Handel. "Do you think you can look into the fountain's old pipes and drainage and such, get it goin' again?"

Handel was clearly surprised. "I-I can at least look at it, yes. I'm sure it'll be a lot easier now that it's not actively causing mayhem. Whether or not I'll be able to fix it, though..."

"Suppose we'll cross that bridge when we get to it," Thunder replied, the silence having spoken for itself. "Well, then. What's up next, Hunter?"

"Our second missive is more of a report than anything else, stating that reforestation is going well; almost all of the sick trees in the woods to the east have recovered. As is easy to tell, much of our grass has grown back in a lovely yellow-green hue, as to be expected in our section of the desert, and I've received word that a few scholars from the City of Garnet will soon be embarking here to reintroduce some native flora to the city. The only question regarding this is: will we be doing anything to assist the regrowth of our plant life? Does anyone have any input on this matter?"

Logan was the first to have thoughts on the matter, as usual. "Is there anything we *can* do? I dunno, it kinda sounds like everything is being taken care of."

"It does, doesn't it?" agreed Hunter. "Still, it is something that we should continue to keep an eye on. If we are to be committed to the betterment of this city, part of that will inevitably be intertwined with its appearance."

"I hear you, Hunter. I think the best thing we can do is to let those scholars know when they get here that we're willing to help them in any way that we can," Phoenix said then. "Being that that's an external communication, I'll handle that. Besides, if they're coming from the City of Garnet, there's always that possibility that I may already know them."

Hunter nodded, pulling out a pen so he could update his notes. "Excellent. Then we can proceed to our third missive: regarding the issue that, at current, plagues us most frequently and strongly."

"Ah, yeah. Our anti-fanclub," Thunder replied, with a bit of a sigh. "I just don't get it, y'all. What is it that we've done to warrant such a strong reaction? And what about it makes it so these kids can't just come and talk to us about it? I'm pretty sure we could work through whatever their problems are if they'd just talk to us, but no, they've gotta go gettin' everybody else riled up in the square and destroying things."

"This is the missive that confuses me the most, agreed," Hunter replied. "At least things have been quiet for the past couple of days."

"Yeah, it was pretty normal in the square on our way home," added Logan. "I don't want to jinx it–"

"Then don't," everyone else in the room said before he could continue.

"Ouch. No love for the man on the street," Logan folded his arms. "Fine, I'll just say that if things start getting gnarly again, it'd probably be a good idea for us to address this at some point, in some way. I know, I know, not wanting to engage has kept us silent so far, but I just worry that if we don't do something soon, someone innocent could get hurt."

This, of all things– for probably obvious reasons– was what got Thunder to turn toward Logan. "You know, youngin, I reckon you've got a point, one that's worth investigatin' about. The only place I ever see these guys is the square, though. Is it worth it to just walk around there and hope they'll show their faces? And even more so than it being worth it, would it be safe? Without knowing what their motive is, who's to say what they could be planning?"

"I can try to gather more information about their operations from other citizens," Hunter suggested. "In particular, the merchants that vend in the area should have some level of information about their whole deal. Opinions, if nothing else."

Everyone seemed to agree to that, based on the sounds in the room.

"What's the last one?" Phoenix asked then, looking up at Hunter.

"The last what, exactly?" he asked in return.

"The last missive, Hunter. You said there were four of them," Phoenix reminded him.

Hunter blinked in surprise. "Oh. Yes. Right, the fourth and final bulletin for us to discuss is the matter of the strange distortions that have been appearing around the world. Since we've last discussed them, we've heard word of two more occurring–"

"Might as well make that three," Logan interrupted. "Arrigan and I saw another one on our way back here just now. It was just as unsettling as I've heard."

This made Hunter sit down and ready a pen. "This is the closest you've been to one, right, Logan? How would you describe how you felt when you were around it?"

"How I felt? Uh..." Logan thought. "It's... I think 'distortion' is an uncannily good word to describe these occurrences, because when I try to explain what being near one is like, the thing I think of the most is that my body kind of felt like it was being pulled in multiple directions at the same time; like if there was a piece of taffy sitting in the middle of this table, and we all grabbed it and tried to pull it to our resting positions. That, as well as that feeling in my chest that was a bit fluttery, a bit crushing, a bit fragmented– as if I would have trouble breathing for long if it continued on, but luckily it stopped."

"How disturbing," Phoenix said softly.

"No kidding," agreed Thunder. "How consistent is this with any of your research of the human body, Phoenix? Have you ever run into anything like this when you've treated people?"

A pause. "Off the top of my head, absolutely not," she replied. "This is something that I'll have to consult the books about, for sure. If there's ever been a similar instance of something like that happening and it was medically induced, it'll be in one of them."

Thunder nodded. "And if it ain't, I guess we'll have to entertain other ideas of what could be causing the ruckus– but let's cross that bridge when we get to it. Well, that was all that was on our itinerary. You got any parting words for us, Hunter?"

The question, for whatever reason, seemed to startle the redhead. "I have nothing further. Just– to restate the obvious– be sure to update me with any progress that is made, so that I may update the logs. If that is all, we may adjourn."

Everyone stood then, ready to return to their places of residence.

What They Don't Know...

With February came a vast chill over most of the United States. The frigid winds and dusting of snow over every exposed structure was certainly typical of the Midwest. Usually, during this time of year, a lot of people would leave their houses as infrequently as possible– and their friends understood, when this happened– but that didn't stop the Pagliardi sisters from hosting a sleepover at their house on one especially cold Friday night.

It had been a long time since the girls had been able to host such an event, and this manifested in a bit of anxiety for them both; but some level of excitement, as well. Mishaela, the younger, had convinced their father to take her to the grocery store to be sure they had only the best snacks available for the planned movie marathon. Chiara, the elder, stayed behind with their mother as they hashed out dinner plans; although snacks were essential to a sleepover, real meals were also important. Chiara also took on the role of making sure there were enough blankets and pillows for everyone, so that no one would be cold or uncomfortable. These were her friends, but she would always be nervous about accommodations.

When Mishaela announced her return home, the two girls sat in the living room to go over their plans for the night.

"Dad was asking me a lot of questions about allergies, and it made me realize that I don't actually know everyone's food sensitivities," Mishaela admitted as she began to pull the snacks she bought out of their bag. "I mean, I know that Jaiden would be fine with anything, but I still didn't get anything with peanuts or chocolate, just in case."

Chiara nodded, her eyes falling on the bag of sour gummi worms that now sat on the table. Everything else was fine, now that she saw those; she'd be digging into that bag as soon as everyone got settled in.

"Right, and I also picked up some playing cards in case movies get boring," Mishaela continued. "I think I can still remember a few card games that are fun for the amount of people we'll have. Now, should we start rounding up the blankets?"

"Oh, I already did that," Chiara replied.

Mishaela blinked. "Really?"

"Yes. They're right over there, on the other side of the couch. I located the pillows too. I also discussed dinner plans with Mom; she's giving us money for pizza," replied Chiara. "The floors have been swept and mopped, the rug vacuumed, and I cleaned the TV too, just in case."

"Chiara, you know I would've helped you with all of that," Mishaela said then. "I– I feel bad that you felt you had to do that all on your own."

Chiara waved a hand. "It's not that I felt like I had to. Well, I guess it was in a way, but it's not a way that believes you wouldn't have. It's just, since you were out taking care of things with Dad, I would've felt bad if I just sat around and waited for you to get back. Taking care of everything here made me feel... what's the word I'm looking for? Vital. Useful. It is a very good feeling to feel, Mishaela."

"Yeah." And Mishaela knew that Chiara was always looking for ways to be useful, lest the persistent voice of anxiety in her head would convince her that no one wanted her around. "What's done is done, anyhow. How are we doing on time?"

No sooner had she said that, the doorbell rang. The first guest of the evening! "I'll get it!" Mishaela volunteered, her walk progressing into a bit of a jog by the time she arrived at the front door; where, somewhat expectantly, she and Chiara's small blonde friend awaited.

Although originally from the Portland, Oregon area, Brecken Islington had bounced around the entire United States more than many other seventeen-year-olds due to her parents' work. Because of this, it had historically been difficult for her to make friends; it had always felt like, by the time she was finally getting used to a place, it was time to move again. This time, though, the move had been beneficial because it ended up bringing her closer to the Pagliardi sisters. She'd become close to them during their time fighting off magical zombie creatures; especially Chiara, since they had a some-what similar temperament.

"Brecken, you're so early." Mishaela inwardly cringed the moment she said this, worrying that it was too harsh.

"I am," Brecken nodded, the motion making her blonde ponytail bounce. "I placed an order at the bakery near my house, the one that makes the really good cookies, and I misjudged how quickly they would be done; by then, I don't think I'd have had enough time to go back home, so I thought it would be best if I continued on. I hope that's okay?"

Mishaela smiled. "Sure. Come in, it's too chilly outside to stand there in it. Chiara and I were just finishing the setup, I think."

"Already?" Brecken asked. "Well, if you're not quite done, I don't mind helping. Dad always says that, if you arrive early to a function, the best thing you can do is ask the organizer if they need any help. It makes sense, so that I won't be in the way."

They turned into the living room then, where Chiara was busy pouring the snacks that Mishaela had bought into bowls, so they would be easier for everyone to grab and pass around. When she saw Brecken, it was easy to tell her mood was instantly lifted. "Brecken! Welcome to our home!"

It was a bit of a silly sentence, as Brecken had already been to the Pagliardi house plenty of times at that point. She'd been a guest often enough that, before she'd gotten her own car, her father had learned enough Italian to exchange pleasantries with the girls' moth-er whenever he came to drop her off/pick her up. At the same time, though, this would be the first time she was visiting while neither of the Pagliardi parents would be home.

"Thank you, Chiara. I brought cookies from my favorite bakery near my house," Brecken replied, placing the box on the table. "There are chocolate chip, sugar, and peanut butter. How are you doing with preparations? Can I help in any way?"

"I think we were getting ready to configure the specifics of our sleeping arrangements," Chiara explained. "I brought the pillows and blankets down already, but we didn't get a chance yet to work out where everyone will be–"

The doorbell rang again, then.

"Why don't the two of you hash that out, while I go see what's happening at our door?" Mishaela suggested. "I won't be long, I promise."

Briefly stopping at the shoe rack near the door to make sure there was enough room for the incoming pairs of shoes, Mishaela opened the door again, and couldn't help but smile at the sight of two of her favorite people.

Mishaela had always been amiable, and easy to get along with, but that hadn't always guaranteed her friends because she was naturally on the introverted side; this had all changed in the fifth grade when she'd met her best friend, Jaiden Winchester. The two had become close because they were the two with "unusual" origins– Mishaela being the daughter of an Italian immigrant, and Jaiden having a Black mother and Irish-American father– and at this point, the two were virtually inseparable.

It was Jaiden who had introduced Mishaela to Lulu Madrigal, the girl that was currently with her. It would not be technically incorrect to say that Lulu and Mishaela were dating, in a very literal sense of the word. However, there were quite a few external factors making it difficult for the girls to have an established relationship. Mishaela remembered, on the day she'd been in shambles confessing to Jaiden that she realized she was bisexual, her biggest concern was how to tell her parents and sister. While there had never been any explicit incidents that indicated either of the Pagliardi parents would be homophobic, the thought that the conversation even had a chance of not going well was enough to make Mishaela fear it happening at all. And, even when Chiara revealed that she had already known this about her younger sister, it hadn't instilled much more confidence within her.

The situation was similar on Lulu's end. She didn't talk much about why, which led both Mishaela and Jaiden to think things would turn out even worse on her end if her family found out she'd been dating a girl.

The two of them lived close enough that Jaiden's mother had brought them both over. Mishaela waved to her, seeing her sitting in the car, presumably configuring the GPS for her next stop. Mrs. Winchester rarely stayed in one place for long.

"Are we early?" Jaiden asked just as her mother pulled off.

"The more I ponder that question, the more I realize the line between 'ready' and 'preparing' is really blurry," Mishaela replied. "Come in! You can leave your shoes here on this rack, and the coat rack is behind you. Chiara and Brecken are in the living room."

"Oh, so are we just missing Madeline, then?" Jaiden asked. "I am zero percent surprised by that. For as long as I've known her, she's had a lot of positive qualities, but timeliness has never been one of them."

And this was something that Mishaela would know arguably better than Jaiden did; she and their final friend, Madeline Navarro, had known each other since they were very young because their parents had attended the same high school. This meant that she was very familiar with all of Madeline's particular eccentricities, and... she certainly did have a lot of those. Whether it be her bright, neon, bordering on garish sense of fashion, or her steadfast belief in the existence of aliens, one scarcely needed to worry about sticking out too much as long as Madeline was present.

"Do you think I should call her and make sure she's still on her way, though?" Mishaela asked, just as she made it to the living room with two more guests. "It wouldn't be the first time she straight up forgot about a prior commitment."

Everyone in the room affirmed in various ways. Somehow, even with not hearing the beginning of the conversation, both Chiara and Brecken knew this was about Madeline.

"Oh, and hi, Jaiden and Lulu," Brecken added then. "It's so weird, even though we go to the same school, it feels like it's been forever since I've seen either of you. How have you been? How are things?"

"Things have been well, Brecken, thank you," Lulu replied. "And it's always good to see you, Chiara. Mishaela's told me that the two of you are shopping for prom dresses– I hope that's going well."

Brecken and Chiara exchanged a look. "It's... going," Brecken was the one to reply. "I think that story would only bore you to sleep, though."

"We're loathing the lack of choice," Chiara added softly.

"I think it's just like that when it comes to going to a store to get a prom dress, so don't start thinking you're being impossibly picky or anything," Lulu said supportively. "If it's within budget and other possibilities, you could look into ordering something online or working with a tailor! That way, you also make it impossible for someone to show up wearing the exact same dress! Well, if you wanna go the tailor route, I have a tita in Detroit that does beautiful work when she's not busy with her desk job."

"Oh! Could I have her contact info, then?" Brecken asked. "I'll have to run it by my dad for budget purposes, but that sounds so amazing. I know prom is only one night, but the idea of having something made especially for me makes me so happy inside! What do you think, Chiara?"

The characteristic pause before Chiara spoke reared its head. "I think I'll wait until I see what our stop next weekend yields."

"Right, we were going to another place next weekend," Brecken realized. "Well, nothing is set in stone, right? We can go there, and then make decisions based on that. After all, we still have plenty of time. Prom isn't until May."

There were footsteps in the hallway then, and five heads turned to see the Pagliardi parents preparing to leave, grabbing their coats and hats and scarves, preparing to brave the blusters of a Midwest winter. As he pushed his arm through the sleeve of his coat, the girls' father walked back to the living room, taking a moment to digest the faces he now saw staring back at him. "I see we're starting early," he said with a smirk. "Chiara, Mishaela. You have my and your mother's numbers if you need anything. If something happens where you need an adult immediately, you can call either the Thomases or the Michalskis– those numbers are on the kitchen counter along with the money for pizza. Is there anything else that you girls may need before we head out?"

The room was quiet as everyone thought.

"I don't think so, Dad, but thank you for everything," replied Mishaela. "We'll call you if that changes, I'm sure. Um, you and Mom should have lots of fun though, all right?"

"Of course." He nodded. "Don't tear the place down, girls." He affectionately pat Chiara's head on his way out.

After the door had closed, there were a few seconds of silence before Jaiden said, "Whoo! The parents are gone! As much as I like the Pagliardis, we can finally unclench."

Indeed, it was like everyone in the room exhaled, and became less tense.

"We can't order the pizza until Madeline gets here, or else she won't have any input in what will go on it, so now what do we do?" Mishaela asked.

With impeccable timing, the doorbell rang.

***

"Sorry about the lateness, my dudes, but I didn't wanna show up to this party empty-handed," Madeline said as she sat a container on the coffee table. "The idea was to stop by Jess' place so her mom could help us make queso fundido– which we did, that's what's in the pot– but I got so distracted by this new book that Jess and her sister were telling me about that it wasn't long before I forgot I had somewhere to be... ha..."

Madeline stood by the table now, with her shoulder-length light brown hair situated in a loose ponytail and a neon pink knitted hat pulled over the rest of her hair– presumably, to hide how messy it was.

"It looks delicious, even so," Mishaela said then. "Thank you for bringing it, Madeline."

"Yeah, no problem. I know I'm usually the queen of having my mom make whatever German snack she's willing to make, but she didn't have the time to do it this time, so I thought I might have my dad make something... just to remember he's one of the most vanilla Mexicans in the city, so I had to outsource this one." Madeline sat on the couch, before immediately standing back up and grabbing a pillow. "Should we pull out the pullout first?"

Jaiden smiled and replied, "Gee, you already started, might as well." But, even when teasing her, she went over to help with the transformation of the couch. When it had been fully let out, every-one gathered to sit together and eat snacks– but not too many, for there was still pizza to be devoured.

"It looks like we have sixty dollars to contend with," Chiara said as she returned from the kitchen, placing the money on the table. "But remember that we need to account for taxes, delivery fee, and the driver's tip. With the exception of Brecken, I think we are all fairly familiar with the available pizza places at this point, right?"

"My only contribution to this conversation is that we do not get Domino's," Lulu said then. "I hate their sauce, it's so bland and yet it still gives me heartburn. If I'm gonna suffer it could at least be for flavor."

"Oh! Are we slandering Domino's?" Jaiden asked. "Worst wings. Consistently. We got some one time when we were in Boston visiting my brother and I was almost impressed at how the wings were still just as bad as the, like, three different locations I've ever eaten at in Chicago. Er, Chicago and Harwood Heights I guess. What are our other options, who's got the list open? That sounds like a you thing, Mish."

Indeed, Mishaela did have the list open on her laptop. "We have Papa John's, Lou Malnati's... I think we could place an order for pickup at DiMaggio or Cucina Biagio. Little Caesars–"

"Ew," Madeline cut in.

"I like Little Caesars," Lulu replied.

Madeline stared at her. "I think that is possibly the most Michigander thing you've said since I met you."

"Honestly, I don't mind it either," Brecken said. "That is, if I'm remembering the right place. If I am, though, it also means it's been a while since I last had their pizza."

"It is also the most economical option, so keep that in mind," Mishaela pointed out. "At the same time, there are only six of us with no dietary restrictions; it's not like we need to order more than one pizza at all unless anyone's feeling particularly finicky today."

"Hey, that's a good point," Jaiden realized. "There's no need to be economical in that case. Let's get some of the good stuff. Pepperoni, I'd assume."

"Yeah, pepperoni is good," Madeline replied, the other girls assenting in various ways as well. "I would assume one of the sisters here is going to call, so in the meantime, why don't we start sorting through these movies to see what we should put on first?"

Once that was all settled, the teens arranged themselves onto the couch to get ready to watch the movies that had been prepared for the night, all excited to be able to spend time with their friends.

...Could Never Possibly Hurt Them

I t had been a long week, and yet at the same time it had felt so short.

That was always how it felt when one left their home for longer than a couple of days. And it was certainly how Spencer-Lynn Cambridge felt as she rode the train from Dublin– where her school had just finished an educational trip– back to her home city of Belfast. Although she was eighteen years old, Spencer-Lynn was currently in her final year of secondary school because she'd lost a year and a half of progress when she was eleven years old due to her experiencing a traumatic event, so all of her classmates were younger than her. It was something that had weighed heavily on her mind when the Cambridges had moved back to Belfast from Japan when she was thirteen, but these days, she was more so ready to be done with school.

As she rested her head against the window, watching the raindrops cascade down the glass (because of course it was raining), she reflected on how the past week had gone.

It had mostly been boring school stuff, but that hadn't been all that it was. After all, the dorms that everyone had been staying in were very nice; it was like having an apartment complex full of classmates. After class, the students had free range of the city, so long as they were in by curfew. Spencer-Lynn's older brother Liam lived in Dublin– he'd moved shortly after getting married– so she'd had the chance to visit him and his wife and her baby nephew, and that was always good. There would be so much to catch everyone up on once she got home: the sights, the food, and everything she'd learned on the trip.

One thing she would *not* be telling family about, though, would be the very cute girl she'd flirted with while the class was visiting the National Gallery of Ireland. Spencer-Lynn had known for a few years now that she was attracted to girls and boys, but had never acted on her attraction to the former until that moment. She'd unfortunately learned moments later that the girl was just in it for fun and had a boyfriend, but at least this was a hurdle she'd finally surmounted– so she was telling herself, anyway.

Her phone vibrated then, a text message from her friend Gavin Harplein, a sixteen-year-old Londoner. *How's the commute? Made it home yet?*

She smiled as she texted back. *Not just yet. Within the hour, likely– don't worry, we're still on for today.*

It would be difficult to not be able to tell that Gavin was a bit of a lonely person; he didn't have very many friends in London, and none of them were so close that he'd spend too much time texting them, if he even had their numbers. He was, obviously, closer to the group of people he'd first experienced the magic world with– Jaiden, Mishaela, Madeline, Jasiela– but there was also the time difference to contend with. So while he frequently spoke to them, he about equally frequently texted Spencer-Lynn, and also had regular video chats with her since they were within the same time zone. This was the plan they had made for this evening, once she was home and adequately rested.

When she finally disembarked from the train and got to the outside of the station, she looked around hopefully, but no– still raining. Damn Belfast weather.

"Do you need a ride home, Spencer-Lynn?" one of her classmates asked as she departed the station with what looked like her parents. "I don't believe we're in too much of a hurry, so we can make a wee stop for you."

Spencer-Lynn wanted, so badly, to turn her down. To say, "no, I can walk, I don't live far," even though she did, and to continue on on her own– but minutes later she found herself awkwardly seated in the back seat of the car, wishing she'd had the resolve to finally walk somewhere alone. *Damn it all. It's been seven years. My classmates are two years younger than me and they have no problem walking places alone. What am I going to say if people start noticing and asking questions?*

"You don't have to be so closed off from everyone all the time, you know."

"What?" Spencer-Lynn was taken by surprise, before she remembered that she was sitting beside someone. "Oh, um, sorry, Eileen. It's not intentional. I– it's complicated."

"I see." She nodded. "Well, I guess it's not like it matters too much whether or not you're friendly with our classmates, at this point. We've not got a lot of time before it's GCSE season. The light is at the end of the tunnel, aye?"

"So it is." Spencer-Lynn smiled, despite herself.

When she was dropped off in front of her house, Spencer-Lynn waved, deciding that the ride hadn't been all bad; Eileen had always been very kind to her (to everyone in their year, really) and her parents were able to make the ride as least awkward as possible, which was certainly a task when it came to parents of teenage girls. All the same, she was glad to finally be this much closer to her room, and to her bed. Gavin wouldn't hold it against her if she took the tiniest of naps before she videoed him, would he? She was suddenly being hit with a wave of fatigue, when she remembered how comfy and inviting that bed was...

It took a maximum of five steps into the house for her to hear the implications that she wouldn't be getting that anytime soon; she was able to hear the sounds of a conversation in progress the moment she closed the door.

"...quite a cumbersome thing, truly, but it isn't as if we don't have the space, Kate. With only a few exceptions, that room's not been touched since it was vacated."

"That's not the point, Murph, and you know it isn't. Would it have killed you to give us some warning that you'd show up here like this? Just because your father has a soft spot for you doesn't mean we're always going to be able to drop everything to accommodate you and whatever disaster you've brought in with you this time."

"Wow, okay. You make it sound like I'm not also your child. What crawled up your arse and died?"

Spencer-Lynn could hear her parents speaking (her mother mostly), but when she heard the third voice, she couldn't stop herself from leaving her rolling luggage at the door and quickening her pace to the living room. It was difficult for her to process who she'd heard speaking, and was still in disbelief; nevertheless, she was elated the moment she saw the person sitting on the couch opposite her parents. The full, somewhat round figure, the freckles on her arms, the long, curly, dirty blonde hair pulled into a chaotically messy bun. Maceida Cambridge, her older sister.

Her older sister that no one in the family had seen in about four years.

"Maci! Is that really you?!" Spencer-Lynn asked, interrupting their mother in the middle of a sentence she hadn't heard the beginning to.

She turned around immediately– despite having a slightly rounder face than the last time the two had seen each other, there were the warm brown eyes she remembered, eyes that lit up when it registered who she was looking at. Maceida was the larger of the two in both height and weight; she was often teased as "the only chubby Cambridge." Regardless of anyone else's opinion on that, Spencer-Lynn liked this because it meant she gave the softest, warmest hugs.

"Spence! Oh, you're back already! And you look different." It was such a comfort to hear Maceida's voice– Spencer-Lynn had always loved its eccentricities, like how high-pitched it was despite her size, and her words occasionally meshing together in strange ways (this had been caused years ago when she'd worn braces and didn't want her tongue to touch them, and never stopped when the braces were eventually removed, resulting in a fairly noticeable speech impediment). "I wasn't expecting to see you so soon. Mum and Dad said you were in Dublin for school." Her arms, as freckled as Spencer-Lynn's face– if not more– hesitantly opened, welcoming her into one of those warm hugs.

"I was. I only just now got back," she explained as the two hugged. "It's so good to see you! What are you doing back in Belfast? You've got at least another year of university left, right?"

"Ah. Yeah, about that. I do, but that's... a long story," Maceida replied, and it was easy to tell it wouldn't be a happy one either, by her tone. "I can tell you– I *want* to tell you– but..."

Privacy, clearly, as she subtly gestured toward their parents. Spencer-Lynn awkwardly waved to them, realizing she hadn't greeted them. "Hi."

"Glad you noticed us back here," their father was the first to speak. There had always been something about his sarcastic nature that felt like home. It was difficult to put into words, but this sentence made Spencer-Lynn feel the same amount of warmth as if he'd also given her a hug to greet her.

If only the same could be said about the matriarch of the family.

"...how did you get here, Spencer-Lynn? You didn't walk here."

He said this as a statement, but there was a bit of a question there as well. "I didn't. One of my classmates' parents dropped me off. She offered."

"That was nice of her." He nodded.

"Aye, so it was," Spencer-Lynn agreed. "Oh, by the way– that reminds me. When I get unpacked, Liam sent a few gifts for the house; I'll bring them back down with me."

Both parents exchanged a smile. Sometimes, Spencer-Lynn felt jealous of how much both of her parents openly loved their first-born.

"Well, go on then. I'm sure there's a lot that Maceida wants to tell you, but don't forget about your dinner either."

Both girls smiled at each other. "We'll be back for dinner, promise!" Spencer-Lynn called as the girls started down the hallway. "Oh, wait, I need to grab my suitcase."

It was a brief walk up a flight of stairs and to the end of the hallway before they got to Spencer-Lynn's room. Maceida's old room had been across the hall, and she stopped in front of it, placing her hand on the door. It was then that Spencer-Lynn realized what was differ-ent about her; despite her size and somewhat abrasive personality, Maceida tended to dress like she'd fallen into a bowl of cotton candy. Lots of pinks, lots of pastels, and it was rare to ever see her in jeans. But jeans were what she was wearing today, along with a rather plain band T-shirt. The... Silversun Pickups? Spencer-Lynn would have to ask her about them later; she had never heard of them.

"What's in here?" Maceida asked then, startling Spencer-Lynn.

"What's in where? Oh, your old room. Nothing, as far as I'm aware. Your old bed is in the basement, and Dad gave your old wardrobe and stuff to Liam when you moved out." Spencer-Lynn had always had thoughts about that, but had kept them to herself at the time.

"So it's empty." Maceida turned to her. "Can we sit in here instead?"

If one were to ask her later, Spencer-Lynn didn't understand why she felt she needed to go along with the idea of sitting in an empty room, on the bare hardwood floor, but there was something about her sister's demeanor that made her feel as though she needed to humor her. Maybe it was the fact that, thus far, she'd been uncharacteristically quiet. It was rare that a room was quiet whenever Maceida was in it, but she hadn't spoken as much as usual since Spencer-Lynn had first seen her. And so, after the grabbing of a few pillows and blankets, the two sat together on the floor.

"I don't really... know where to start."

Even now, Maceida was having trouble looking at her younger sister.

Spencer-Lynn tried to reassure her with one of her brightest smiles. "From the beginning is usually regarded as the best starting point."

"You little shit." Maceida laughed a little, and there it was: her usual demeanor, or shadows of it at the very least. "Fine, then, but the issue with that is that I don't really know how to tell where the beginning *is*. I guess I can start with telling you that I dropped out of school, effective immediately– that's why I'm here now."

This was a shock. Maceida loved living in Montreal; even if she hadn't said so multiple times, it had been evident in the photos she'd share on social media, and the way she raved about her classes and the politely rude demeanor of the quebecoise. There had to be more to the story, which must have been why she'd said she was going to start with this.

"It's immediate, but it isn't permanent. If there's one thing I'm confident of, it's that I want to finish my degree. But not right now. Right now... it's too much to deal with."

When she was silent for an uncomfortably long time, Spencer-Lynn asked, "How so?"

"That's the part that's difficult to put into words," she replied. "It's one of those things where I can only really tell when things became too much to bear, and that was a few months ago, when I was told I wasn't on track to pass one of my music classes."

"Oh." Spencer-Lynn couldn't keep herself quiet about this. From a very young age, Maceida had been obsessed with music, specifically the composition side of things; she'd been playing the viola since she was six, and now played four more instruments in addition to having begun training as an opera singer when she'd first moved to Montreal. She had even placed in some moderately prestigious strings competition in Japan when she was twelve. Basically, it was impossible for Spencer-Lynn to believe that Maceida would ever not ace any assignment related to music, let alone fail one.

"Obviously, upon being told this, I went to see my professor to find out what the hell happened, and I– Spence, I swear to whatever gods are out there, I will never know how this happened, but somehow the file that I sent in for my final wasn't the finished product; it was a version right before I'd made some pretty major changes to it. I was so certain that the file I'd sent was the correct one. I still am! I checked it thrice before sending it even, but of course, you can't tell a professor that in a way that doesn't make it sound like it's all been fabricated to buy yourself extra time. So I had to try and think of a way to undo that whole mess, because my pride when it comes to musical projects wasn't the only thing at stake– mainly, my scholarship, after failing that English course. Twice. Now, I'm only telling you this next part because I trust you more than anyone else– you cannot tell anyone else in our family this, but you know how bad my judgment gets when I'm under a lot of pressure. I went to my professor's office and I... *kinda* agreed to some things that would get both of us booted from the school if anyone ever found out, if you get my drift."

Spencer-Lynn blinked. "What in the–"

"...at my insistence," Maceida added softly. "Look, it was absolutely a bad situation and probably somehow illegal– but he was hot, okay? What else was I supposed to do?!"

"Say no? Report him to the dean? Holy shit, Maceida, anything but agree?" Spencer-Lynn replied.

"I know! I wasn't thinking straight at the time, okay? Besides, miraculously, the next day, my grade was fixed and the correct file was uploaded to the database... and I have to admit the dick was good. Excellent even, but mentally, at that point the damage was done. Like, even though it's illogical– given that there would have been no way for the other file to have at first been there unless I had been the one to submit it– there's still this little voice in my head that wonders whether he specifically set that up so that he could have the opportunity to fuck me, or if my composition work isn't good enough, and looking back, I think realizing that I'd never know the answer was what kind of sent me into a spiral. Even when the new semester started, I stopped going to class. Stopped leaving my dorm, really. Nothing seemed worth it anymore. My friends would call me, but I wouldn't answer. You may have noticed that I wasn't texting you, either."

Spencer-Lynn had noticed this, actually, and it had been something that had made her incredibly sad– not only because her sister hadn't been talking to her, but because she'd had no one else to talk to about how sad it had been making her. Maceida's personality was polarizing enough that most of the family didn't particularly enjoy her presence, and they were pretty obvious about this too, so they probably wouldn't have been able to empathize. Even now, learning the reasons behind the silence, it made her feel sad in a different way.

Maceida's eyes began to trace the lines in the hardwood flooring. "I... started seeing a therapist."

Now, this was big. Both of the sisters knew how staunchly anti-therapy their parents were– to the point that one could argue Spencer-Lynn received way less than she needed after her traumatic experience as a child– and this was something that had carried over to all their children. Maceida, particularly, had been very vocal in her opposition to the idea of speech therapy, even with how obviously her speech issues bothered her.

"Yeah? What did they say?" Spencer-Lynn asked.

"Well, the depression diagnosis wasn't a surprise at all. Saw that coming from a mile away. We talked about some other suspicions she had, but we didn't have enough time to really get to the root of any of it before I had to come back here. Still, I've got a lot on my mind as the result of our talks, and I'm likely going to be thinking about it all for a while, as I try to find a therapist here in Belfast that can pick up where we left off without our mum and dad finding out; that being said, I think it is also quite possible to make the most of being with my sister again."

This made Spencer-Lynn smile. There did not seem to be a lot of good in Maceida's life at present, but it was still good to be seeing her again. Even if they had texted regularly while she was away, there was this unparalleled warm and inviting feeling that came with them being in the same room.

Before anything else could be discussed, though, Spencer-Lynn's phone vibrated with the reminder to get ready to video call Gavin. Had the time really passed that quickly?

"Maci, I'm so sorry. I was supposed to video call a friend in London when I got settled in, but I didn't know that you'd be..." she trailed off.

"Don't worry about it, then. It can't be helped," Maceida replied, standing with a great grunt of effort and holding out her hand to help Spencer-Lynn up. "You go and take care of that, and I'll see about tracking down a bed so I have somewhere to sleep tonight."

"Are you sure they're going to let you stay? That's what they were arguing about when I came in, right?" Spencer-Lynn asked.

This made Maceida laugh. "Do you honestly think Dad would ever turn me away? Mum can nag all she wants, but I think we both know this is something she can't bitch and moan about in a quantity that matters."

A perk of being their father's favorite, surely. "You've got the right of it," Spencer-Lynn agreed. "See you at dinner, then?"

"Count on it." Maceida smiled, "If I don't see you down there in a timely fashion, I'm gonna start eating off your plate."

***

When the call connected, Spencer-Lynn was faced with Gavin dressed as neatly as usual, his wavy brown hair perhaps grown out a bit longer than usual because some of it was pulled back into a ponytail. It hadn't been long enough for that before, had it?

"Hey, sorry if I'm a wee bit late, family stuff," Spencer-Lynn said as she waved. "How are things, Gavin?"

"It would seem that 'family stuff' is the name of the game," replied Gavin. "I just found out literally ten minutes ago that one of my brothers has been hospitalized."

Spencer-Lynn gasped. "Oh my god, Gavin. Should you really be here, then? I can let you go– we can reschedule."

Gavin waved it off. "I have less feelings about it than you'd expect. This is my brother who's spent most of his young life openly being an antagonist, so in all honesty, I'm surprised it's taken this long.

I convinced my parents to let me stay at home because someone's got to tell my sister when she finally gets here. She had a lacrosse game today, so she won't have had time to check her phone or notice someone was calling."

"Oh, I see. I guess, then," Spencer-Lynn replied. Even with her dubious opinions on some of her siblings, she couldn't imagine not rushing to the hospital if she ever heard that any of them were there.

"So, what's your family business?" Gavin asked. "Unless you don't want to talk about it! I should've... said that first. My apologies. You don't have to answer that."

"It's fine. It's actually a good thing, sort of. I may have mentioned to you before that my older sister lives in Canada– er, lived in Canada. She's back. She dropped out of... I don't think that's the correct turn of phrase to use. She's currently *on hiatus* from university. I'm glad to see her again, but there's... there's a lot surrounding her whole situation, so I don't know that being happy that she's back is the correct way to feel about it."

"The correct way. Hm." Gavin repeated, marinating on that last sentence. "That's an interesting thing to say."

This intrigued Spencer-Lynn. "Is it? How so?"

"No, it's just, it's a rather odd thing to say– that you don't know if you should feel happy to see your sister again," Gavin replied. "It's been years, right? Even if the circumstances surrounding it aren't the best, my humble belief is that you can still be happy that you can work through the issues with her, together, without worrying about contending with time differences and such."

Spencer-Lynn thought about this. "Suppose you've got the right of it."

"How was your school trip?" Gavin asked then. "I believe we were discussing how excited to see your brother you were, the last time we had any communication."

"My brother." Spencer-Lynn exhaled slowly. "I certainly did visit him. Well, it's like I've said in the past. Liam's got a maximum of two active brain cells at any point in time, but to his credit, he seems to be an excellent father. The tenderness I saw in his eyes whenever he looked at my nephew was something I'd have never thought him capable of, before now. It was very heartwarming. I can't possibly express how happy I am for him."

Even with the lowering clarity due to the environment getting darker behind him, it was easy to see that Gavin had smiled. "That's so lovely. I can only aspire to be the same way someday in the future, if I ever become a father."

Spencer-Lynn placed a hand at her chest. "Gavin. That's adorable."

"Yes, well..." he replied, bashfully. "Oh! You also visited the National Gallery of Ireland, right? That's a place I've always aspired to go to! I remember you mentioning it because I got so jealous when you did. How was it? I hear the architecture is something to behold."

Honestly, Spencer-Lynn couldn't remember much about what the architecture was like. "Sorry to disappoint you, but I don't remember much, because I didn't have the best time there. The gallery itself is quite grand, but..."

"What happened?" Gavin asked, clearly concerned.

"I met the most lovely lass whilst I was there. Long blonde hair, very feminine, rather lithe, and I could tell she was also from NI somewhere because of her accent. The artsy type, I could tell by the way she talked about all the exhibits with me. I thought we had a real connection, you know? I was just about to ask for her number so we could go out sometime before I had to come home, but right before I could get it out, we were approached by this painfully average lad, who she introduced as her boyfriend. At this point, I was probably visibly disappointed at least, if not hurt, and the way she smiled at me as they departed– it was almost as if it amused her that I felt that way. It was like having something tear straight through my heart."

Gavin was silent for a few moments before voicing his thoughts. "That sounds awful. I'm sorry you had to go through that. But, Spencer-Lynn, I didn't know that you're– I suppose you being a lesbian makes *sense*, but I can't believe I never picked up on it."

"Bisexual, actually. Have I really never said so?" Spencer-Lynn frowned in thought. "I thought for certain that I said so at some point, but the fact that my parents don't know probably kept me from explicitly saying it aloud. Then again, I always thought it was pretty obvious," she shrugged. "Maybe that's just how I view it from the inside looking out."

"Perhaps so. One's orientation is something very personal to them, so I think we get in our heads a lot when it comes to how obvious we are in our presentation," Gavin replied.

Spencer-Lynn had a thought about how much Gavin had said "we" in that sentence, but was distracted by a knock at her door.

"Dinner's ready!" she heard her younger sister call before hearing her feet speed back down the hallway.

"There's the dinner call," she explained to Gavin. "I've got to be off."

"Have you really got to?" Gavin asked, clearly not liking the idea. There it was, that residual loneliness.

"I have. Listen, Gavin– maybe someday we could arrange for you to come visit? I'm sure your parents would be less wary than when you went to the States since we're so close, in comparison. And I'm quite sure that, at the very least, Mumford and Maceida will like you. That's already half of us."

Gavin laughed at this. "That's a lovely idea, Spencer-Lynn, and I'd love to plan it out a bit more in the future– but for now, you should probably go eat dinner whilst it's still hot."

***

Dinner at the Cambridges, in the past, had been a messy jumble of cups and plates plinking around the table as nine pairs of hands did everything they could to ensure they left the table with a full and satisfied stomach. This changed as the siblings gradually got older and began to leave the nest, but tonight's dinner still retained some of the echoes of the past, because it was the first time in years that almost everyone was back in the dining room. The chicken and rice that had been marinating in the slow cooker all day also made everyone just as excited, as they began to take their seats.

No one had told the two youngest siblings that their eldest sister had returned, so needless to say, they were shocked to see her in the dining room. There was Nicole– more often called Nicky– who was twelve, and Colin the youngest at six, and their faces lit up with both surprise and confusion before running to their sister for hugs.

"You've both gotten so big on me!" Maceida said, smiling as she held both the smaller ones in each arm. "You look away from the weins for four years and they become different people. I'll let you go now, but I can't wait to hear all about what you've been up to."

Being released meant Colin quickly ran toward the food, but Nicole stayed behind. "Are you gonna be staying long, Maci? I would really like it if you taught me how to braid my hair really pretty like you do yours."

This made Maceida smile; even before she'd left, her youngest sister had been following in her footsteps when it came to her personal style. Very colorful, very feminine, and at this point they probably had a similar length of hair as well. "Of course, Nicky. Once I'm settled here again, I can show you all manner of very cute ways to style your hair."

Everyone sat down then, as Murph, the patriarch of the family, began to lead the family in prayer. Spencer-Lynn bowed her head in respect, her hands folded in her lap, but then did what she always did– lifted her head slightly and looked over at her younger brother Mumford, just in time to see him do the same to her. There was that knowing smirk they always exchanged whenever their father did this.

Oh, the way it would rock their worlds if they knew about their queer atheist children.

"...and those who they love, who will have to be separated from their loved ones for an indeterminate amount of time. Lastly– but certainly never least– for our second-eldest Maceida, as she takes time to restructure her young life after some major setbacks; our Lord, please bless her as well."

Mumford glanced up at Spencer-Lynn again, as if to say, *I don't think any god is watching over our elder sister, least of all our father's.*

When everyone began to eat, Kaitlin, the family matriarch, turned to her eldest daughter. "We didn't get to that part, did we– what is your plan from here, Maceida?"

"You believe she has a plan?" Vincent asked– sotto voce, but Maceida was sitting right beside him, so she heard him anyway.

"Keep on like that and I'll end you, Black Parade," she replied. "But... as much as I hate to admit it, he's right. I haven't got a plan yet, but then again, I've only been back for three hours, about. Is there something wrong with me taking a moment to catch my breath? It's been four years already and I've hardly gotten a chance to slow down before now. What have I missed here?"

"Attempted assassination of the secretary of state on 29th October," Mumford replied without missing a beat.

When the room was silent, Vincent added, "He's not kidding, by the way; that really happened."

"If memory serves, it wasn't even worth the attempt because she was in London at the time," Spencer-Lynn added. "Never a dull day in Northern Ireland, though I'm sure Canada has been much more exciting."

"What's it like in the country of maple leaves and hockey, anyway?" Vincent asked.

"Oh, you know. Standard fare for a former colony." Maceida paused here, most likely to decide what story she could tell that was family-friendly enough. "Before I had to leave, even though I'm not a reli– uh, a very *reticent* person, yes that is definitely the word I intended to say, my local friends knew how much I'd been studying Canadian culture and history, and made sure we could make it up to Trois-Rivières to see the Notre-Dame-du-Cap Basilica–"

"Do any of these things have English names?" Colin interrupted.

"Har munnen din en av-bryter?" Almost immediately, Maceida switched to Norwegian, as she sometimes did to annoy her siblings. "Trois-Rivières. Three rivers. It's literally in the name."

"You are arguing with a six-year-old," Kaitlin reminded her.

"He's old enough to get roasted if he's old enough to talk shit," Maceida replied, but only then realized her mistake, and sighed. "God damn it. Yeah, I know, no swearing at the table, don't take the Lord's name in vain, et cetera, et cetera. I'll be going to my room that *has nothing in it*, thanks for that."

Spencer-Lynn held in her laugh, not at the fact that her sister had nothing in her room, but at the fact that even with the shift in ages nothing had changed in the Cambridge dynamics.

"I do not know what we're going to do with that girl," Kaitlin said then. "Do you see what I mean, Murph? We can't keep coddling her like you always want to do."

"I hardly think Maceida's been coddled, Kate. No one else at this table has been in the military, or decided to go to a completely different continent to study all on their own," he pointed out. This was what Spencer-Lynn had wanted to say, but didn't want her mother yelling at her; that there were a combination of very unique reasons that Maceida was the way she was– and even so, she was nowhere near as bad a person as their mother liked to pretend she was.

She'd never understand the specific brand of borderline hatred her mother had for Maceida.

"Well, *I'm* glad Maci's back," Nicole said then, reaching for her water unsuccessfully before Mumford nudged it closer to her. "She came back at just the right time! Do you think she'd be able to translate that manga I got for me?"

"That's why you're glad she's back?" Vincent snarked. He could see that he'd hurt his sister's feelings, though, so he immediately added, "I'm just messing. But, no, she probably won't be able to. Why haven't you asked Spencer-Lynn or Mumford? They're still the best at reading Japanese."

At this reminder, Spencer-Lynn's stomach tightened, as it always did whenever she was reminded of the years her family lived in Japan. Yes, she was still fairly conversational and could read some kanji– but it would be much better if she did it on her own terms. Otherwise all she'd be able to think of...

"I'll see what I can do with it, Nicky," Mumford volunteered, knowing that Spencer-Lynn would have such an adverse reaction to the idea; plus, he was the most fluent in the family by far. "You'll have to understand that, if it's a long one, it might get eclipsed when I have to begin my GCSEs, though."

"Yeah! I know!" She was still beaming over the idea, of course.

Spencer-Lynn hesitated a moment more before standing and picking up her plate. "Thanks for dinner, Mum and Dad, but I'm not very hungry at the moment. If it's all the same to you, I should like to take the rest of this upstairs in case the mood strikes later?"

"Hm? Sure. Get as much rest as you need, child." Murph was the first to agree. "There'll be leftovers if you get hungrier still." It was easy to tell there was a second part to the sentence that he hadn't said aloud: *tell your sister this too.*

Back upstairs, Spencer-Lynn gently knocked on Maceida's door, before coming in and placing her food in front of where her sister was sitting against the wall. "Here. I barely ate any of it, so don't worry."

"Thanks. Aren't you hungry, though?" Maceida asked, struggling for a moment to configure the fork and knife in her hands before she found the sweet spot for both.

"Not particularly," she answered. "Maceida, I know you just got back, but I worry about if this is the best place for you to be. Most of the things you're going through right now are mental, and we both know your mental health always suffers whenever you're exposed to our mum."

"It does, but I didn't really have a choice. I didn't want to cause any visa issues, which unfortunately ties me to the country of my birth," Maceida gestured around the room. "It's going to be a struggle, but my hope is that it's at least bearable until I can at least figure something else out, even if that something is living with our grandmother in Norway."

Both laughed then, recalling the days where the threat of being sent to live with their grandmother in Norway was the quickest way to get them to behave.

"Well, you sound sure of yourself. But remember that you've got Dad in your corner. Dad and me, at the very least," Spencer-Lynn smiled.

Maceida returned her smile. "I appreciate it, I really do. Now, as long as you're here, and speaking of family members in my corner, you saw Liam recently, aye? Is he sound? Has he dropped the baby yet?"

Spencer-Lynn could only laugh again before she began to tell the story of how visiting their older brother had gone.

Anti-Resistance Sentiment

"So, you'd think things would be over then, right? I did. But no! That, my friend, is where all the interesting things began to happen."

Logan recounted the tales of the past year and a half to Arrigan as they began to leave their university, descending the stairs of the former palace. Of course, Arrigan had already heard the gist of what had happened– it would be impossible to have not, at this point– but it was always more enlightening to hear things recounted from a local. And even more so from Logan, who always had a flair for the dramatic whenever he had the floor.

"That's when the infestation of holzomen came in, right?" Arrigan asked. "It's so strange how something like that only affected this particular city. You'd think it would be an epidemic before long."

"I do not even want to *think* about that." Logan shuddered. "It was a hard enough time just keeping them under control here. Although, I suppose if they'd tried to take over Andesitia, the locals would've just thrown 'em in the volcano."

Both of the men laughed then, imagining the vile zombie-like creatures being thrown into lava.

"Even from a far enough distance that I wouldn't have to worry about the situation affecting me, it was still scary to read about," Arrigan said then. "I read about it in the newspaper as soon as updates became available because I was so anxious about it, even. How in the world did you guys manage to work through that?"

Logan took a moment to think, then, and was reminded of how nervous he was back when he'd first been taken out to the field to fight the holzomen. He'd quickly found a groove with which he was able to effectively fight them off, but it hadn't always been that way. "This may surprise you, but in the beginning, I think we were all a little afraid of those things. You never had the displeasure of being in close quarters with one, but there was something deeply unsettling about the particular way they toed the line between human and inhuman. They looked like us, you know? Especially from a distance. But seeing them up close– the sickly skin, the soulless eyes, the noises they made in place of speech– that combined with the way that killing them only expelled dust from them rather than blood, it's so disconcerting. I envy you for never having to have beheld it."

Arrigan nodded silently.

"There is something to be said, though, about how quickly we were all able to work past that, which I dare to say was a positive for everyone involved so we could defend our town. Which we did a pretty good job of. Well… there was that one day that didn't go so well."

"That was the day that inspired that memorial monument just outside of the square, right?" Arrigan asked.

"The very same." Logan nodded somberly as they reached the bottom of the stairs, continuing on through the marketplace in the square. "As you may recall, it's also the reason why some of the people who live here have reservations about trying to turn the fountain here in the square back on. The last time anyone touched that system, it resulted in the entire area flooding enough that it, combined with an unfortunately-timed horde of holzomen, meant that…"

He exhaled here, remembering how awful everything had felt at the end of that battle. The sound of Flavian's anguished scream. Thunder's face as he tried to console him, the looks on Spencer-Lynn and Brecken's faces as they began to understand the state this world was in, and Logan struggling to keep himself from either passing out or vomiting when he saw Lisandra working on patients as her own clothes were stained with blood that wasn't hers– a fifteen-year-old having to do that– these were things etched into Logan's memory, things that the new and improved Compositora could never make him forget.

"It was too much," he said then, suddenly conscious of how long he'd gone without speaking. "We fought with everything we had, but in the end, that horde was too much for us. There was so much destruction, too much death."

Arrigan knew, somehow, that when Logan said this he meant it in a similar way that his father always said: "One death is one too many."

"You know, I don't think I ever read about how that whole situation ever got resolved," Arrigan realized then. "Not in detail; just that it was. Which I don't doubt because nothing like that has happened in the six months I've been living here. But how in the world did you guys manage to get everything under control if it was that big of a problem?"

"As one always does: with a little help from their friends," Logan smiled. "The 'friends' here being some very interesting people from the other world and literally a goddess, but with their help, we were able to find the witch causing all the mess, and put them to pasture."

"Whoa, an actual goddess!" Arrigan said in awe. "That's so cool that you got help from one of them! What's more, you say it so casually that it sounds like that's more or less a normal thing here."

"Is it not in Trelana?" Logan asked then.

To answer this question, Arrigan required a moment to gather his words. "Sometimes, my mom says that the price we pay for Trelana's advancements in innovation is the goddesses having forsaken us. As a kid I thought she was just being dramatic about it, but as I get older– and especially now that I'm living somewhere different– I think about that idea a lot."

"It's such an interesting notion to consider," Logan said as he stopped at a food stall making crepes. "Did you ever ask her why she says that?"

"No, never. I always just accepted it as some kind of weird parent thing," Arrigan replied. "You know, like when they talk about having to walk miles to get to school. I'm not sure if I've ever told you this, but my mother isn't native to Trelana. She's from the city of flowers, Rima Dahlia, so I guess a lack of the goddesses' presence would be easier for her to feel since that's supposed to be an especially mystic place."

"I see. Thank you," Logan said to the clerk as he was handed two strawberry-banana crepes, and as usual, handed one to Arrigan. "If I had the time and resources, I'd ask my grandparents what they thought of it. I'm sure they'd have some idea."

Logan had intended to expound upon that idea, but got distracted by hearing the unmistakable sound of a person speaking through a megaphone. At present, they were too far away to distinguish any of the words being said, but they seemed to have a sense of urgency within them. He was beginning to get that feeling he'd always get whenever something bad was about to happen.

Evidently, Arrigan felt it as well– because his next words were, "I don't know what's making me feel this way, but I think we should see what that ruckus in the distance is."

"I really wish I didn't agree with you," Logan sighed. "Let's get going. If we don't check it out and something bad ends up happening as a result, it'll eat at me for the rest of my life."

The two hurried deeper into the square, where a notably-sized crowd was now forming. It was difficult to make their way through because, as both soon noticed, there was no movement within the crowd. Everyone who was a part of it was stoically fixed in the direction of the speaker, as if in a trance; as if nothing else mattered, other than the words that were being spoken.

More so than the entire audience being seemingly in a trance, there was something indescribable about the atmosphere of the area they both now stood in. Geographically, they were still in the square, but this felt nothing like the square that Logan felt was home at this point. The air was warmer and more stagnant; it was impossible to hear and smell the typical elements of an afternoon in the market-place. It almost felt like they had been pulled into another part of the world just by coming into this area.

Logan carefully reached out for Arrigan's arm to stop him from going any deeper into the crowd as he turned his attention to the podium. They were close enough now; no need to draw attention to themselves.

"...and only then will we be able to experience true liberty! Are you with me?" the hooded figure on the podium spoke, raising a fist to the sky. The audience mirrored this action almost immediately, causing Logan to scramble and halfheartedly raise a fist as well, so he wouldn't stand out too much.

"Why should we attribute the development of our esteemed city, which every single person here has contributed to– directly or oth-erwise– to any one group? I know this, you know this, we all do; so, then, why does the Resistance not balk at such grandeur? It is a small detail, but one that contributes to the bigger picture when viewed alongside all of that group's other shortcomings."

At this point, Logan was squinting at the person speaking; not because he felt slighted (he did), but underneath the black robes they were wearing... that voice was beginning to sound *very* familiar. Even with the amplification and slight distortion of the megaphone, he *knew* he had heard this person speak somewhere that wasn't this overcrowded section of the square. But remembering where was a task that felt impossible at this point in time. Had it been in class? While he was helping build things here? Someone back home, even?

"Friendly reminder that I cannot see anything," he heard Arrigan say then. "What's happening?"

"Happening? Uh..." Logan turned back to the podium.

"We have to stick up for ourselves!" the speaker was now saying as they raised a fist again. "We have to decide what's best for ourselves, without the interference or influence of a select few! Are you with me?!"

The crowd also raised their fists again in solidarity, yelling their affirmation.

Logan closed his eyes, sighing, before tapping Arrigan's arm, a signal for them to make tracks.

When they had exited the square area, Arrigan asked, "What in the world was that?"

"A rally, I'm assuming. Correct me if I'm wrong, but they've never had one of that particular flavor in the square, have they?" Logan sighed, "They're becoming ever more bold. We're going to have to discuss this at home for sure."

***

Upon arrival back home, Logan and Arrigan took turns relaying everything they'd seen and heard to the rest of the Resistance members.

"But there's something... I can't explain it, but I *know* I must have met the leader of the anti-Resistance faction somewhere before," Logan was saying then. "There's something about them that sounds and feels way too familiar. But without being able to put my finger on what it is that feels familiar, I have no way of knowing if this is a classmate, or some random person I stopped to talk to back in the City of Garnet."

Hunter placed a hand under his chin. "Let's suppose that was the case. If you had been acquainted before, would this person not have recognized you two today, Logan?"

"We weren't very close to their podium," Logan replied. "And even so, in a crowd like that, I don't think we'd be very distinguishable as affiliated with the Resistance. Plus, I look a lot different than I did a month ago, and Arrigan is new here."

"Camouflage without even trying," Thunder replied with a chuckle. "What else was happening at the time, boys? Was there anything especially unusual or concerning in the area?"

The two exchanged a look. "Honestly? No," Arrigan replied. "But I think that's... how do I explain it? Logan and I both felt as though we should check the situation out because it was causing a ruckus in terms of sound, but once we got to the main crowds, the energy was so bizarre."

"Yes, it was as if everyone else was enthralled by that person who leads the faction," Logan agreed. "I know that people will be attentive if a person is a particularly good speaker, but this felt different from that. I'd be willing to claim that magic was involved, but is that possible; does such a spell exist?"

"Almost definitely." This was the first time Phoenix had spoken; for a moment, Logan had forgotten she was present. "But it's not something that would be of my repertoire, so I'd need to reach out to a few friends that would know more about that kind of thing. A little later, I'll need you guys to give me an extremely detailed recollection of what the scene was like so I can describe it to them, though."

"Could you do that now, actually?" Thunder suggested. "Best to do it while things are still fresh in the boys' heads. Hunter, let's give 'em some room."

"Yes, of course," Hunter nodded. "I'll be in my room."

After the two older men had left the room, Phoenix turned to the younger ones. "You heard the man. Start explaining everything you saw, with as many details as possible."

Brighter Pastures

What was the point of having a large family if you were still able to hear your parents fighting amidst the discord?

This was the thought that constantly repeated itself in seventeen-year-old Jasiela Alfaro's mind, as she sat at the desk in the room that she shared with her younger sister, hearing her parents arguing yet again. What was it this time? It didn't sound intense enough to be another of their spats about money, so at least there was that to be thankful for. This also meant that it was probably something dumb that they were fighting over, though, so she couldn't be bothered to strain her ears to determine what it was.

Not that she would have to before long, knowing that the disagreement would only increase in volume from here.

Sitting on her bed, Jasiela opened her phone and absentmindedly scrolled through her Facebook feed. As much as she adored her friends here in New York, she had to admit, there was a certain level of nonchalance when it came to her complaining about her parents and their arguing. It hadn't been said explicitly, but something widely believed in the group– most likely because they could all relate, because all of their parents would also constantly argue– was that this was just how things were, so there was no use complaining about it. And for a long time, Jasiela had agreed, but when she'd returned home at the end of the summer it sunk in that she hadn't heard Madeline's parents argue at all. Jaiden's parents had a disagreement once while she was present, but neither adult raised their voice. And even seeing Mishaela and Chiara's mother raise her voice at their father that one time, he didn't yell back. She'd even apologized later.

Why, then, was she expected to accept less than what her friends had?

Realizing what she wanted to do now, Jasiela opened the group chat that Madeline had made a few months after their second adventure, aptly titled "The New And Improved Savior Troupe." Gavin had insisted on adding a "u" to "savior," but he had been predictably outvoted.

Anyone around? Jasiela texted the group.

Almost immediately, there was a response from Madeline. *I'm always around, neverending, omnipresent*

Yeah, okay. Jasiela laughed. It was difficult to be in a bad mood when Madeline was around. *Well, for everybody that's around, I could use some uplifting words.*

Almost immediately, Mishaela was the one to respond. *Did something happen?*

It's not so much that something has happened. I just need to vent, and I feel like you guys are the only people in my life that would understand.

Vent away. Gavin and Spencer-Lynn are probably asleep, but the rest of us can help I'm sure. Now Brecken was also chiming in.

Jasiela took a breath, trying to arrange her thoughts in a coherent manner before beginning to type them out. But after a while she knew she wasn't going to be able to, and decided to take the approach of typing out everything and then rearranging them in an order that made sense.

Everything sucks.

Did she really have to start this message in a way that was so stereotypically teenage? Whatever, she could come back to it later.

When I'm at home, my friends and I find comfort in venting about our families, especially our parents, because we're all in a similar boat. There's varying levels of toxicity in all our parents' relationships, and the feeling of having people who relate to you is unmatched. But the downside to that is the expectation, I guess, that this is the way things have to be.

Except, meeting you guys and getting the opportunity to spend time around you and your parents taught me that it is not the way things have to be. Now I'm in a weird spot where I can't get my local friends to understand that the toxicity is not the way things have to be and I wish it was no longer there, and I can't explain to you guys the extent and still have you understand how it affects me, because it's so many worlds removed from what you're used to.

What's a girl to do?

After typing all of that out, Jasiela decided she didn't have the strength to go over and fine-tune it. If anyone in the chat got confused, they could just ask for clarification. The overall message was clear enough, she decided as she pressed "send."

And now to wait for everyone to read and digest that. In the meantime, luckily, things seemed to have calmed down in the other room. It was completely quiet in her room for the first time in years, since her sister wasn't currently home. Jasiela wasn't sure where she was, but also didn't worry about it, knowing that if something was amiss, her parents would've found a way to blame her for it. The dilemma of being a middle child– constantly infantilized, and yet somehow still expected to be responsible for one's younger siblings. Maybe someday, she'd vent about that too; but one family issue at a time was more than enough, she was sure. After all, the only other middle child in the chat was Spencer-Lynn, so she'd have to rant at a time where she was awake for the best results.

The sensation of her phone vibrating brought her back to it with a start.

That is a predicament, isn't it? It was Mishaela who had responded first. *Is there truly absolutely no one who can understand the intricacies of your current situation?*

If that's true, you're not alone in that, almost immediately came Jaiden's addition. *There's some issues I can't really talk to you guys about, and I'm ok with that but it does get really lonely sometimes.*

"Huh." Jasiela said this out loud, having never thought about whether or not someone would be able to relate to the general feelings she was having, even if not being able to relate to the situation exactly.

I guess it does help to know that I'm not alone in the feeling, even if the situations aren't the same. Is this about the whole nonbinary thing?

...oh. I was talking about being Black and having almost exclusively white friends, but now that you mention it, yeah.

Jasiela laughed. She had a point.

Anyway, you can pick my brain about that feeling any time you want, Jas. We as a society don't talk enough about how crushing loneliness can be so let's try to help each other out of it, together!

Madeline was the next to respond. *Could that motivational message have been any more anime?*

Multiple laughing emojis from just about everyone were sent then, before Madeline continued.

I'm with it, though. That's what friends are for, right? If we're ever able to help one another, we do that for each other. That's what I would do for anyone in this chat, unless it greatly damaged my reputation. Sorry, but I need to look super upstanding and cool whenever our alien overlords come and claim this planet as our own.

If there were a camera, Jasiela was sure she'd be staring into it right about now.

Of course, Madeline. We would never ruin that for you. Ah, Mishaela. Ever so kind.

Well, thanks for being such great friends guys. But I should probably start seeing about the possibility of dinner. You know, hour ahead of you guys and all. I'm starting to get a little hungry here. Ttyl as always

As she grabbed the step-stool to look in the cabinets for food, Jasiela thought about how she and Gavin had been able to convince her parents to visit everyone in the Midwest last summer. It had been relatively easier to do then because school had been out for the season; there was no way she'd convince them to let her disappear in the middle of February.

If only at least one of them lived on the East Coast.

Unexpectedly, Jasiela's phone vibrated again, so she picked it up and saw that Gavin had texted the group chat. *Have you eaten dinner, Jasiela? Remember that being fed makes many things more bearable.*

Of course, if anyone would be reminding her to eat, it would be Gavin.

I'm looking for something to eat now but jfc dude it's like 1 a.m. over there, shouldn't you be asleep?

Judging by the amount of times her phone vibrated while she was continuing to look for dinner, Jasiela assumed that now, everyone else was grilling Gavin about being awake so late. She would too, but decided it probably wasn't smart to try to text and walk; that would be a recipe for walking straight into a wall, and she knew that at least one of her siblings would never let her live that down, or at least not for the rest of the night.

Or would, if anyone was in the kitchen at the time. It wasn't often that the Alfaro kitchen was completely vacant, and especially not at this time of day, so Jasiela wasted no time in looking through the cabinets for something to eat. Her father hadn't been grocery shopping in a little while, so there wasn't much to comb through.

She sighed as she reached for a packet of noodles and didn't feel one; she had been hoping to eat that with an egg and some sriracha. She checked the time on her phone then; was 6:30 too late to ask any of her friends if she could come over for dinner?

Hey does anybody have food I'm starving here

This would be the way she found out, apparently.

Jasiela's main group of friends were the ones she had collected from her drama class she'd taken her first year of high school. There was: Alessandra, or Alex for short, a tall Italian girl with masses of wavy brown hair and brown eyes to match; she was usually the one to initiate dinner invitations when it did happen. Caitlyn, a fair-skinned Puerto Rican non-binary person with brown eyes and short hair that was this pale green color, who didn't often invite people to their house because of the general dynamics between the people who lived there. And Devin, Jasiela's fellow Mexican, more fair-skinned than her and not quite as short, who kept his brown hair cut short.

It's like 7 pm Jasiela. Even before reading who sent that message she knew that was Devin, just based on the general rounding up of time.

She responded back: *I asked for dinner not the time keep up here Devin*

A picture was sent then of a pot full, almost overflowing, with a very Americanized form of spaghetti. To its credit, it did look really good, which was all Jasiela could think as she read Caitlyn's message. *As long as we bring this to a location that is not my house I will literally feed u all pls help*

This, Jasiela was sadly too familiar with. That last message carried the tone of all the other messages Caitlyn had sent when things were actively bad inside their home. This could range from them or one of their siblings being screamed at to one of her parents (usually their father) physically abusing someone else in the house. Jasiela always wished there was more she could do to help her friend, but what could one seventeen-year-old living with nine other people in a five-bedroom house possibly do to help anyone in that kind of situation?

Oh shit, come on over then friend, bring the spaghetti or don't we just need you safe. That was Devin again, but Devin was also an only child and did not have a lot of space in the apartment where his parents lived, as a result. *Or maybe we could show up at Alex's place.*

True, Alex would never turn them all away, especially if they brought food and explained what was happening.

Say no more, I'm on my way. I'll bring... something. Jasiela texted the group, before looking around the kitchen, hoping to see some kind of snack, before she noticed a bag of plain pork skins. She didn't particularly like the plain ones, but it was at least something she could share with her friends. She was pretty confident that Alex had barbecue sauce at her place, so they could always eat them with that. Jasiela would, though, need to explain to her parents where she was going– but knowing they wouldn't like it and not wanting to hear their arguing yet again, she settled for leaving a note in the kitchen explaining that she'd be at Alex's house for dinner and the rest of the night. If nothing else, it was usually a lot quieter there; it would be nice to have a brief break from all of the chaos of home.

As she put on her shoes and grabbed her coat, Jasiela opened her group chat and sent one more message: *I'm bringing chicharrones, I guess. Prepare the barbecue or hot sauce. See everyone in 45 minutes.*

Another Promise, Another Seed

On this particular day, Phoenix arrived at the meeting room at home for the weekly Resistance meeting, and was surprised to see Thunder already there with an unfamiliar– and very thick– binder. He was looking through it as if it was the most interesting thing he'd seen in a long time, so the closer she got, the more curious she became about its contents. Stepping farther into the room, the sounds of her shoes on the hardwood floors got Thunder's attention, and he looked up at her.

"If you keep arriving at these meetings so early, it's going to make the rest of us look bad," she teased, punctuating her sentence with a laugh.

"Could say the same thing about you, couldn't I, young'un?" he asked with a laugh of his own. "Last I checked, we're not gettin' this show on the road for another twenty minutes."

Phoenix smiled as she took a seat beside Thunder, turning to face him. "What's that you're looking through? It looks new."

"It is, or new to us, at least. Nice lady dropped it off a couple of hours ago," replied Thunder. "I haven't gotten through a lot of it yet, but from what I've read, this seems to be an extremely detailed plan for the railroad system, the one that connects us to other towns. The one we have now is doing wonders when it comes to getting us to the cities nearest us, but it would be nice to eventually have something that will connect us to every major city in the world, and some of the smaller ones too. Course, that'd require cooperation from those places too, which would be the hardest part."

"Agreed." Phoenix nodded. "Well, it helps that we have Herman in our corner too. I've only known him for a few months, and I've noticed that it's practically impossible to say no to him. Then again, I probably don't have to tell you that."

"No kidding. That's how he got his ladykilling reputation back in the day. You think anyone was saying no to that man when he asked them on a date?"

Phoenix smiled as she turned her head, hearing the shower in the other room switch on. That had to be either Logan or Arrigan, based on what time it was. Hunter was the type of person who showered as soon as they woke up; and it was just like him to rise with the sun, as well.

Speaking of the redhead, Phoenix was now realizing she hadn't seen him, so she asked, "Have you seen Hunter at all today?"

"Yeah. Not very long ago, actually. He said he was gonna run down to the market and grab some stuff. Said he knew of a certain stall that was gonna be running a special on their herbs, which is always nice to come around."

Phoenix nodded. "Yeah. You know, I came down here because I was thinking of when Logan was talking about that meeting that he and Arrigan stumbled upon. Remember when he said it felt like everyone who was part of the crowd was in some kind of trance, as if they were influenced by some type of spell? Between consulting with some of my friends and reading some of my magic reference books, I still haven't come across anything that would yield that kind of result, but I realized last night who probably would know that kind of information offhand."

They said at the same time, "Lisandra."

It was a realization that came with a bit of a sigh from both; Lisandra was indeed very knowledgeable about magic and its effects, but she was also sixteen years old and in high school at the moment, in the City of Garnet, which was about two hours away by train.

"You don't think her parents would let her go for a couple of days, do you?" Thunder asked.

"If I know my aunt and uncle, hell no," Phoenix replied. "They've always been so overly strict about her. On one hand I get it, but you also can't help but wonder how badly it's affecting her. Anyway, we'll get by. What kind of Resistance would we be if we let our success hinge on the knowledge of a teenager? Even one as unusual as my cousin."

Thunder nodded. "When you're right, you're right."

Footsteps approached the room then, before the door creaked open. "Hey, everyone." Logan walked into the room, hair still damp from the shower he'd taken. "Do we still have some time before the meeting starts? I'd love to take some time to get a start on my homework."

"You've got a good twelve minutes, so I don't know how good of a start that'll get ya," Thunder replied. "Then again, we can't actually start until Hunter gets back. Any of y'all seen Arrigan today?"

"He's in the kitchen, I just saw him," Logan replied. "Oddly warm today. What's going on with the weather? I hope that's not something else we have to end up fixing. We already have so much going on."

"Don't jinx it, dummy," Phoenix replied as Logan sat beside her.

Not long after, Arrigan took a seat with his bowl of cereal, as usual sitting in a way that made it obvious he was trying not to draw too much attention to himself. Before he could even speak, though, the front door crashed open loudly enough that it drew all four of their attention.

And then Hunter ran into the room. "Everyone, I must apologize for the crudeness of my entry, but all of our presence is needed in the square! There is currently some sort of... fracas happening, in which many innocent people could possibly be hurt!"

Immediately, Thunder stood, walking over to where he kept his dual pistols. "Say no more. Let's get going as soon as possible, everyone."

"Uh, my sword is at headquarters," Logan pointed out. "I don't think I have time to go grab it."

"It's a good thing you know how to defend yourself without it," Thunder replied. "You're right; no time to go that far out of the way. We've gotta get moving."

The other members of the Resistance quickly grabbed their weapons before hurrying out of the door.

***

Before the group could officially arrive within the square, the shouts and clamor of a disturbance met them halfway. It was something that immediately put them all on guard, even amidst the confusion that came with hearing that kind of thing in a fairly residential area. It was disconcerting; and, knowing how many people frequented that area, worrying.

Logan was the first to speak. "Not the best day for me to not have my sword with me, I assume."

"Let's hope you're wrong," Thunder said with a sigh as he picked up his pace. He knew that Logan wasn't wrong. When it came to matters of combat, he rarely was.

Arriving at the square meant the group was faced with a battle of admittedly smaller scale than the last time this had happened in the square, but large enough for it to be concerning. The most alarming part of this occurrence was that most of the crowd was composed of confused civilians that seemed to have no idea what was going on. This, clearly, was the most worrying part of the incident because it was difficult to see where the actual fighting was happening for the extra crowding.

"What's the plan, boys?" Phoenix asked.

Instinctively, everyone turned to Hunter, the strategist. "I do not believe we'll have much success unless we head right into the thick of it. Do you feel comfortable attempting to shepherd some of these people to safer terrain, Logan?"

"Since I don't have a weapon, absolutely," he replied. "Stay with me, Phoenix. There's always the possibility that a few of these civilians may have been hurt."

"A capital idea," Hunter agreed. "Thunder, Arrigan, with me. We need to be swift."

The older men were off in almost an instant, but Arrigan was hesitant, nervously holding his polearm with both hands. He hadn't had a lot of practice with the thing, but holding it did usually at least boost his confidence. Usually.

"Arrigan, you should get going before you lose the others," Phoenix called out to him. "You don't want to get swept away in the undertow."

No, he didn't, because that had happened the first day he'd arrived in Compositora, and it had been a borderline traumatizing experience. It was one of the reasons he was so attached to Logan whenever he had to leave the house. Come to think of it, this was the first time since then that he was faced with the town without Logan at his side.

This was not helping his already nervous state of mind.

Heading into the thick of battle, Arrigan wondered why he was so chronically unlucky; immediately, he was pulled into a small twister that pulled him off his feet and spat him out so fast that he wasn't able to parse what had happened until he landed on his back. With a sense of urgency, he used his polearm to get back to his feet; he knew it wasn't wise to stay on the ground too long, or else it would be impossible to get back up. Even so, and even when he was able to rise back to his feet, there was a moment of dizziness he needed to shake off before he was able to proceed farther, toward what he was relatively sure was the mastermind of the whole operation, since Hunter and Thunder were also headed in that direction.

The trouble with that was that Arrigan wasn't able to do so in a straight path; his small stature meant that, in an active battlefield, it was too easy for him to get repeatedly elbowed. Once, twice in the stomach, once in the chest, and in the face from a taller person before he decided he'd had enough.

"I don't know why I didn't do this before," he said softly to himself as he clasped his hands together, summoning the magic from within.

It was almost an instant, the way the magic began to form; a purple-pink tinted viscous, expanding mass of jelly that conjured just a few inches above Arrigan's head of brown hair, before spreading, eventually covering his entire body in a protective layer. Once it had covered his entire form, the layer became invisible– but it was then that the effects could truly be felt, as well.

This part always felt comforting– like the perfect warm blanket over his entire body.

With the spell to boon and an added layer of confidence as well, he hurried to where the others had run off to just as the leader– if when he and Logan had been in the square that day was any indication, this was the leader– had tackled Hunter. This clearly caught the redhead off-guard, but he was able to recover fast enough to use the shift in both their weight to flip himself over and land on his knees, effectively using one of them to pin the mysterious leader to the ground.

This motion also made the hood on their robe fly off, which meant that Hunter gasped when he saw who it was, faltering when it came to pointing his gun at them.

The first thing he said to Hunter was, "You look like you'd be a lot heavier than you are."

"Flavian! What are you doing here, you could get hurt!" Hunter replied, as if he hadn't heard him, as he removed his knee and stood, offering a hand. "I feel as though it's been months since I've seen you. We have to get to the bottom of…"

It was only then that it sank in.

"I don't think I'll be needing any help from your kind, thank you," Flavian replied, standing on his own and dusting off the black robes he seemed to wear devotedly these days. The tumble on the ground meant that a few stray twigs had gotten stuck in his white hair, braided as it almost always was, but at the moment this was the least of his concerns.

This was when Thunder came around, and stopped dead in his tracks. "Flavian?!"

"Oh! The mastermind!" Flavian smirked, but there was no joy within him doing this; sarcasm, if anything. "I was wondering when you'd finally show your face around here."

"What are you talking about?" Thunder asked.

"I mean that the next time you do, you may not get off as easily as we're going to let you do today," he replied, rubbing his shoulder, clearly affected by the tackle. "This is just a... a demonstration, if you will. But we'll be back, again, and again– as many times as it takes, until I am sure that we'll be able to ruin you."

With a sweeping turn, Flavian and the other anti-Resistance members dashed off into the distance.

Almost immediately after, Arrigan and the Oliveiras caught up with the others. "Hey, what happened? That crowd thinned almost immediately," Phoenix said as she looked around. Indeed, the area was even quieter than usual. Most of the merchants in the area fled when the fighting had begun, so now that the crowd had dispersed, everyone was left with silence.

"It's... a long story," Thunder replied simply. "Let's get y'all home and then we can start analyzing what's all happened today."

Why Will You Live?

- -

Why hadn't Thunder expected this?

The Resistance, as an organization, had existed for more than a decade at this point. In hindsight, it was a miracle that they hadn't attracted this level of bad press so far. They'd been helping the populace– they always had– and he'd have understood if there were people in town that had been so brainwashed that they revolted against their efforts of goodwill. This had indeed happened a few times, but never so often that those people would be numerous enough to form an entire faction.

But someone who had formerly been a part of the Resistance would have more potent, more polarizing ways to describe their disdain for the organization, and would be more convincing to the everyday citizen. It was one thing to develop one's own suspicions about the Resistance's motives, but an entirely different thing to have been told by a former member that they were not the benevolent organization they claimed to be.

The timing was also not the best; now that disaster had been averted twice, and the general region that Compositora rested in was becoming more and more prosperous, the Resistance wasn't as vital to daily life as they had been before. While this didn't really mean it was easier to think unfavorably of them, it did mean that it would be more difficult to convince the general populace that they were necessary. With this being the case, would there be any popular opposition to the anti-Resistance faction?

It was all a veritable mess; one that, for the first time in possibly forever, Thunder wasn't very sure how to fix.

"Oh. Are you busy?" Hunter had entered the room so quietly that Thunder hadn't noticed him until he spoke; or had he been that preoccupied?

"Not so busy that I can't hear you out," Thunder replied. "What's going on, Hunter? I hope it's not more bad news."

Hunter smiled then. "No, no, I– well, I confess that I don't know just yet. However, if my hypothesis is correct, I think you'll agree that it is very good news indeed. Are you in the mood to accompany me on a walk?"

***

The sun was beginning its descent behind some of the two- and three-story buildings bordering the square of Compositora, and the crowds that frequented the area had already substantially thinned.

This was post-midday in the town; the cooking stands would sometimes start another small round of food for the remaining shoppers, and the aromas floating from their cooking fires meant that no one would be able to resist their wares. Bits of conversation floated upon the air in many different languages: the excitement of getting a deal on a cute article of clothing, the satisfaction of that first bite into a delicious snack; and isolated conversations regarding school, work, family, and everything in between.

It was at this time that five teenagers were unknowingly brought into the madness.

"What *is* this place?" Jaiden asked, looking around. "I realize that the last two times I've asked this question, it's been the same place, but this looks nothing like that."

At Jaiden's side, as usual, Mishaela looked just as confused– but more introspective, which was also about usual for these two. "I thought the same at first, but the more I look around, I don't think it's completely accurate to say it's nothing like that. There are way more buildings than we're used to, but if you look further on that way–" she pointed– "I think I can see some of the stands that we're used to seeing in the market. I can also see what I think is that fountain that's in the middle of the square, but I'm not completely sure about that. We'd have to get closer."

Jaiden shrugged, and turned to the others. "Does anyone disagree with heading toward the, uh... the huge stone thing that Mishaela thinks is a fountain?"

Brecken, Madeline, and Chiara seemed to still be recovering their wits, but after a moment, they all shrugged as well.

"Wait, so is this really Compositora?" Madeline asked, as they all began to walk. "I mean, other than everything looking completely different, I have another concern! The past few times we've been through this stuff, it's required us to go through a door. There was no door this time! I remember perfectly well that my butt was situated firmly on these two's couch! How do you explain that, huh?"

"Oh. I think you're right, Madeline." Jaiden stopped walking, and turned to her. "As far as I remember, we weren't really doing much of anything, were we? The last thing I remember is us trying to decide on what horrible 80s movie we were gonna watch, so we could laugh at it."

The whole group laughed then. "Yeah, we were definitely doing that," agreed Madeline. "So then, what gives? How did we get here all of a sudden?"

"I think that's something we're not going to find the answer to for a little while," Brecken said then. "That was how it went last time, after all."

"Right. There's also less of us than usual, so that's something else to look out for," Mishaela pointed out. "It wouldn't be too out of the ordinary to find Gavin and Jasiela and Spencer-Lynn here. Well, using 'out of the ordinary' extremely loosely here."

"Yeah, no kidding," Jaiden agreed as the group began walking again.

Meanwhile, farther into the square, one of the food stalls was visited by a couple of young women that definitely seemed foreign to the area in a way that no one could quite articulate. They were paying customers, though– even though their currency was strange and unfamiliar– so it wasn't so strange that anyone complained. Still, the clerk stared after them as they made their way to one of the tables near the fountain.

It was an interesting turn of events where before, Maceida had been the one to dump a lot of exposition on Spencer-Lynn about how her school life had been going; now, the younger Cambridge was explaining to her older sister everything she could about the magic world and the adventure she'd gone through last year. It was something that she'd have gladly told her before now, but even disregarding the period of time where Maceida had gone completely silent, the distance between them had made it pretty much impossible. This, after all, was not the type of thing one explained over the phone.

"So– hold on, there's still one thing I don't quite understand. Well, other than the overall... everything, all of this," Maceida said, waving her arms in the air. "Why is it that... the witch or whatever from the last time you were here, how in the world would they know about what happened to you? That was almost a decade ago."

"You know, that's one of the things I never got around to understanding myself," Spencer-Lynn confessed. "It's not just that, there were other little things that I– and everyone else I was here with– noticed, that kind of implied that this world and ours are connected in ways we'd not even scratched the surface of. There were just more pressing matters at the time."

Maceida nodded. "I'm still a wee bit on the fence regarding whether or not I believe all of this, but one thing is for certain: wherever we are now, it is *not* Belfast. These noodles are more flavorful than anything I've ever eaten back home. Damn, Canada spoiled me," she laughed.

Spencer-Lynn gave her a half-smile, before something in the distance caught her eye. She squinted a bit to keep the sun from her eyes, in an attempt to ensure her sight was correct, before deciding she was okay with potentially embarrassing herself if she was wrong about this– and using her entire arm to wave at the group of people. "Hey!" She called.

Meanwhile, a few feet away:

"Who is that person waving at us?" Mishaela asked. "I feel like I should know, but they're just a teensy bit too far away for me to tell."

Jaiden, Madeline, and Chiara immediately turned, but Brecken took a little longer to realize where Mishaela had seen this. "That's a good question," Madeline replied. "Do you think we should be on guard? What if it's another of those weird zombie things?"

"Were they capable of waving?" Brecken asked rhetorically.

Madeline thought for a moment. "That's a good point. I don't remember that being part of their skill set."

"You know, I have an idea of who that might be, but she looks different if I'm right," Jaiden answered. "Let's roll."

When the two groups converged, the silence lingered for just a bit too long before anyone spoke.

"Hi! I'm so surprised– well, not *surprised* to see you, but happy to!" Spencer-Lynn finally said, before realizing that she might need to remind them who she was. "It's Spencer-Lynn. My hair's different."

"Yeah, no kidding!" Madeline agreed. "You look great! Also, if you feel like dropping the hair care routine that helped you grow your hair that fast, I'm listening."

Spencer-Lynn laughed at this. "It's refreshing to hear yousins in real time again."

"Who's your friend?" Jaiden asked. "Hi. Jaiden. This is Mishaela, Madeline, Chiara, and Brecken." She then gasped, "Wait! Is this the girl you mentioned flirting with? Are you guys on a date?!"

The disgusted looks from both of the Cambridge girls made everyone go silent again. "Uh, no," Spencer-Lynn replied. "This is my sister, Maceida."

"Oh! *Oh*. That... yeah. This is awkward," Jaiden said. "Sorry. Didn't mean to 'Sweet Home Alabama' you guys."

"Wait a second." Mishaela suddenly realized, "You're the one who's studying in Montreal, right?"

"Er, was. It's a long story," Maceida replied. "At present, I'm living with my parents in Belfast again until I get a better idea on what my life is, I suppose."

"Oh, that makes a lot more sense then– I was confused as to how you ended up here, but I guess if you're in the same location as Spencer-Lynn, it makes a little more sense you'd be transported together," Mishaela replied. "It's nice to meet you!"

"Still, it doesn't make a *whole* lot of sense, but I guess it's similar to how Chiara ended up with us last time, but wasn't with us the first go-around," Madeline added.

"Maci, these are the friends I made the last time I was here," Spencer-Lynn explained. "Or, some of them, rather. I can't help but notice the crowd's a wee bit thinner this time; have you not come across Gavin and Jasiela, then?"

Madeline shrugged. "We literally just got here. The only reason we decided to come this way was because the fountain looked familiar, and we wanted to confirm that we're where we thought we were, you know?"

Spencer-Lynn nodded. "It does look a lot different than it did last time, doesn't it? The changes are grand, though. The particular aesthetic they're going for here is so visually pleasing."

Most of the historic buildings were in the square, so when the newer buildings to supplement them were built, they were done in a way that tried to emulate how the older buildings looked. There were telltale ways to discern them– the windows were probably the easiest way, the newer window frames weren't quite as ornate and detailed, and were a lot more clean– but overall, the scenery was cohesive and enjoyable.

"Where do we go from here?" Brecken asked. "More so than that, where *can* we go from here? This town isn't as navigable as it used to be, with all the new buildings. I wouldn't know where to even start, which direction to go in."

"You have a point. Well…" Spencer-Lynn gestured toward the empty seat at the table. "Whilst we have no idea where to go, you may as well have a seat. These noodles are delicious, if you're hungry; plus, it's difficult to brainstorm on an empty stomach."

***

At the very heart of the industrial district of the town stood the warehouse where many of the necessary materials were manufactured that were used to improve the town. Magic and machinery combined in remarkable ways to create benches, panels, window panes, the bricks that the average Compositoran walked upon for their daily commute. And at the helm of it all was one large, brown-haired man, who had alerted Hunter that he may want to come to this part of town.

"Place is always so dusty." Thunder coughed as he and Hunter entered the building.

"Sorry about that, but the dust tends to accumulate faster than we can clean it up when we're handling larger projects. We're finishing up the last sectors of the old palace so that the university can finally make full use of the entire building."

The air was slightly tense when the two came face to face with their former comrade-in-arms, because of the way they had gone onto separate paths; however, it didn't mean the communication was going to be impossible. On some level, it was the opposite; with no bad blood remaining, on some level it felt good to be reunited again.

"Y'all have certainly got your hands full here, Anton," Thunder said, looking around the warehouse where the workers were busy creating materials to fulfill their tasks. "So much so that I wonder why it is that you asked us here. Now, I apologize, but I'm not gonna be too useful in any construction projects. Too old for that. My back's practically giving out just at the thought."

This made Anton chuckle. "Don't worry, you won't have to lift anything. At least, not anything that I'm aware of. I just wanted to let you all know that, when some of the guys and I were out gathering some wood, we came across some of those kids you like keeping around. Gavin, right, and... one of the girls, the tiny one with brown hair. Wasn't the best at remembering their names, sorry. I told them I could get ahold of you if they wanted to wait, but they refused. I don't blame them after the way things went down between us– plus all the dust isn't exactly inviting. So I asked them to at least stay in the area until you got here, but I have no idea of knowing if they listened."

"Really?" Thunder looked at Hunter, to Anton, and then back to Hunter. "That don't exactly bode well."

"What do you mean?" Hunter asked.

"Even with how busy we've been lately, with all the different tasks we've taken on, there hasn't been a point where I felt that things were impossible, like the first two times the kids showed up here," Thunder explained. "That they're here now, again... it kinda implies that we're in a worse way than we thought."

For a while, all that could be heard was the sound of saws, drills, and magic casting.

"You're correct, this certainly does *not* bode well," Hunter agreed after the silence.

"Well, gee. If there turns out to be anything the Restoration Effort can do to help, you know where we are," added Anton. "Although I guess that would depend on what exactly is threatening life as we know it this time. Still, if you need something built– or just some extra pairs of hands– you'll have them. After all, this is all of our home."

"Indeed." Hunter nodded. "I'll check the immediate area; hopefully, Gavin and Jasiela will have not wandered too far at present. Thunder, might you stay here for a few moments longer, in case they return?"

"Sure can. I got some stuff to discuss with this kid, anyway," Thunder agreed, nodding toward Anton.

Hunter smiled. "Of course. I'll try not to be gone too long."

Turning on his heel, the redhead set out to explore the streets of the industrial district, hoping that he wouldn't have to look far before he found the two runaway Earth-dwellers. His rationale was that the unfamiliar surroundings would deter them from doing too much wandering; however, as he walked around, he had to admit that another deterrent would be that the industrial district was not particularly inviting. The dustiness of the Restoration Effort's building was not at all out of place in this area of empty dirt plots, haphazardly built wooden buildings, and the odd sandy patch due to this being on the outer ends of the city, going further toward the desert highlands.

This area was not a popular destination for much of anyone for this reason, but Hunter found a sense of peace whenever he came here. If he had to guess why, it was likely because there was something about the emptiness and warmth that reminded him of his childhood; while his memories of the first decade of his life were scant, he found that he could more readily recall the general feelings he felt during those years in this area.

If Gavin and Jasiela were around, he hoped that they were feeling that same sense of peace.

"Oh! Excuse me, kind sir!" Hunter waved down a burly man walking in the opposite direction, his blond hair short. Based on the way he was dressed– a simple white t-shirt and dark blue overalls– it wouldn't have been a surprise to learn he was heading to the Restoration Effort's warehouse. "Have you, by chance, seen a couple of teenagers with a peculiar aura in this area?"

This made the man squint. "Teenagers? In this area? That alone would make 'em kinda peculiar, don't ya think?"

The guy had a point. "I suppose so," Hunter agreed.

"Why don't you tell me what these kids look like, and that'd help a little more, especially if I mistook 'em for adults."

"Right– and given that they're around... sixteen or seventeen years old, I suppose that would be quite possible," Hunter nodded. "There are two of them, a boy and girl. The girl is a brunette, very small, with skin the color of the sands right outside our fair city. The boy is a brunet as well, and speaks with a particular accent. It would strike you as unusual if you were to hear it."

The man was thinking about it now. "Nah, I think I'd remember seeing and hearing a pair like that, but I got nothing."

"I see. Apologies for interrupting you, then," Hunter replied. "Enjoy the rest of your day."

Hunter was now near the very small entertainment section of this district. It housed a bar, a sporting area, and a theater. As could be expected, these were mostly frequented by the people who worked in the area, hoping to grab a bite to eat or entertain themselves after a hard shift at work. Although he'd never eaten at the bar, Hunter recalled that it supposedly had amazing burgers.

"Listen, I already told you, I can't accept your foreign money," he heard the person at the theater's box office saying. "You can head over to the currency exchange building about 20 minutes north of here and then come back."

"This is ridiculous. Why can't you just go there at the end of the day and exchange the money, since you know where it is?" That was a girl's voice.

"How stupid do you think I am?! You give me a fraction of the money for admission, and I wouldn't know until you're already long gone! Plus, do you really think I get paid enough to be doing extra tasks for this damn company?"

"No, no, he's right– our apologies, sir. Sorry to have bothered you."

Hunter recognized that voice; and picked up his pace to make it before his target was on the move yet again. "Gavin, Jasiela!" he called.

This confused the two, both turning around hesitantly. The confusion persisted until Hunter rounded a corner, clearly winded. "I... I've been searching for... apologies, I'll need to catch my breath first."

"Hunter! Where the hell are we?" Jasiela asked him. "Is this really Compositora? The desert areas look familiar enough, but I don't remember any of these buildings being around. Still, finding Gavin and then you– we can't be anywhere else, could we?"

"Indeed," Gavin agreed. "What exactly is going on?"

Putting a hand up to indicate he'd need just a few seconds more, Hunter took a final deep breath before standing up straight. "Thank you. That was embarrassing. I will try to answer your inquiries to the best of my abilities, as usual: yes, this is Compositora, but the reason you do not recognize these buildings is because we currently stand in an area of the town that did not exist eight months ago when you were last here. This is the industrial district, which is responsible for most of– if not all– the development you will see as you wander about the town. If I may interject a question of my own: are you two alone?"

Jasiela and Gavin exchanged a look. "Alone?" she asked.

"Oh, I think he's asking if anyone else was brought here with us," Gavin realized. "I don't think we can be quite sure of that just yet, Hunter. I only managed to find Jasiela because she happened to be on a bus that only narrowly missed hitting me. It wouldn't be surprising if we weren't alone in our arrival, though."

"I'd be more concerned if we were," added Jasiela. "It'll be nice to see everyone again!"

Hunter nodded. "I see. Although I feel I know the answer already, I feel I must still formally ask, so as not to purport that I intend to take advantage of your good graces: will you be cohabiting with myself and the rest of the Resistance during your time here?"

"Dude, why would we not?" Jasiela asked, laughing. "You've always been good people to us. And you guys will know your way around too, so it benefits us 'cause that way we don't get lost. So. Where we headed?"

"Oh, thank goodness," Hunter sighed in relief, turning back the way he'd come. "Follow me. We have to circle back and retrieve our captain, and after that, we will likely return home to discuss everything further."

"Everything? You mean, why we're here," Gavin asked.

"Indeed."

***

Another productive day in classes meant that Logan and Arrigan would likely stop for a bite to eat before beginning the walk home; and, indeed, after getting far enough out of the building, Logan paused to take in all of the complex and delectable aromas floating from all of the food stalls. This was something that he was sure he'd never tire of.

"What's on the menu today?" he asked as the boys walked. "I wonder if that one stall is cooking again today. I wouldn't object to more of those pierogies."

"Pierogi is already plural. The singular form is pierog, it–" Arrigan stopped himself. "Sorry."

Logan waved a hand. "No apologies. I made a mistake, and you corrected me. Would you not expect the same from me if we were speaking Portuguese?"

"I... guess you have a point," Arrigan reluctantly agreed. "Sorry. I just get worried about sounding too mean."

"Not mean. You're the authority here," Logan reminded him. "Also, you apologized again."

Before Arrigan could reflexively apologize for apologizing again, Logan was already on his way to a stall with baked goods. He hurried to catch up, for the goods on display did indeed look delicious. Seeing them up close would only make them look even better, he was sure. And by the time he got close enough for Logan to see he was there, he had already fixed his sights on one of the tarts being offered.

"Are these the winter buns? Oh! I had no idea those were still in season. Can I have five of those, please? And, uh, one of the apple turnovers. Oh! And the– what did you want, Arrigan?"

"Could I have the..." Arrigan trailed off, his attention being directed to the scene behind the stand, it causing him to tilt his head just a bit sideways.

Logan turned to him. "Is everything all right?"

"What? Oh, the– um, egg tart, please. Sorry, I was distracted by the scene back there, that group of people. I've never seen such a distinctive style of dress, not even back home," explained Arrigan.

"Really?" Always one to be intrigued by eccentric styles, Logan looked in the direction he'd seen Arrigan look in. "Can you take care of the tab this time? I'll be right back."

"Oh– uh, sure, I guess," Arrigan replied, unable to get the full sentence out before Logan had wandered off. He bashfully turned to the person running the stall and said, "Sorry about that. I'll pay for everything the dark-haired man that just ran off asked for, and one egg tart."

Meanwhile, Logan walked observantly, hoping to find the group of people that Arrigan had seen. He was starting to get a little disappointed in how typically everyone in the square was dressed, but when he rounded the side of the fountain to the left of where he was, his eyes lit up, and he ran as fast as his legs would carry him, hoping he could catch up to the group of people– this group of people he now recognized– before they decided to move.

"...so that, if it turns out that no one here can get a grasp on the overall geography of this place because it's changed so much, at the very least we'll have located a place to stay for the night before the sun sets. That way, if the entire day passes before we can find any of the places you remember, we can try again tomorrow with a fresh– why is there a man running toward us?"

Six heads whipped around just as Logan came into earshot, waving as he approached the table they had congregated at.

"Hey! Hey, I wanted to be certain I got here before you started moving," he explained, taking a breath. "It's been a while!"

Immediately, Brecken (who was standing the closest to him) recognized his voice. "Oh, Logan!" she replied. "It's so good to see you again!"

"You sure did decide to change your look, huh?" Jaiden asked.

Logan shrugged sheepishly. "It turns out I accidentally cut my hair a few times during that larger fracas we had some time ago. I couldn't quite get it even myself, so I decided to just have most of it cut off when I visited my parents last. And it is certainly good to see you all as well, Brecken, Jaiden, all of you! But I notice this crowd is slightly different than I recall it being when last we all met. Are we not missing one... or two people here?"

This made everyone laugh. "The dynamics of the group are a little different at this point, yeah," Madeline agreed.

Before she could start, though, Arrigan had finally caught up to Logan, his hands full with the bag of bread and pastries Logan had ordered at the stand. "Logan, was there any reason you needed to buy all of this stuff? Will we even be able to eat all of this before it goes bad?"

"Ah." Logan smiled then. "Something tells me that we won't have to worry about that at all, with what I've just learned! Everyone, we have a change in dynamics on this end as well. This is my dear friend, Arrigan Navarrete; he lives with me, my sister, and Thunder and Hunter as he attends Compositora's university. It's a long story that probably sounds better on his end, if you want to hear it as we start on the way home."

"Sure!" Madeline was the first to approach Arrigan, holding out her hand to shake before realizing he couldn't because of the large bag he was holding. "Ope, sorry about that. Don't worry about it! So, Navarrete– that's a Spanish last name, I'm assuming your family is some kinda Hispanic descendant?"

"Yes, it–" Arrigan stopped when he almost dropped the bag. "My father's side of the family, yes. I'm impressed you know that."

"As it turns out, same hat," Madeline replied. "I think we are gonna get along great!"

Meanwhile, Logan had decided there was another matter he wanted to get to the bottom of, as he walked beside Spencer-Lynn.

"I see I'm not the only one here who decided they wanted to get a new look, hm?"

"Oh! Um, I suppose not," she replied, clearly startled, and smiling nervously. "It's... something that I'd been debating for a while, but didn't really commit to until months ago. There's reasons behind it, but I'd feel more comfortable giving them whilst I'm sitting– and not within mixed company."

Logan nodded, immediately understanding what she meant. "Indeed. In any case, it was a good call; you look positively radiant."

"Do I?" Spencer-Lynn blushed ever so slightly. "Well, you, um... you don't look so bad yourself."

"So who is this gentleman, then?"

Both the young adults jumped at the sound of a third voice, but relaxed when they saw who it was. Spencer-Lynn explained: "This is Logan. When I told you the story of the witch and the zombies– sorry, the holzomen– he was the one who assisted us most when it came to understanding this place's history and customs, and had plenty of combat tutelage as well; arguably one of the most useful people in the operation, if not *the* most useful. Logan, this is Maceida. She shares the unfortunate fate of having the same parents as I do."

"Oh! It is a pleasure to meet you!" Logan's smile practically radiated sunshine as he shook Maceida's hand. "I noticed you, of course, but didn't quite know how to ask who you were; that being said, I could tell there was a reason you were already so comfortable with the group. Now I know why!"

"I think 'comfortable' is being a wee bit generous," Maceida replied. "But I have no reason to be on high guard, at the very least.

Spence has always been very discerning when it comes to the people she keeps company with. If she's determined you can be trusted, I have no reason to argue."

The group had now reached the block that Thunder's house was on, the lines of houses feeling foreign but fitting at the same time. The sparse grass gently blew in the wind as they walked along, footsteps echoing upon the brick pavement.

"Wait, so you guys live in an actual house now," Jaiden noted.

"Most people do. We still have our HQ, but one can only live underground for so long without feeling the adverse effects of vitamin D deficiency," Logan laughed. "We're the larger house over here. I'm sure everyone will love to see you again."

***

"We're home!" Logan called, the moment his foot crossed the threshold into the house. "I bought bread! And some sweets, too!"

"Good, I was planning on making soup tonight; we can have the bread with it."

The sound of approaching footsteps could be heard until the group was faced with a familiar round face and black curly hair. Upon seeing the group of new faces in the living room, though, Phoenix froze both her sentence, and in her tracks.

"Have things become this dire?" is what she finally decided to say.

"Admittedly, I hadn't even gotten to that point in my thought process," Logan admitted. "I think we should at least let everyone get settled before we begin to hash all of that out. We have enough room for everyone here, right?"

Phoenix thought about this for a moment. "We should. There are two extra bedrooms, and the basement is pretty expansive," Phoenix replied. "Hold off until the rest of the boys are back, too. They left about an hour ago; Hunter said he had something important to show Thunder, and they left before I could ask them where they were headed."

"Oh?" Logan raised an eyebrow. "Interesting. For now, everyone, feel free to have a seat here. I'm going to check the extra bedrooms and basement to be sure they are fit to host guests. Be back!"

Everyone began to sit down in the living room then, feeling relief at being able to get off their feet for the first time in a little while. "Phoenix, may I ask you a question?" Mishaela asked as she took a seat on the couch.

"Always, Mishaela," she replied. "What's on your mind?"

"It's just..." Mishaela paused. "Logan said, when we were on our way here, that this is Thunder's house. In that case, I can understand why you and Logan live here; I think I've heard both of you mention him being like a father figure to you both. And I know why Arrigan lives here with you, based on the information Logan shared when he introduced him to us. What I don't understand is, why does Hunter live here?"

Phoenix nodded. "I think the best explanation for that is because we all– Thunder, Logan, and I– just happen to really like him. He doesn't have any family he can live with..." she stopped here. "Now that I say that, I'm realizing that I don't know if it's because they're all dead, or if he's not welcome home– but, regardless of the circumstances, having no family remaining is not uncommon among Resistance members. Those in that position who don't live at HQ anymore seem to have shacked up with their friends, so Hunter is only doing the same, when you look at it that way."

"Right," Mishaela agreed. "Well, then, I'm happy he has a place to call home, amidst people who care for him."

There was a crash in the kitchen then. "Everything is fine!" Arrigan called almost immediately.

Phoenix just sighed. "I'll be back."

No sooner than she had left the room, the front door opened, and Thunder's arrival with Hunter, Gavin, and Jasiela was marked by seven faces staring back at them.

Thunder could only say, "I'm less surprised than I want to be."

***

"Where do you think we should start?"

Later, with bowls of soup and bread, everyone congregated in the living room, ready to be brought up to speed on the current situation. It was a bit of a crowded situation at this point, but not so congested that anyone was uncomfortable; it merely meant that there was a lack of seating, if nothing else.

"Well, what have we missed?" Spencer-Lynn asked. "Don't worry about recapping what we already know; I'm working on getting this one up to speed, but she already knows the gist of what's happened here before," she gestured to her sister.

Thunder turned to Logan, wordlessly asking him to pick up the exposition. "As you could probably assume from how differently everything looks around town, there's a lot going on here, these days. Of that, though, there are two large things that continue to draw our attention. They're both, uh, equally confusing. It appears that, even with all the good we've done– continue to do– for Compositora, there exists a group of people who oppose our actions and mission, and have made this obvious."

"And the newest development is that this group is led by someone we know," Thunder added. "If you all will recall, there was a battle in the square a few days before most of you got here; Brecken, Spencer-Lynn, you were present for it. This was a battle where we lost both civilians and some of our own; and of that latter group was the partner of this man. It has fueled him with such a hatred that... I can't say it's completely out of left field, but it is still complicated nonetheless."

"Because of the mixed emotions that come with knowing some-one who you were friends with– or at least worked with– turned on you?" asked Jasiela.

The room became silent then.

"I believe the situation may be even more complicated still," Hunter replied.

"It definitely is," Thunder added. "That's a part of it, yes. And I don't condone Flavian's actions up to this point, but as a person who's been through the pain of losing the person I loved most in this world, I understand where he's coming from. And it's because of that, that it makes it hard to decide what to do in response to all of the trouble he's causing."

Hunter raised his hand. "That and the other issue."

That made everyone turn to him. "Other issue?" Brecken asked.

"Yeah, at the same time this is happening, there have been very odd things happening with our world itself," Phoenix replied. "It's difficult to describe if you haven't seen it yourself yet, but there have been these strange distortions appearing at random, and not just in Compositora– apparently, everywhere around our world. The best way I can describe it is that, for a few seconds at a time, you'll be able to see something that's starkly out of place– usually sparkly– and you will feel affected physically by it as well; we've heard everything from dizziness to fainting. At this point, we're still struggling to figure out what is causing these occurrences, and what they mean."

There was a silence, as if everyone was taking everything in.

"This is the first time we've been here that there's been two things going on at once, isn't it?" Mishaela was the first to say.

"Yeah! And not only that, but two things that are complicated! We're really gonna have to thunk our heads together to come up with a solution to this one, huh?" Madeline asked. "But at the same time, it doesn't sound like that would be impossible to do. I mean, look at us! This is the most people we've ever had working together, so we've got a bunch of bright minds all together here!"

"Gotta love that optimism of yours, Madeline," Thunder replied with a smile. "But since we do have such a large group this time, maybe that's to our benefit. Boys, why don't you take some of these kids out so they can see what a mess Flavian and his crew have been makin' firsthand, and Phoenix and I will stay here to work on the other issue."

"A capital idea," agreed Hunter. "Everyone, divide yourselves into two groups, and Logan and I will be on our way with one of them."

Industrial Revolution

During this current walk through the streets of Compositora, somehow, the air felt thicker and more pointed than it usually was. The closest it could be likened to was that electric day in which the Resistance had first met Spencer-Lynn, but even that had been different. That had been electric in a physical, trembling way. This current atmosphere was electric as well, but in a way that felt much more hostile.

"I feel like I'm being stared at," Madeline said softly. "More than usual, even. Is this how things are here now?"

It was a quieter day in the city, likely because it was midday, and one of the chillier days as well. Not so chilly that it would require the layers of a Midwest winter, but the wind blew with more bite than usual.

"Unfortunately, it seems that everyone has been more guarded ever since that whole anti-Resistance outfit began causing trouble," Logan replied. "Regardless of whether or not one agrees with them, they can be a nuisance, especially when it comes to their rallies. That's usually when stuff starts getting broken."

"If it's that much of a nuisance, why don't you guys do anything to stop them?" Jasiela asked.

Hunter raised a hand. "I can answer that. The situation ensnares us in something of a paradox, you see. Since its inception, the Resistance has stood for– among other things– the ability to live freely according to one's own moral code. If we were to directly oppose this group, who appears to stand for the same, what message would that send to the rest of the citizens of Compositora?"

There was a silence then. The situation, admittedly, was complicated.

"So then, where do we go from here?" Gavin asked. "Although I suspect that that's the question you've all been asking yourselves these days."

"It is. And it's one we haven't gotten far on answering just yet," Logan replied. "Part of it is because of the aforementioned nuances, but it's also that there are multiple pressing issues at this present time. There's the rebuilding effort, the reforestation effort, the extension of the educational system–"

"Logan?" A voice called.

"There's more, I promise," he continued, waving a hand, before turning to the source of the voice. He allowed his gaze to extend until his eyes settled on a familiar figure: a woman with olive skin and wavy dark brown hair, wearing a long blue and green dress with a matching scarf to– presumably– protect her skin from the sun. When she drew closer, she saluted everyone in the group with a wave.

"I'm sorry for calling you from so far away, but I had to catch your attention before I ended up losing you. For better or worse, I think we are all familiar with how easy it is to lose sight of someone within the stands. Actually, I saw you in the square a few days ago and tried to get your attention then, but everything became so frenzied after so long that it was more wise for me to return home and wait until I saw you again."

Logan nodded. "Everyone, this is Kaveri; she is one of the citizens here that we helped during the flooding battle in the square. What seems to be the matter? There is urgency within your voice."

Kaveri nodded. "Actually... I would feel a lot more safe if we were to discuss this within my home, if that's all right. It's not very far from here."

"Of course– as long as everybody here is okay with that?" Logan asked, turning back to everyone. When there was no dissent, he nodded. "Lead the way."

***

The degradation of the older buildings in the square came into more obvious view when the group entered Kaveri's home. The floors, which were constructed with dark wooden planks, were decorated with intermittent holes and cracks. The wallpaper on the walls– which once may have been a lovely, bright floral print– was dingy and peeling, and even the ceilings didn't seem completely stable. The furniture inside had certainly seen better days, as well.

However, none of this seemed to dampen the sunny disposition of the young girl sitting on the couch, in her sunny yellow short-sleeved dress, grinning and kicking her legs as she realized that there were visitors in the house.

Logan was the first to notice her, and gave her a warm smile back. "It's lovely to see you again, Inaya, and in such high spirits! You've been recovering remarkably."

She gasped. "Logan!" she responded, reaching out for a hug.

As the two hugged, Spencer-Lynn kneeled beside them. "You're the little wein we saved in the square," she realized now that she was closer. "I thought so, but I wasn't certain until I got closer. I'm glad you're all right."

"I'm a what?" Inaya asked, looking adorably confused.

"Oh, a…" Spencer-Lynn paused. Remarkably, this was somehow the first time anyone had asked her to explain something she'd said. "Wein. A 'wee one,' a small person..?"

"This is Spencer-Lynn. She looks different now, but she's the woman who helped me make sure you and your mother got home safe on that day, remember?"

"I remember!" Inaya smiled. "Thank you for making sure me and my mama were safe!"

Spencer-Lynn smiled back. "It was my pleasure, and what anyone else would've done, I'm sure."

It was then that Kaveri returned with a pitcher of ice water and multiple glasses for the guests. "Thank you for accommodating me on such short notice. I wouldn't ordinarily impose like this, but there's the… subject matter."

Her eyes, then, fell to her young daughter. She didn't say as much, but it was clear: they would be discussing subjects not suitable for young ears.

"Don't worry, I got this," Jasiela said then, immediately picking up on what was happening. She sat beside Inaya and said, "Hi there! I'm Jasiela. What's your name?"

"Inaya! I'm seven years old!" she replied proudly.

"Wow, that's so cool! I'm new to this town, Inaya. Could you show me around? I think your mom would be okay with that," Jasiela replied.

When it looked like Kaveri was going to object to the idea, Logan quickly interjected, "They won't wander too far. Jasiela is quite familiar with caring for young children, so she is aware of the amount of care that must go into watching over them."

"She's probably the best person out of all of us to be looking after a kid, really," Jaiden continued to reassure her.

"And if that does not assuage your very justified concerns, I will accompany the two young ones," Hunter volunteered, standing. "This way, in addition to having a chaperone that is adept at childcare, you will also have one that is knowledgeable about the city."

This was what made Kaveri agree to the idea, as she gave the trio a hesitant nod. "Be on your best behavior, Inaya. I don't want to hear that you caused any trouble for our friends here."

"Okay!" she agreed as they headed out of the door.

When the three had left the room, Kaveri turned back to her guests. "Now, what was so important that we needed to be indoors for it?" Logan asked her almost immediately after the door had shut.

"It is a concern for the way our town has been changing," Kaveri replied, her voice indicating that these changes were ones that she was not comfortable with. "Such changes are impossible to ignore if one spends enough time in the city center, which is easy for me to do, living in the area. I must stress that I do not feel totally unsafe in the area, but even so... I cannot say that I feel completely safe here, either, and it is almost completely because of that band of hooligans that's seemed to make this area their base. How has it come to this? How have we allowed our once great city to fall so far?"

"Well, we..." Logan paused, struggling to be as eloquent as Hunter had been when he'd explained the complexity of the situation. "There isn't a whole lot we can do as it is–"

"Nothing you can do? Are you not the same group that managed to save our home from a horde of seemingly insurmountable undead creatures? The ones that, after years, were able to free us from a decades-long oppressive regime? And a group of wayward delinquents is where you draw the line?!"

Logan took a few breaths then, not fond of being borderline yelled at over this, but knowing he had to be calm in this situation. "When I say there's nothing we can do, I don't mean that in a physical way. I'm sure many people would be overjoyed to find out the Resistance has finally put down the threat to peace here, but I think we are all also acutely aware of what that would look like in a place where it wasn't very long ago that we *did* experience problems with a dictator. We must be careful to not go down that path again, or even appear to be going down that path again, which means affording people their right to voice contrary opinions."

Kaveri sighed. "Yes, but that aside, I didn't ask you here just to complain. My main motivation is what I saw yesterday, on my way home from grocery shopping. As you may be aware, occasionally there will be people in the square working on the fountain, so that it can be turned on again someday, hopefully soon. Yesterday was the first day that group has actively gone into the fountain to– I think– repair its plumbing and structure, and it was then that I could see one of those hooded hooligans approach them, and begin arguing with one of the maintenance crew."

"Does the fountain hold any cultural significance here?" Spencer-Lynn asked. "It seems a wee bit strange that this, of all things, would be something they'd pick a bone about."

"There is some historical significance, but I think they'd be more incensed by the fact that the maintenance team is routinely assisted by a member of the Resistance," Logan explained. "Handel has been very hands-on with the whole process, because he was the head of the team that, ultimately, stopped the flooding during the battle in the square. What became of the argument, Kaveri?"

"After the two groups exchanged words for the better part of five minutes, the maintenance team ended up leaving the area. Once they had completely vacated the area, the one that started the argument walked off and began speaking to a person who... I know it is not wise to make judgments of others based on their appearance, but this person seemed the type to almost definitely be affiliated with the underworld."

A stunned silence overtook the room. "Underworld?" Madeline repeated.

Kaveri explained, "For years, there have been rumors of a society that lives underneath our own. These have been merely rumors because no one has ever been able to find significant evidence of their dwellings or their society at all. It is not unheard of to have buildings that extend underground, but these rumors suggest that these people live completely underground, never having to be seen above ground if there's no explicit need."

"I've never heard of this," Logan said then. "Please excuse my ignorance as someone not native to Compositora. Could you explain further why this could potentially be a bad thing?"

"The existence of an underground society, in itself, is not necessarily a bad thing; but, these rumors have always been intertwined with those that there were a litany of indecent dealings happening under our feet. Rumors of stolen valuables, a black market, those kinds of things. In this town, these stories are told in a way that an adult would give them as much thought as the other stories they were told as a child to keep them obedient. To think that they may have been true all along... the thought is unsettling enough to send a chill up my spine."

"Yeah, I could see how that would give somebody the heebie-jeebies," Madeline agreed. "So what do we do from here, then?"

Logan shrugged, being thrown off because of this new information. "Entertaining all ideas from here."

"Hmm. So we have a group of troublemakers, actively making trouble, who could possibly be affiliated with a different group of troublemakers who haven't caused any trouble yet– potential troublemakers, I guess," Jaiden tried to summarize the current situation as best she could. "I know you said the Resistance is preferring to stay neutral when it comes to that first group, Logan, but aren't they directly interfering with you guys' work at this point?"

"Yeah, if nothing else, you guys are probably gonna have to give them some words about leaving the fountain alone," added Madeline. "But at the same time, I don't see that going over without some kind of fight if they really have that much animosity for the Resistance."

"If I may ask a potentially redundant question," Kaveri said then. "Have you all not had a chance to converse with one another regarding your differences and why this group suddenly has such a level of disdain for the Resistance? It's never made any sense. My husband and I cannot wrap our heads around why anyone would hate the people who have done so much good for us and all the other people here."

Logan shook his head. "Not for lack of wanting to. This comes up a lot in our meetings; that we'd be more than happy to discuss any differences we have with these guys, but they haven't been open to it at all. Also, because of recent developments, I personally believe they never *will* be open to it."

"Can't we just bonk some sense into 'em?" Madeline asked, a touch of exasperation in her voice.

"I think it would be most wise to consult with Thunder before we make any major decisions," Gavin suggested. "He's always urging all of us to not endanger ourselves, so if the rumors about this underworld are true, that sounds like something we would need to plan more extensively for."

"Right, that makes sense," agreed Spencer-Lynn. "Then I suppose we'll be on our way when Jasiela and Hunter come back."

With the agreement to wait for any further decisions, everyone went back to sitting silently, occasionally drinking their water, or observing the decor in the house.

"By the way, is your husband well?" Logan asked, turning to Kaveri. "I've only met him once, but I recall he had been wounded in the battle in the square and was not quite ambulatory at the time."

Kaveri smiled at the mention of her husband. "While he will likely not regain the ability to walk as freely as the rest of us do, he has been able to find work with the Compositora Restoration Effort that does not require him to stand; he assists with the magic needed to create the bricks for our streets and sidewalks. He says it's an enjoyable line of work, knowing he's contributing to the beautification of our city; and that the man in charge of everything there seems to be very passionate about that mission."

"He is. That man is a former member of the Resistance– my personal feelings about him aside, it can be argued that anyone that has ever been a part of our ranks probably has a certain level of love and devotion to this fair city, even those of us who don't originally hail from here. And he's– they're all– doing such good work," Logan smiled then.

The door opened then, signaling the return of one man and his two young charges. "We're back!" Jasiela announced. "And all in one piece!"

Indeed, Hunter and Inaya both were holding large pretzels, both looking particularly satisfied. "Shall we be on our way, or do you require more time?" Hunter asked, taking a look around the room, as if to see if he could find the answer to that question by the look on everyone's faces.

"I think that'll do," Logan replied as he stood. "Thank you for sharing your knowledge with us, and inviting us into your home, Kaveri."

"It's like I always tell you, Logan– nothing will ever be enough after you potentially saved my daughter's life," she replied. "Get home safe, all of you."

"Bye!" Inaya waved, her mouth half full with the pretzel she was eating.

Logan laughed and waved back as he ushered everyone out of the door, before following behind himself.

The Underworld

As soon as the group that had left the house arrived back home, Logan wasted no time in addressing everyone: "All right. So we found a lot of stuff out, and now we need to decide how we're going to use it all."

This was a statement that everyone could agree with.

"It should have been obvious that a place like this would have a whole underworld, but hearing of it so plainly is still a wee bit shocking," Spencer-Lynn was the first to say. "As if yousins didn't already have your hands full with the people causing the ruckus in the city and the weird magical things happening, you've got this potentially waiting under the surface as well."

"Do you think they're connected?" Arrigan asked then.

Thunder turned to him. "All of it?"

"Maybe not all of it. I'm still struggling to understand where the fissures fit into it all, if this truly is the case, but..." Arrigan paused to think. "I don't believe it's too farfetched to think that the underworld may have something to do with the sudden uptick in disturbances, especially when you consider that they've gotten progressively more violent."

"If that's true, how would we go about proving it, though?" Logan asked. "And even more so, would it be worth it to? It's a good hypothesis, one that makes a lot of sense, but in order to do anything with it, that would require us to encounter those supposed members of the underworld. That is a step that we'd have to seriously consider if it's worth it– especially considering that our manpower is not what it used to be."

At the mention of the Resistance being smaller than it once was, there seemed to be a collective sigh among its members.

"At the same time... would it be possible to ignore the possibility of the alleged underworld affiliation?" Phoenix asked then. "If they're as dangerous as we're led to believe, wouldn't that mean it'd be even worse to be ambushed by them in any way? We don't want to be going about our business just to be caught off guard by anyone, but I also don't think it would be wise to completely ignore it. I guess the question is, then, how to not completely disregard the idea while also not devoting too much manpower to it."

"The good thing is that you guys have a few extra hands here now!" Jasiela pointed out. "And I would imagine that's why we're here again. We can help you guys... somehow, I guess."

Gavin turned to her. "But how, exactly?"

"We don't want to put you all in harm's way, but on some level, all of our predicaments have the capacity to be dangerous," Hunter said then. "While I do not doubt that all of you would be willing to assist us to the best of your ability, to ask you to– again– put your lives on the line personally makes me feel ill. It would simply not be right."

Logan appeared to be about to say something, but shut his mouth, deciding to keep it to himself.

"Well..." Thunder stood up with a grunt of effort. "It's been a long day for just about all of us. I think the best thing we can do right about now is get some rest. We can continue hashin' this out when we've slept and eaten breakfast and all that– and not a moment sooner, y'all hear me?"

Scattered assent echoed around the living room.

"When everyone's ready, I can show you all to the available rooms," added Logan. "There's one room up here, and the rest are in the basement. Section off as you wish; the room up here is warmer, if that will sway any of your opinions. You may wish to give some thought as to who will be residing with whom for your stay."

With that last sentence, Madeline turned to everyone. "Well? You guys know I'm okay with shacking up with whoever needs a roomie, but the rest of you guys probably wanna put more thought into it, especially those with siblings or best friends or people we've otherwise become incredibly emotionally attached to."

"Can we get the grand tour while we decide, Logan?" Mishaela asked.

In response, the man in question stood. "Of course. If you'll all follow me, I will be happy to show you all around."

***

"Are you doing all right, or have you been overloaded at this point?" Spencer-Lynn asked her sister, as she held out a glass of water. "Rest assured that it'd be perfectly normal, if you were."

Maceida hesitated before taking the water, giving it one small sip before deciding it was palatable, and gulping it down. "You're being awfully cavalier about this, aren't you."

"Eh. It's part me having been here before, and part you fortunately having a far more welcoming introduction to this place than I did," Spencer-Lynn laughed. "I know that landing here always does a number on people's brains, but at least you didn't have to fight off a horde of some of the most unsettling things you've ever seen in your life, the minute you got your wits about you."

The two were sharing a room with Brecken and Chiara, the room on the main floor of the house. At this point, it sounded as though everyone had gone to bed, or at least gone to their rooms for the remainder of the evening. The night was quiet, and a gentle, refreshing breeze was blowing through the sole window in the room, under which Brecken was seated, reading a book. There was a bathroom attached to this room, and Chiara was currently taking a shower there.

"Everyone here seems so kind," Maceida said then, placing the empty cup on the nightstand beside the bed she'd claimed. "Is that how it's always been? It almost feels too good to be true."

Spencer-Lynn had to think about this, as she sat beside her sister on the bed. "Well, if you'll recall, me being pulled into this whole ensemble wasn't the first time something like that had happened, so even then it felt as though I'd missed some things– since I had.

From what I'm told, not everyone is nice here; we just got extremely lucky, when it came to being affiliated with the most well-liked organization in this town."

"They are lovely people," Brecken piped up, not looking up from her book.

"That's something I never questioned during my time here," agreed Spencer-Lynn. "As I mentioned before, my arrival here was extremely disorienting, but I think it would have been even worse if I had been found by a different group of people. Between Thunder knowing everything there is to know about this town, Phoenix being as knowledgeable as she is about healing people, Hunter's ability to strategize, and Logan..." There was a notable shift in the conversation when she got here, "Logan, from the beginning, was always nothing but kind to me, and I appreciate him so much for it. Whether it was bringing me up to speed on the way this world works, or making sure I was all right, physically and mentally... he's just, he's sound."

"Oh, I'm certain. I can tell by your tone," Maceida said then, being acutely aware of her sister's tonal shift.

Chiara entered the room from the bathroom then, a cloud of steam escaping from the area when the door was opened. She looked incredibly cozy in the pajamas she'd grabbed from the closet in the room a few minutes prior to going into the bathroom. Judging by the grand sigh of comfort she sighed as she entered the room, she had clearly enjoyed her time in the shower.

"Nice and cozy?" Spencer-Lynn asked her.

She nodded. "It's so good to get all the sand and dust off my skin and out of my hair. I remember it being this way last time, too."

"Huh. I think that's the most words I've ever heard you say," Maceida said to her.

This, predictably, made Chiara begin to turn red. "Oh! I, um, I-I guess so..."

"Maceida." Spencer-Lynn just sighed.

"What? Oh, am I doing that thing where I talk too much again? I've been working on it! I've been quiet almost all day!"

Spencer-Lynn looked over at Brecken and Chiara, silently asking them if this was true for the time that she'd been gone. The expressions on their faces let her know that it was debatable, but most likely false.

"B-but it's not–" Chiara started. "It's not a problem. Getting to know new people means you have to learn the way they communicate, right? I can retrieve some of the courage I had here last time. At least it's not as scary here as it was back then."

"Yeah, no kidding," agreed Brecken. "I don't have to try very hard to hear the sounds of those creatures in my dreams."

"Let's not think of that when it's so close to time to dreaming once again, aye?" Spencer-Lynn suggested. "Is it not your turn in the shower, Brecken? Maybe take that time to take your mind off of such things."

Brecken stood, sitting her book aside. "Yeah, that's a good idea. See you guys in a few."

When Brecken left, Maceida noted, "So the three of you are quite close, then."

"For all three of us, it was our first time experiencing this world," Spencer-Lynn explained. "Between that and us all being a wee bit older than the ones that had been here before, I guess it's not entirely incorrect to say there's a relative closeness between us, aye. If you cannot trust anyone else in this house with your feelings about how new and disorienting being here is, Maceida, you can certainly trust Chiara and Brecken."

"How *are* you feeling, now that it's been a little while?" added Chiara.

Maceida took a moment to reflect on her feelings about the place she currently found herself in. "I can't say. There's a large part of me that refuses to accept that any of this is real; that I'm having an overly elaborate dream, or that I've hurt myself somehow and am currently in the hospital. But I don't think... I don't think that some of the circumstances would be the way they are if this were of my imagination. Regardless, I wouldn't know the first step to returning back to reality– or if I'd even want to, so I'm fine with riding this wave to see where it goes."

"That's exactly the kind of answer I'd expect you to give." Spencer-Lynn smirked at her.

"Are you calling me predictable?" Maceida asked, nudging her.

"I'm not. I'm just trying to say that it's good to have my sister back."

As Chiara watched the Cambridge sisters interact, she wondered if this was how Mishaela had felt when she herself had been brought along for the first time. In some ways, she still felt as though she'd been in the way and caused more work for the Resistance, but it really had been nice to have an opportunity to bond with her sister like that, even when things had gotten dire. This world was able to create situations that Earth never could, and as a result, the way they got to bond was just as unprecedented. Chiara would not hesitate to think– or at least hope– that she and her sister were closer for it, even with them never being far apart.

She wished upon the stars twinkling in the sky, then, that the same would happen for Spencer-Lynn and Maceida.

***

"It's still so surreal that so much has changed here."

From the window, Mishaela gazed at the streetlights shining down on the brick paths of the block. It was dark now, and from this basement bedroom, this was all that was visible at this time. The subtle shimmers of the pavement just past the grass were enough to captivate her long enough that she hadn't realized how much time had passed until Jasiela sat beside her and asked, "What's so interesting out there?"

"Huh?" Mishaela turned quickly, very clearly startled. "Oh. Please don't startle me like that, Jasiela. My poor heart cannot take it."

Jasiela gave her a look of disbelief in response. "Always so dramatic."

"To answer your question, I find myself staring at the pavement here. Especially now with the streetlights shining down on it, you can see the subtle sparkles even more; they're not so subtle anymore. It's very pretty. I wonder how they got it to do that?"

"Oh! I think I may actually know the answer to that." Jasiela put a hand under her chin. "After me and Gavin ran into each other here, we ended up at the warehouse where everybody makes all the bricks and wooden planks and everything else to build all the infrastructure here. Now, I'm no expert, but I know that– in the brief time we were there– I saw some of those people using magic to put these materials together."

"Really." Mishaela said this as a stunned statement. "I'm reminded, suddenly, of when the Resistance was telling us that the reason the palace was falling into disrepair the last time we were here was because it had been made completely with the magic of men. It would seem, then, that you still can use it in the process of building– it just has to be supplemented with other materials. This is all so fascinating!" She grinned. "Now I understand why Chiara would read all about these things well before either of us ever knew there was a magic world!"

This made Jasiela turn to her. At the moment, they were the only two in the room; neither knew what Jaiden and Madeline had gotten up to. "Do you think we could get an even more in-depth explanation about things in this world now? I mean, we *are* practically experts on how all this works by now."

Mishaela gasped. "You're right! We should ask tomorrow! It's going to be so difficult to sleep now, I'm so excited!"

"Don't get too excited, or else you'll be so tired you won't remember to ask," Jasiela pointed out as she began to walk away. "There's nothing like a good night's sleep, right?"

"Right! That way, my brain will be nice and primed for new information!"

In her bed on the other side of the room, Jasiela smirked. She wouldn't ever let it show, but the idea of learning more about how magic worked excited her just as much as it did Mishaela. Well... *almost* just as much.

***

The next morning, it rained.

"Wait, I think this is the first time I've seen it rain here," Jasiela said to Mishaela as they both got dressed for the day; Jaiden had already left the room, and Madeline was curled up in her bed, sleeping. They both knew it would be a while before she woke up. "I mean, I guess it makes sense since this is desert land, but you never know if magic will subvert things like that, you know? Even so, seeing it rain feels weird."

"It does, doesn't it?" agreed Mishaela. "It almost feels wrong in a way."

Opening the door, both were able to hear the unmistakable clatter of plates, bowls, and cutlery. There was a certain aroma very vaguely wafting from the upper levels, but neither of the girls were able to distinguish what exactly it was; it was not a familiar breakfast scent. This was exciting in a way, discovering a new type of breakfast.

Meanwhile, upstairs, Jaiden had volunteered to help with breakfast, so she was busy giving Hunter a hand with that as Logan, and Arrigan set the table. There would almost definitely not be enough room for everyone to sit at the table, so they would have to be creative with ensuring everyone would have a comfortable place to sit and eat. It was doable; after all, they'd had more difficult tasks than this.

"Has it been a big adjustment, going from headquarters to an actual house?" Jaiden asked.

Hunter glanced up briefly, before placing the bowl he had been holding on the counter. "Indeed it has. I do believe it is a positive, overall, for many reasons; but it is very different to be so much closer to the heart of the city, and to have actual streets, roads, streetlights. It almost reminds me of–" he abruptly stopped himself here, turning to the refrigerator to open it.

"Reminds you of..?" Jaiden asked, noticing the omission.

"It is of no importance. My apologies." Hunter shut the door then, placing the items he'd grabbed on the counter: butter, what looked to be some type of spread, and two cartons of eggs. "Do you think two dozen eggs is enough? Would it be more proactive to go to the market for more, just in case?"

Whatever the topic had been, it was clearly something that he didn't want to continue talking about. Jaiden was mature enough to recognize that. "It should be enough, right? After all, there will be other things to eat, right? You might have needed more if we were eating *just* eggs, but that doesn't seem like a very good breakfast at all."

Hunter smiled, then, clearly amused by the thought. "You are correct once again, Jaiden. The more I am able to converse with you, the more I am able to understand why you were the one the goddesses chose to give their blessing, the first time you visited us here."

"Oh. Yeah, that did happen, didn't it." Jaiden was clearly a bit flustered at this level of praise. "I mean, I didn't forget. It's just, since the most instrumental person in that plan was Mishaela, it never really felt that important, you know? And no disrespect meant there, either– I think we'd probably have used the blessing to our advantage if we'd known it existed. Why do you think Thunder and company never mentioned something like that, anyway? It would've made things *so* much easier."

Hunter closed his eyes for a brief moment, before picking up a whisk. "I cannot say for certain, because while this was all transpiring, I was still confined to my librarian post; however, just knowing my companions in the Resistance, I do think the only person who would have ever considered the blessing would be Logan, to start. And even then, this thought probably did not cross his mind still because... well, when you think about it, would it not be rather odd to obtain the assistance of those from a world not of magic, and then consider the possibility of them having capabilities pertaining to our own world? It would make one wonder why we'd go to the effort, for one."

Jaiden nodded. "That does make sense."

"Even with this being the case, though, I am certain you are aware of how rare it is for the goddesses to bestow such a privilege upon anyone, even those of this world," Hunter added. "You are a fortunate girl, indeed."

There it was, again. "Not a girl," Jaiden said under her breath, only slightly exasperated. She knew she couldn't hold this against Hunter, but the frequency with which this happened in her life made this just slightly annoying even when the person did have the best intentions.

"Oh? Have I made a mistake?" Hunter asked, raising his brow. "My deepest apologies. I merely assumed, but I won't anymore; thank you for correcting me."

"What?" Jaiden asked, amazed he'd even heard. "So you– you're not gonna argue with me about it? I haven't even explained the concept of being non-binary to you yet."

This only made Hunter confused, judging by his facial expression. "Who would I be, to argue one's gender with them? Why would I ever think I know that more than the person who possesses it? And, furthermore, I am even more confused at– do you find yourself often having to explain the concept of existing outside the gender binary in your daily life? This is not... I cannot speak for this entire world, but we are relatively familiar with the idea here in Compositora; if you will recall the last time you were here, Threnhette was also not a woman."

It had been such a tense situation that Jaiden hadn't given it a lot of thought, but yeah– there had even been a time where Hunter had referred to them as "she," and Thunder had corrected him. How had she forgotten about that?

"You're right. I didn't think about it too much; too busy concentrating on all the fighting and temporary magic powers and getting back home and all," admitted Jaiden. "So, yeah. She or they pronouns are fine, but just don't call me a girl, it feels gross. There's enough girls here for that, right?"

"Indeed." Hunter picked the bowl and whisk back up. "Perhaps, if we are ever able to converse during a time where things are not dire, I'd hope to hear your thought processes about the gender binary, and how you came to realize you did not exist within it; not in an attempt to debate, but... to understand how closely they align with my own thoughts about it."

"Oh!" This took Jaiden by surprise. "Sure, Hunter. Gender is a mess, so if I can help somebody figure out where they fit in it all, I'd be glad to. Now, what's that you've been whisking for like ten minutes now?"

Hunter laughed, being caught off guard. "Phoenix taught me that the best way to get silken, flavorful scrambled eggs is to whisk together a sprinkle of milk and a scoop of this cheese–" he lifted the container that had looked like a spread– "and a dash of assorted spices of the chef's choice, before finally adding the eggs. However, getting the cheese to the desired consistency requires a level of arm strength that I am afraid I do not quite possess."

"What, is that all? Hand it over," Jaiden held out a hand. "You can focus on something else while I do this."

***

Phoenix was in her room, lying on her back, staring up at the ceiling when a knock sounded on her door; she didn't move, and this was enough for a second, smaller knock before the door slowly opened and Logan's head peeked through the crack.

"I was going to tell you that breakfast will be ready soon, but then I realized you'd know that," he explained. "Can I come in?"

She glanced at him before her gaze returned to the ceiling. "If I say no, I know you're just going to come in anyway."

"That I will!" Logan chuckled as he came in and shut the door behind himself. "Is everything all right? To be in bed so late, and not even getting up to see what's cooking when you can start catching its scent, is very unlike you."

"It is, isn't it?" Phoenix agreed. "Sorry if I worried you. There's been a lot on my mind since I woke up a few hours ago."

"I see." Logan nodded, taking a seat in the chair opposite Phoenix's bed. "Would you care to talk about it?"

Phoenix sat up then, so that her conversation with Logan would feel more open and collaborative; she couldn't stand feeling like she was about to dump a pile of emotions on her younger brother, of all people, but she also knew that she should give him more credit than that. Logan had always been very good at understanding people, and being respectful of others' feelings; these qualities didn't mean less just because he happened to be two years younger than her.

"Dad and I were able to speak a few days ago," she began. "We were able to coordinate a time to use the telephone; did you know they have them there, as well? I guess it's not really surprising, when you think about it. We were talking about everything happening here, and that's when he mentioned his parents being really frantic lately over the whole random weird fissure thing. He hasn't interacted with them enough to know if they're frantic because they don't know what's happening, or because they do and it's that bad, but neither of those inspire confidence."

"It sure does not," agreed Logan, knowing that it was much more likely to be the latter. Phoenix knew this too, but neither was brave enough to say so out loud.

"I don't know when to mention this to the captain, if I even should," Phoenix continued. "We've already got our hands so full with the whole predicament with Flavian. I know it has to be addressed eventually, but when would be the right time? How do I bring it up? It's just... it's so much, Logan. How is it that the Resistance is going through it this much after our main objective was accomplished?"

Logan sighed in agreement. "I'm no strategist, but I think we could probably at least not mention this until we've had our talk today about what we're doing about our antagonizers. When that matter appears as though it is at least arranged with a game plan, that would be the earliest time I would recommend bringing this up. That way, perhaps in the meantime we can find a way to ask our grandparents what all the fuss is about. The fact that Dad is describing them as 'frantic' worries me. That sounds very unusual of them."

"I noticed that too." Phoenix nodded, before turning to get out of her bed. "Well, if that's the plan, let's get some breakfast before it gets cold."

***

At breakfast, as one could expect, the first few minutes progressed with everyone eating and not much other noise. There was a point, though, where everyone was clearly ready to get to the matter at hand, and this was when Hunter politely raised a hand to direct everyone's attention to himself.

"Thank you, everyone. Now that we have all been able to get some rest, I believe the time has come to further discuss the predicament we find ourselves in. To summarize the current crossroads we find ourselves at: we have recently discovered that the force against us is led by a former comrade, who is harboring some resentment toward us all, particularly our leader, Thunder. We also have reason to believe this faction he leads may currently be in league with those who live in the alleged underworld, which makes the situation delicate not only because we do not know how dangerous these people may be, but because, even if we discover they are harmless, it would not bode well to see us in opposition to the poor and downtrodden of this city. After all, one of the most prevalent arguments of our opposition is that the Resistance is on its way to becoming a dictatorship; we cannot take any actions that would lend itself to that belief."

"A right pickle," Thunder concluded. "I thought about this all night, as y'all could probably assume, and there's one thing I know for sure: however we decide to approach the situation, we cannot do it with all of us at once. We're a nice sized crowd, now, enough to put anyone on edge if we approached them this way. And that's before you get into the debate of whether or not Flavian is in his right mind right now, but we can save that for a later time. Now, as for today's happenings, me and Hunter will go and poke around the area where all that shady stuff happened– Logan, you got the location, didn't you?"

"Of course." He nodded.

"Good. Now, it'd be great if one of you three young'uns could stay here, just in case anybody comes knocking, lookin' for trouble. Or help." Thunder turned to everyone else. "As for the rest of ya, as much as you've helped us before, I don't think you could be as helpful until you get used to the way this place is now. I think you should all take the day to refamiliarize yourselves with Compositora. I think you'll like some of the changes, even. My only real ask about that, is that you all stay in groups, or at least pairs. We don't want any of ya gettin' lost, you hear?"

Madeline raised her hand in a show of comprehension. "Copy!"

With everyone dispersing, Logan turned to Phoenix and Arrigan. "So, who's keeping tabs on the house today?"

"I can't. I promised that I'd check in on the fountain's progress today," Phoenix replied. "Today will be the first day that it'll be on, so I'm sure that the amount of data and concerns that Handel will bring to me will keep me busy for the better part of the day."

Arrigan turned back to Logan. "If you wanted to rest today, then, um, I'd kind of like to finally see the fountain in working order."

This made Logan smile. "Of course, Arrigan! It'll be good for you. I can't remember the last time you left the house without me– not in a bad way, of course, but I am glad to see that you feel confident enough in your ability to navigate the city, that you'd be the one to propose heading out without a local to guide you. But I do suggest you take at least one of our friends here along, just in case. It is very easy to get turned around these days."

"Of course." He nodded. "I'll ask around after I get dressed for the day; I'm sure no one would say no to rediscovering the city."

"It sounds like the two of you have that settled, then," Phoenix said as she turned toward the door. "I'll likely be gone for most of the day, but if you need me for anything, I think most of that time will be back at headquarters. Don't tear the place down, Logan," she waved, before setting off for the fountain.

In the city square, not quite as busy as usual because of the rain, Handel was waiting just in front of the fountain with a clipboard in his hand; when he saw Phoenix, he waved excitedly. "Good afternoon!" he said, before looking up at the highest point of the fountain. "It certainly is magnificent, isn't it?"

Phoenix looked up as well, at the streams of water cascading from the top tier of the fountain onto the plateau below, then falling like a waterfall to the lowest point of the fountain, the base. The walls of the base were tall enough that one had to be a fully grown adult to see the pool of water inside; because of the maintenance and cleaning, the floors of it were clean and pristine. Somehow, already, a few coins dotted the area.

"Everything seems to be going just fine," Handel said then, sifting through the pages on his clipboard. "It's been running for about an hour now, and even with the rain, there have been no signs of flooding. I do have some notes of concern, though, regarding the sound and efficiency of a structure like this; those are more so for its longevity than any immediate, pressing issue, though."

"That's good." Phoenix smiled. "I'm really glad you and the guys were able to get this thing up and running again. It really does bring a certain aura to the city, doesn't it? And it'll look even prettier on the days where the sun is out, I'm sure, and the water can refract the sun's light."

"Oh! Light! You've just reminded me of something else." Handel flipped to a page. "We found out that there are lights on this fountain, on the pillars as well as on the floor of the plateau. However, we weren't sure how to get them on and working without the water interfering somehow. We were thinking there may have been some type of magic that allowed this to be, based on how it was mentioned in the book we found it in."

"The book, which I'm assuming is at headquarters?" Phoenix asked.

Before Handel could respond, Phoenix could feel some kind of unwelcome presence behind her, and quickly moved to be able to dodge whatever was coming. Her quickness meant she was able to catch the person's arm before they could grab her.

"Quick one, huh?" they said, frustrated.

In one move that was not as graceful as she would have liked, Phoenix was able to turn and fold the person's arm behind their back. "I'd say so. Now, do you want to explain what makes you so bold as to try to grab a woman in broad daylight–"

The stranger wasted no time in hitting her in the face with a fan, but before he could take advantage of the situation, Handel had hit him with a roundhouse kick to the face, knocking him to the ground. The two wrestled for a bit as Phoenix recovered, taking a moment to cast a healing spell to relieve the pain around her nose. Once she felt normal again, and had a clear shot, she hit the stranger with a small lightning bolt, not strong enough to electrocute him but enough to stun him, for sure. Realizing his chance, Handel created a magic rope to secure his arms and legs.

"Damn it! Let me out of here!" he complained. "I thought you Resistance people were supposed to be pacifists."

"You hit me in the face!" Phoenix reminded him. "Did you expect me to just take it? Desenmerda-te, a coragem de algumas–"

"We'd be willing to let you go if you tell us what this little episode was about," Handel cut in, realizing that their assailant probably didn't understand Portuguese. "And while we are largely a pacifist organization, don't take that to mean we're pushovers."

"Oh? Threatening me?" the stranger asked, a smirk taking over his features. His face was turning red around where Handel had kicked him.

"Not threatening. Informing you that your aggression will be returned in kind."

The two men stared at each other rentensely.

"It's not like there's anything you can do about it anyway," the stranger finally said. "You'll be going up against the type of magic that us mere mortals can only dream of. You could never defend yourself against it."

Hearing that, Phoenix ran up to where the two were. "Whoa, whoa. What do you mean by that?"

A haunting laugh, then. "Even I don't know the specifics, but if I were you, I'd start reconsidering my allegiances. All I know is that, for anyone who's affiliated with the Resistance, the boss is planning on raining down a world of hurt."

"The boss." Phoenix repeated this.

"Yeah. You've probably seen him around. Average height, thin, beautiful white hair. He doesn't get into too much detail about what he's planning, so if you really wanna know what's happening you'd have to get to him. Not that that would be a very smart thing to do right about now. Now can I go?"

Handel glanced at Phoenix, who gave him a stiff nod; he then made the ropes disappear, and the man ran off toward the riverwalk.

"I don't like this at all..." Phoenix said then, as she and Handel began walking back toward headquarters. "But I guess that, if there's one positive to all of that, it's that it sounds like Flavian is working alone, as in 'not with any other dangerous groups.' That's the implication, but... how can we be sure?"

"Outside of tracking him down, I'm not so sure we could," Handel replied. "What do you think that man meant when he said, 'the type of magic that us mere mortals can only dream of?' Correct me if I'm wrong, but I don't remember Flavian's magic being particularly potent."

"No, I don't think it was," Phoenix agreed. "That's probably something we'd need to do research on. Ugh, this is a mess."

"It is." Handel looked over at her, "Are you all right, by the way? You got hit pretty hard with that fan."

"Yeah. I've taken worse," she laughed.

At this point in the walk, one would turn if they wanted to go to the residential district where Thunder's house was. Phoenix hesitated here, wondering if she should make a stop there and tell Logan about what had transpired. He'd probably have some bright ideas, as always. But, upon hearing that his sister had been in a fight- and got hit pretty badly at a point- would make him worry, and right about now, that wasn't something she was equipped to deal with. First, she needed to try and process everything that had just happened. Then she could deal with her brother's fretting over her.

With a sigh, she continued on toward headquarters.

The Runaway

Compositora's streets were already confusing for pretty much everyone because of how new they were, so it stood to reason that they would be even more confusing to people who had only recently taken their first few steps into the city at all. This was the fate that befell Arrigan and Maceida, as the two of them tried their best to navigate the maze with very little prior knowledge. Even with Arrigan's knowledge of his route to and from school, Thunder's house, and the marketplace, they found themselves lost quickly.

They did eventually make it to the marketplace, long after the rain had stopped and the sun had come out once again. This was good– the stands were usually a good landmark to keep track of where one was; being in the marketplace meant being in the center of the downtown area, and having the ability to get to pretty much anywhere else in the city. This was easier to do when Compositora was little more than a desert frontier. Now, there was so much. So many stalls and buildings and people, that it was difficult to keep track of what direction one was heading in.

As the two approached the fountain in the center of the stands, Arrigan sighed as he stopped walking. "I think I'm ready to admit we're lost."

"Oh, you've only done that just now? I accepted that about five minutes ago." Maceida hopped up onto the edge of the fountain to sit. Arrigan watched wistfully, knowing he wouldn't be able to get up that high; his options were to sit on the ground or try to shift his weight to alleviate his aching ankles, and he weighed both options for a little while before deciding on the latter.

"Really? Thanks for not rubbing it in, then."

"I would, but I don't think we've yet reached the level of friendship where I do that," she replied. "Unless you want me to? My, my, Arrigan– I had no idea you were such a masochist," she giggled.

"Ah–" Arrigan started, embarrassed. It wasn't that he minded Maceida's teasing, but he didn't think he'd ever be used to it.

The two were silent then, watching the people in the square go about their business: shopping at stalls, going in and out of buildings, exchanging hellos with acquaintances that they just so happened to run into. Now that it had stopped raining, it was a mild day, fairly breezy and just a bit hazy, so these were pleasant conditions in which to amble about.

"It really is a different world here, huh?" Arrigan said then.

"Yeah." Maceida kicked her feet from where she sat, but then realized what had just been said. "Wait a minute. I thought you were from here?"

"From this world, yes, but not from Compositora. I've only lived here for about six months," Arrigan explained. "I'd always been told that this town is different from what I'm used to, and this is one of those times that I'm noticing it myself, firsthand."

Maceida hummed softly. "Then, what's it like where you're from?"

To answer this, Arrigan gathered his thoughts. "Well, Trelana's a place that, for years now, has always prided itself on being innovative. My dad likes to tell everyone about how we were the first major city to have railroads, for example. If you were to go there now, you'd see... lots of tall buildings, steam-powered locomotives and automobiles, streamlined shopping experiences. They're currently building a... what do you call it? One of those big buildings with lots of stores and stuff inside?"

"Oh, a shopping center!" Maceida nodded.

Arrigan frowned. "I don't think that's the term my father used. Well, anyway, the point is that coming to live here has felt like falling back in time, and I can't even tell if I mean that in a positive or negative way. It's like, while it is a bit inconvenient to learn to do things manually that I've never had to, there's a certain type of... authenticity in the people who live here. As much as I love my hometown, it wouldn't exactly be incorrect to say that a lot of people who live there have an inflated sense of self because of how advanced we are. But here, it's– after interacting with people here enough, you kinda begin to understand why the Resistance is so well-liked. That level of caring for one's fellow man is something I'm not used to, but at this point, I'd hate to be without."

Maceida nodded slowly. "And I suppose that it makes it all the more strange that there's a group of people who hate the Resistance, when all they've done is help everyone."

Arrigan, initially, wanted to agree. After all, Thunder had accepted him into his home without a single complaint, and everyone there immediately had treated him like family. Logan had practically adopted him as his little brother at this point. But it wouldn't be entirely wrong to say that his experiences came from a place of privilege. Would he be able to tell the same story if he didn't have a personal connection to the Resistance's leader? The fact that he couldn't say was what kept him quiet.

"It's... more complicated than that. Isn't it?" Maceida asked then.

Arrigan looked up at her, shocked. "How did you know I was gonna say that?"

She shrugged. "Back home, I dropped out of school and will be living with my parents for a while, after about four years of being away. I told them it's 'cause I'm overwhelmed and depressed, and that is part of it. But the big picture is so complicated that I don't think I have the words to explain it all to them because they weren't there when a lot of the important parts happened– so it'd be hard to make them understand. Likewise, I wasn't here for... anything, really. So it'd be hard for you to convey things in a way I'd understand."

Over the time he had known her, Arrigan had gotten so accustomed to Maceida's playful and boisterous exterior that it was surprising to see her be so introspective. She was right, of course. Especially with how rapidly the world had changed within the past year and a half or so, how would one even begin to explain things to someone who had only known of its existence for two days?

There was a shift then, the type of shift in the air that made one's skin prickle; Arrigan turned back toward the crowd of people in the market, who seemed to suddenly be walking just a bit faster, and speaking more urgently. Everything suddenly felt more pointed and brief. He couldn't put it into words, but somehow he knew something about the atmosphere felt very, very wrong.

"Something's not right," Maceida said then, hopping down from her perch on the fountain. "The whole aura of this place has changed somehow."

Arrigan nodded wordlessly.

"Oh! I assume this is the part where we go and investigate the area, right?" asked Maceida, pointing a finger knowingly.

"You read my mind," agreed Arrigan. "Let's go. You should lead, since you're taller. I'll be right behind you; that way, I can protect you if something happens."

"Good man, good plan!" Maceida smiled, before both headed into the crowd.

***

Now, the market was buzzing with activity, so much so that before long it became difficult to keep going forward in one direction, especially when it came to Arrigan not being able to see through the crowds very well. It was as though he couldn't take five steps without accidentally bumping into someone. When this frustrated him enough that he was ready to admit it did, he called for Maceida to stop so he could catch his breath.

Both of them now knew for certain that something was very wrong.

"Can you see anything out of the ordinary?" Arrigan asked, but almost immediately realized what a futile question it was. Everything here would be out of the ordinary to Maceida, given that she'd only been here for a few days.

Indeed, she shook her head, but then added, "No, but I still know for a fact that something is amiss. What bothers me the most is how sudden the change in this was. I didn't hear anything that would cause this kind of reaction– you know, like an attack, an explosion, things like that– so what happened then?"

"I don't know. But I *really* don't like this."

Just as Arrigan turned to walk another way, he nearly collided with a girl that was just a bit shorter than him, her brown hair swishing in his face before both of them regained their footing, ready to apologize to each other. This was, of course, not to be when the two realized that they knew each other.

"Arrigan!" The girl said, pointing.

"Lisandra? What in the world are you doing in Compositora, don't you have school or something?" he asked.

Judging by the look on Lisandra's face, she'd been expecting him to say that. "I mean, yeah. I guess. But did you really expect me to just sit there when I started feeling the seriously bad vibes that are radiating from this town... again? Come on, we both know I wouldn't do that."

"So what *did* you do then, just ran off here?" Arrigan asked. "I'm going to assume, without telling your parents?" Truthfully, he had questions about those "seriously bad vibes" that could apparently be felt from so far away, but part of him felt he should get to the bottom of how Lisandra was here first; she might just end up answering his question before he could ask.

"I had to! There's no way of knowing how much time we have to figure this out," she insisted. "If I had said anything to my parents, they would've forced me to stay at home– but some things are more important than school!"

Maceida, who had been quiet until now, raised her hand. "You know, I've got to agree with the wee lass on that one: there are many things more important than school. Hi, by the way. I'm Maceida."

As Lisandra shook her hand, she stared from her to Arrigan. "Lisandra. Nice to meet you. Uh... Arrigan, have I been gone for so long that you managed to find a girlfriend?"

"No!" Both objected immediately. Arrigan quickly added, "I-it's not that she isn't a lovely lady or anything. She's great. I'm just... not really... look, I can explain later. The most important thing is that you were able to sense that something's up here all the way from another city, which means we were right to think something's wrong. I don't suppose you can follow that feeling, like a signal?"

Lisandra huffed. "No, and that's the part that sucks! I mean, I figured if something big was happening it'd most likely happen in the square, so that's why I made my way here. But now that I'm here, I don't really know what to do! What about you two, you got any bright ideas?"

The pointed, confused silence was shattered by the loud, discordant clanging of metal. It pierced the air so significantly that all three of the party's heads immediately turned in the direction it had come from. "That certainly doesn't sound good," Arrigan said softly.

"We've gotta go! Let's go!" Lisandra said, with urgency in her voice, already running into the crowd in the direction of the metallic clanging, which hadn't stopped. Arrigan seemed to be rooted in place— from either shock or fear, no one present knew— but after Maceida nudged him a few times in the correct direction, they also headed into the fray, quickly catching up with Lisandra and making their way through the confused townsfolk. When they finally emerged on the other side was when the clanging stopped, which was also when they were almost face-to-face with that angry white-haired man again.

"You see? Didn't I tell you? Didn't I tell you all that I would be a force to be reckoned with?" He was saying now, addressing the crowd. "There will soon come a time where none of you have to worry about anything anymore! And why is that? You may find yourself wondering. It is because I've finally procured the means to rid our town— maybe even our world— of a significant thorn in our collective sides!"

Some of the other members of the anti-Resistance crew stepped forward, waving, before opening the two large boxes behind them with crowbars. They revealed the source of the discordant clanging, then: trapped in large cages were none other than Hunter and Thunder.

"Oh, no..." Arrigan said softly as Lisandra gasped.

"Shit. Even I know this isn't good." Maceida turned to them. "What are we supposed to do now?"

Amidst the speech continuing, both girls turned to Arrigan. "Well, I- I don't... I don't know, actually. I wasn't prepared for— this is a mess. This is horrible. What can we... oh! We should probably let everyone else know what's happened. That is a thing we should do. At the very least, Phoenix will know what to do, right?"

"Right." Maceida nodded, beginning to walk. "Let's go ask her–"

"Maceida. Wrong way." Arrigan pointed in the direction of home, which was almost exactly the opposite of where she'd started going.

She turned around. "Right. That is *absolutely* the way back. I knew that."

"Well, I'm coming with you guys!" Lisandra volunteered, hurrying to keep pace with them. "And I won't listen to anything otherwise. You're gonna need me!"

"More so than that, the last thing we need is someone who knows you're related to important people in the Resistance scooping you up for ransom," Arrigan replied. "Come on. We gotta get back as quick as possible."

Just as Lisandra finally caught up to the two adults, Maceida noticed a figure dressed in black somewhere behind Lisandra, coming toward them. She struggled to get out the words to warn everyone, and frustrated, she settled for running into the path of the figure and extending her arm to punch them right before they would have been able to grab at the smaller girl.

"Ow! Shit!" the person complained, their hand rushing to their face; there was not any drastic damage, but the side of their face that had been struck was noticeably red, and would probably begin to swell in some time.

"What the hell is your problem?" Maceida asked, her voice shifting from her usual carefree tone into one much more serious. "There's no way you could possibly rationalize chasing after a child that doesn't make you sound like some kind of creep. What are you doing, lurking around like that?!"

When the person heard this, they chuckled, still holding their face. "Well, well. I could ask the very same thing of you."

Almost as if on cue, multiple other people similarly dressed in black clothing began to emerge from behind the trees and buildings in the area. It wasn't long before they outnumbered the Resistance trio, and the area began to feel much more sinister as they were cornered.

"Noticed the three of you snooping around the square," the first person continued, menacingly. "Now, why would you all do that? You shouldn't go around looking for answers to questions you don't quite understand, you know."

Trying his best to calm the nerves that he was sure had him shaking at this point, Arrigan responded: "This is our home. Do we not have the right to come and go as we please? I thought the era of dictatorship had ended more than a year ago."

"Quiet, wise guy!" one of the other people yelled, brandishing their machete dangerously close to Arrigan's jawline. He noticeably flinched, causing them to laugh.

This is awful. We're outnumbered. There's no way we can take on all of these people. Maceida and Lisandra will get hurt too, and there's a chance it'll be my fault, for not being strong enough to protect them. That's not fair to them at all. They're not even part of the Resistance.

A few of the strange people in black began to talk among themselves then, and just when Arrigan was about to whisper to Maceida for her to run and carry Lisandra with her, she leaned over to him, gesturing toward a slender gentleman holding some type of gun. "Hey. How well do you know guns?"

"Not very. They're still pretty new technology here– but Maceida, you have to run. I'll cover you, but you have to take Lisandra and go."

"What? No way! There's no fun or valor in that! Besides, I'm not leaving you behind."

The person with the gun turned toward them. "Hey! Pipe down!"

"You have to," Arrigan insisted. "It's okay– it is the way of things. I'm part of the Resistance now; it's my job to help protect civilians."

"I said be quiet! Don't make me come over there!"

"Yeah, well, I'm sorry– but my naval past makes it so that I feel a duty to protect others, as well," Maceida responded. "So either both of us take these guys on, or neither of us do. Take your pick."

The person was now making their way over to the three, and Lisandra audibly whimpered. "Guys, I'm all for taking on bad guys, but this many against us doesn't sound smart. Maybe we should listen to them."

When the gap had been closed, the man pointed his gun at Arrigan first– likely because he was the only male in the group. "Kids like you don't fear death enough these days, that's your problem. Do you think I won't blow your brains out right this minute, right here, right now?"

Paralyzed with fear, Arrigan could only let out a squeak in response.

"I don't," Maceida replied, gazing over at where Arrigan was being threatened. "For one thing, you're holding that gun all wrong. The recoil from firing it at that angle would knock you right onto your arse, and burn your right hand. Rookie mistake, really. Do you even know what you're holding?"

"You shut your mouth, blondie!" the man replied, turning the barrel to her.

"I *really* don't like being called that," Maceida replied, notably more tense– although it was difficult to tell if it was from fear or annoyance. "See, now you're going to make me do something I really didn't want to do. Lisandra, I'm so sorry you had to be a part of this."

Before either Lisandra or Arrigan could object, Maceida had kicked the man with the gun; in the process, he let go of it, and she grabbed it before it hit the ground. Almost as a second instinct, Arrigan conjured a protective bubble large enough to protect the three of them, just in case anyone else had a gun or other projectile weapon.

"I can only hold this for a few moments. Maceida, what the hell are you doing?!" he asked.

"Becoming armed," she replied, holding up the gun. "You've got your polearm with you, right?"

Arrigan glanced down at where the handle from which his polearm extended was; he almost always kept it clipped to his pants. "I mean, yeah."

"Dead on. Lisandra, can you fight?"

Still trembling ever so slightly, Lisandra pulled out her magic ribbon from her jacket pocket. "Yeah... but there's like, fifteen of those guys and three of us."

"Aye. You're capable of taking out five of them, right?" Maceida asked. "And if you aren't, just keep them busy whilst I take care of my five. Plus, you've got magic on your side, right?"

Whatever Lisandra's answer was going to be, neither adult heard it, because Arrigan's hold on the barrier surrounding them broke then, exposing them to the crowd of black-clad strangers set on fighting them. He had to scramble to quickly extend and ready his polearm, but once that had been taken care of, he was filled with a new sense of duty: a duty to protect. After all, he was the one that should be protecting the girls. That was what the Resistance did, right? He dedicated much of his effort into supporting his other two teammates; conjuring a wall if either of them needed time to recover. Lisandra benefitted from this the most, because she wasn't accustomed to using her magic for attacking. The usage of her ribbon– fluttering through the air gracefully as she conjured a symphony of lightning strikes– helped, but she clearly struggled with being able to defend herself while doing this. Maceida fared well, until one of the members of the black-clad group managed to sneak behind her and strike her in just the right spot that all anyone heard was a high-pitched yelp before she fell to the ground with a thud.

Lisandra immediately turned to Arrigan, who had turned to her. "Go, I'll cover you," he said, already knowing what she was about to ask. With a nod, she ran to where Maceida's unconscious body was– preparing to begin one of her healing spells. Not far behind her, Arrigan began to create a magic wall. As long as both of them stayed in sync, this plan would be effective, but something neither of them considered was that it was also very much contingent on Arrigan's ability to both concentrate on the wall, and not be hit himself.

With twelve remaining enemies, it was very likely he would be hit himself.

"ETA, Lisandra?!" he asked as he began to run perpendicular to where she was sitting, in hopes of avoiding a strike from one of their swords.

"I'm almost done!" she replied. "Can you hold them off for like, thirty more seconds?"

"I guess we're both about to find ou-" Arrigan hadn't noticed that he'd gone off the pavement, and had promptly tripped over a medium-sized rock in the bushes. When he got to his feet, winded, he could barely make out the figure of that very first antagonist in black– he knew it was them because, indeed, their face was beginning to swell on one side– before their body was seemingly yanked out of frame by a large man with an axe.

Wait, he'd seen this man before. Somewhere. Not at headquarters, not at school...

"Are you going to help, or just stand there?" he asked. "Come on. I expect better from the Resistance."

Now Arrigan remembered: the man in charge of Compositora's Restoration Effort! He was a fighter too?! And with such an impressive weapon.

"Right!" he said aloud, grabbing his polearm. "Um, my attacks aren't very strong, so I'll go ahead of you and stun a few guys first!" And then he was off, determined to do just that. With now four people on their side, it thankfully didn't take long for the antagonists to turn tail and run, leaving the four where they were a few blocks outside of the square.

"Thank you for your help, Mr. Anton," Arrigan said, turning to him. "But how did you know where to find us?"

"Okay, first off: you don't need to call me 'mister.' I can't be *that* much older than you all." Anton's gaze turned to the square. "And as for how I knew where to find you: I didn't. I came this way because some of the gentlemen who work with me were in the square a little while ago, assessing some of the old buildings, when they heard a ruckus, and saw you all's captain being taken captive. They came back to tell me, because if hell like that is going to continue to break loose, it's going to majorly get in the way of our construction– so I was on my way to see the aftermath for myself."

Arrigan looked over at Lisandra and Maceida– wordlessly assessing whether or not they were okay, and deciding they were– before saying, "I didn't even think about that, but if those guys keep pulling stunts like this, it *is* gradually going to undo all the work you've done here, isn't it?"

"They think of it as collateral damage, I'm sure," added Maceida, rubbing her head.

Anton nodded. "And that is not something I'm willing to sit down and take, so you can consider myself and my team on your side. Listen, you kids need to go tell your friends what happened here. I don't know a lot about the bigger picture of what's happening, but I don't think it will be put to rest in a conclusive way until you're able to shut this group down, and there's a good chance you'll need your captain for that."

"That's where we were headed before we got intercepted," Lisandra pointed out. "But now we need to get there even faster."

"Let's pick up the pace, then," Arrigan replied. "Thank you again, for protecting us in battle. We would've been in a bad way if you hadn't!"

This was met with a casual shrug. "I owe Thunder. This is the least I could do."

Not This Time

Amidst all the feelings of hurt, confusion, and urgency, there was also one of determination; that the Resistance had been in this position before, and they all– or Logan, at the very least– was set to ensure they wouldn't flounder as hard as last time.

"And you're certain that this is what you saw in the square?" he asked the three returnees.

Lisandra crossed her arms. "Yes, but dude, what does it matter? Would we not try to save those guys if they weren't our friends?"

The look that Logan gave her made it easy to tell he was already tired of her, but he quickly shut his eyes and nodded. "It merely means the situation is more delicate. But you've got a point. Lisandra, you know a lot of the Resistance at this point, right? There's a phone at the end of this block; if you can round up a group and have them scout the town for information as soon as possible, I'll be the first to defend you when Phoenix tries to call your parents and tell them you're here."

That was enough for her. "Yes, sir," she saluted, before running back out of the door.

Logan, meanwhile, was readying his weapon. "My sister's currently at the old HQ, so I'm going to go tell her what's going on. Can the two of you handle catching everyone up while I'm gone?"

"Do we have a choice?" Maceida asked.

"Well– you know. I cannot *make* you do anything, but at the same time, none of us know how much time we have before something else drastic happens," Logan replied. "I'm confident that you both have enough knowledge between you to get everyone up to speed, and by then I'll be back with Phoenix. We can pick up from there. See you guys in a bit," he waved before hurrying out.

Arrigan turned to go further into the house when he heard Maceida's voice: "Somebody's going to have to do damage control."

This made him turn back toward her. "What do you mean?"

"The Resistance is the closest thing this city has to any type of government, right? Who knows how many people just saw its captain in a metal cage. Can you think of any bigger sign to start committing crimes with reckless abandon?"

"Damn it. You're right." Arrigan sighed.

"Hey." Maceida nudged his arm. "One step at a time. First, let's go get everyone up at speed."

***

"And so, Lisandra is currently rounding up a group of people to poke around town a bit, and see if they can find any information related to the spectacle that we saw in the square, and that attacked us," Arrigan explained. "Concurrently, Logan went to get Phoenix. Right now, they're the closest thing this organization has to leadership, so they'll be the ones making further executive decisions. So there's not really a lot we can do until they get back, outside of trying to process everything that's happened in the past hour."

Before anyone else could speak, Lisandra entered the sitting room where everyone was holed up, placing the phone book back on the table it usually sat on. "Okay, I was able to get in touch with a few of our buddies, and they're on the case," she said as she took a seat beside Chiara. "What did I miss?"

"Nothing much. We've only just finished recounting the tale of what we saw in the square, and what we dealt with afterward," Arrigan replied.

Lisandra nodded. "Well, what do you guys think?" she asked, turning to everyone else.

"I think the whole situation sucks," Jasiela was the first to speak.

"I don't think any of us could possibly disagree with that," Arrigan said. "On our way down here, Maceida said something I didn't think of until she said so: that with such a public showing, things can and likely will get worse for the everyday citizen here. The fact that our captain isn't around is bad enough, but I can't help but feel a level of personal responsibility for what's going to happen in the city because of what's come to pass. And I know that Logan will feel the same way about it. There's... so much happening that it's hard to know where to start when it comes to tackling it all."

"Why don't we try to evaluate each one separately?" Brecken suggested. "While it's a fact that everything is more or less related right now, if we step back from that and look at each issue on its own, it's very likely that the solutions we come up with will end up intersecting again anyway. Right? Um, I... don't know that I explained that well."

"No, I understand. That was, more or less, the approach we were going to begin adopting anyway," Arrigan replied.

The sound of the door opening upstairs meant that, clearly, Logan had returned with his sister. The few steps it took for them to make it down to the basement felt much longer than they actually were; everything felt so tense, it was difficult to breathe.

Nevertheless, when they finally arrived, everyone present seemed to have adopted their coolest facade.

"I was really hoping that Logan was just messing with me." These were the first words Phoenix said, upon seeing Lisandra on the couch.

Lisandra didn't know how to respond to this, so she settled for a timid smile. "Haha. Hi."

"We'll deal with you later," Phoenix replied. "Everyone, as much as I know you love our long, democratic meetings, I already thought of what needs to happen next while we were on our way back here, so we won't need to preoccupy ourselves with that this time."

Logan, then, held up what looked to be a stack of tickets. "We're heading to the City of Garnet."

Everyone remained silent, for not knowing how to react.

"There are many reasons why we've decided this. There's so much going on in the city right now that we've neglected the pressing issue of the fissures, which is affecting more than just our place of residence; it could be affecting the entire world as far as we know," Phoenix explained. "Furthermore, it's a good idea for Logan and I to be separated for a little while. The two of us, plus Handel and Anton– formerly, Tornado– are now the most prolific people that have, at any time, been affiliated with the Resistance that aren't in solitary confinement; so it makes sense to put some distance between us all."

"Wait. So, you're not coming with us?" Arrigan asked.

"Someone needs to stay here and ensure that the city doesn't burn down, now that it's public knowledge that our captain is out of commission," Phoenix explained. "We decided that it would be me. I have the knowledge and the magic to help anyone who may get hurt as a result of the current state of things. Logan's spent less time away from the City of Garnet, so he'll be able to navigate better than I would; plus, he's closer to our grandparents... and our parents don't hate him."

At this, Logan's expression softened. He said softly, "I don't think they *hate* you, Taylor."

"Didn't I ask you not to call me that in front of people?" she replied, in a voice only slightly louder than he had been. She cleared her throat before addressing the room at a higher volume. "So, that's settled, then. The next train leaves tomorrow morning. Logan has enough tickets for all of you to go, but if any of you would like to stay, I wouldn't refuse the company. That is a decision I'll leave up to you."

This made all the Earth dwellers conference among themselves for a short time. "Are you kidding? A chance to finally see another of the cities here?!" Madeline asked. "None of us would ever say no to that!"

This made both Phoenix and Logan smile. "That's a good point. Well, you've all been through a lot today. Get some rest, so that you can be sure you'll be able to catch your train."

As everyone began to head upstairs to get ready for bed, Phoenix gently grabbed Lisandra's arm to stop her. "Lisandra, I'm not going to lecture you, since as it happens, you're heading back home anyway. I just want to ask you one thing. If you keep being this rebellious, and doing things like sneaking here, are you emotionally prepared for your parents to treat you the same way that mine treat me?"

"I..." Lisandra didn't know what to say, so she took a moment to sit back down opposite her cousin. "Listen. Months ago, when you took me home, I didn't think about the fact that you might see them again. And I definitely didn't know that things were that bad between you guys. I'm not such a brat that I'd naively think things would be different with me, but at the same time, you know the circumstances aren't the same."

"I do know." Phoenix nodded.

"I'm sorry that happened." Lisandra's tone was sincere, and perhaps the most vulnerable Phoenix had ever heard it be. "You don't deserve that kind of treatment at all, and I think your parents know that too– they just don't want to accept it. I mean, you're practically the one reason the Resistance hasn't had more casualties than it's had. You mean something here! I don't get why they refuse to see that."

"Maybe I'll find out someday." Phoenix turned to look up the stairs. "Now, get some sleep. From what I've heard, you've been through a lot today. I think I'll still be asleep when you all leave, so I'll take that farewell hug now."

"Oh! Right!" Lisandra quickly stood back up, hugging her older cousin tightly, before running up the stairs. "See you when I get back!"

"Yeah, I'll see you when you get b– Lisandra! No! Not when you get back! You need to stay put!" But even then, Phoenix knew: she'd be seeing her cousin again sooner rather than later.

The City of Garnet

Logan led the charge to the main transit system of Compositora, which was just outside of the square. It was still a small building, as train stations went, but it was more than efficient at getting travelers to and from the two biggest neighboring cities: Trelana, and the City of Garnet, the latter of which everyone would be embarking to today. The trip was usually around two hours' time, if weather permitted; luckily, today was a sunny day in both cities, so there should be no inclement weather.

The station, like many of the other new buildings, was built with bricks of a tan color, with terracotta-colored shingled rooftops; there were also multiple doors for entry and exit, but the most visually appealing part of this place, hands down, was the large clock mounted above the doors, displaying the current local time. There were some smaller clocks below it, showing times in various other cities that, presumably, weren't in the same time zone.

"Wait a sec. If you can only get to two other cities from here, why are there so many other clocks?" Madeline asked.

"Nothing ever escapes your watchful eye, hm?" Logan smiled. "I believe it is because of the possibility of connecting commutes. For example– although we will not be seeing it on our way– there is a marina in the City of Garnet. There are two major cities on an island to the southwest, which are in different time zones."

"I'm not sure how many people do so, but it is possible to get to the mountains via Trelana," added Arrigan. "And to most every other city on the continent, too. There's an expansive– uh, never mind. I don't mean to go on about how cool my hometown's transit system is, but it *is* really impressive."

Inside this train station, everything was relatively to-the-point. There were tracks and platforms to board trains, a ticketing window, and a small news stand that also appeared to sell water and small bags of snacks. The people inside the station moved with purpose, intent on getting from one place to another, unless they were stopping at the stand. Further on, past the platforms, were the tracks where trains were boarded; a few engines were parked in terminals, looking to be coal-powered and with distinctive, ornate designs on their engines as well as their carriages, evoking a sense of art nouveau.

Taking in the sights of this station brought about a sense of history, as if this was the standard for what train stations had looked like, long before any of this group was born.

"Let's see if we can find where to board our trains. Hello!" Logan waved to one of the station workers standing beside one of the platforms. "Excuse me, sir! When does the next train to the City of Garnet depart?"

The worker pointed behind himself with his thumb, to an engine painted a magenta color. "The train on track 3 is boarding right now; you can catch it if you're fast enough."

"Oh!" That was, clearly, not the answer Logan had been expecting. "Right, then! Come on, everyone! This way!"

***

The City of Garnet was the largest city on this particular side of the mountains, and it was easy to be amazed by its visage upon seeing it for the first time. Its buildings seemed to be reminiscent of the Victorian era, most being painted in sophisticated shades of black, gray, white, and ivory. As a matter of fact, "sophisticated" was a good word to describe the feeling of this city as a whole. Cast iron street lamps and metal mailboxes with the same ornate designs as the trains lined the brick streets; like Compositora, it didn't appear that automobiles were common here, so people walked along the streets, in clothes that were much more elaborate and formal than the average Compositoran would ever possess, let alone wear.

Emerging from the train station, Logan held out his right arm, showing off the view. "Welcome to my hometown: the City of Garnet. We'll be making a stop before we continue on to my grandparents' place, if that's okay. I'm sure you will all enjoy it."

"Yeah, it's already really eye-opening seeing a large city like this. I didn't think places like this existed in this world," replied Jaiden, shielding her eyes from the sun as she looked around.

"They certainly do," Logan replied with a laugh, before he gestured for everyone to follow him. "This way!"

They fell in line then, striving to not get lost in a new locale.

"So this is where you grew up, then?" Spencer-Lynn asked Logan, with a gentle nudge to his arm. "It's beautiful; but I can't say it's what I was expecting. All of the detailed architecture and fashion sense here is really interesting. It feels like I've been transported to a very specific period of time."

Logan chucked bashfully. "Haha, yeah. It's definitely a place, but I promise it's not as haughty as the first impression would have you believe."

"I can believe it. After all, you and Phoenix are from this place, so there must be good people abound."

"If we have the time, I'd love to show you around," Logan replied, smiling. "I can show you all the coolest spots, of course."

"Oh? Well, I couldn't possibly refuse the offer of a tour from a local," Spencer-Lynn responded, returning his smile. "Estou ansioso pelo tempo que passaremos juntos."

This response gave Logan pause. It would have been one thing if Spencer-Lynn had said she was looking forward to it; and she technically had, but she had specifically phrased it as, "the time we'll spend together," which, for Logan, sounded too good to be true. Of course, he'd be looking forward to that too. But what exactly did she mean to imply by framing her sentence that way? As much as he wanted to know... he was overtaken by a sudden sense of bashfulness. He couldn't gather the courage to ask, or arrange his words in a suitable way to do so. This had never happened before.

And so, the group continued to walk.

"Everyone and everything here is so well put together," Brecken noted. "So far, it looks like every mailbox and street lamp are aligned at exactly the same distance, perfectly parallel to one another."

"They are. People get paid to make sure everything in town is like that," Lisandra replied. "Every major city in this world has its own unique quality that draws people to it. For this one, it's the form and function of its architecture, and its people."

"Well, that and the giant chunk of gemstone at the city center," added Logan. "That's where we're headed now. It's on the way to our ultimate destination, so we may as well. I think it'll really help you all understand the more mystic aspects of our society."

After walking for some time, the buildings lining the walkways spread out so that there was a literal circle in which people ambled and gathered. At the very center of this circle was the prize landmark of this city: its namesake, the large piece of garnet so reddish-violet it appeared black at first glance, pointing toward the sky in an irregular, uneven shape reminiscent of rock candy. There were not a lot of people in this area at this time, which made access easier; the group arrived in front of the giant chunk of garnet, and all took a moment to stare at it in awe. There was a small crowd of people around, also admiring it, but the area wasn't so populated that it had been difficult to get close to the garnet itself.

"Are we allowed to touch it?" asked Mishaela.

"As far as I know, yes. I saw children touching it the last time I was here. I'm pretty sure *I* touched it as a child." Logan shrugged.

In response, Mishaela carefully pointed a finger, and hesitated for a second before proceeding to poke the garnet.

"Wow. I honestly don't know why I expected anything different."

Arrigan stifled a laugh, but Chiara walked past him to place a palm on the garnet. Of course, it was hard and rigid, like one would expect a gemstone that hadn't been shaped to be. However, when she tried to pull her hand back, it stayed stuck to the garnet.

"Um..." Chiara looked around; Mishaela was talking about the streetlights with Jaiden and Gavin, Arrigan and Lisandra were talking now, and Logan was having a conversation with the older girls. Everyone was too busy to notice that her hand was stuck. She tried, a second and third time, to move her hand. No go. Sighing, Chiara silently wished– if no one else– that Logan would notice her. He'd surely have a solution. He often did.

The fifth time that Chiara tried to move her hand, it had actually already come loose and the force she used to pull back sent her falling backward. She let out a surprised shout, landing on her butt.

She couldn't tell what got everyone's attention: her shout, or the ominous cloud of darkness now forming around the top of the garnet.

"Wh– what did you do?!" Mishaela asked as she helped her up, a light scolding in her tone.

"I didn't do anything! I just touched it, like you did five seconds before. Logan said it was okay." Chiara's voice became small.

"Is that..." Lisandra was the only one with her eyes on the cloud, and she was now pointing up at it, prompting everyone else to as well.

The ground began to rumble just a bit, as the cloud gradually began to shift shape. Before long, the cloud took the shape of a deep purple-skinned woman wearing a black frilly dress with accents and bows in many shades of purple and gray, her hair being composed of small cloud puffs arranged to mimic a ponytail. She let out a hefty yawn, before blinking a few times, revealing pale blue eyes, as her feet reached the ground, standing in front of everyone.

"That was such a good nap..." the figure said softly. There were a few more words uttered at a low enough volume that no one could distinguish them, before she looked up at the crowd of people in front of the garnet. "Oh! Hiiii~" She waved a bit timidly. "Apologies for the less than graceful entry. I wasn't expecting to be summoned in broad daylight. It directly contradicts my element, after all. The irony is amusing." She giggled. "Still, if I'd slept any longer, I'd probably be disgustingly sluggish. Thank you for waking me, Chiara."

"You're welcome." Chiara smiled.

"Chiara!" Mishaela frowned at her. "You mean to tell me you don't have any questions about this at all?!"

"Well, not really, not just yet. But, somehow, I can tell that our guest is esteemed," Chiara curtsied.

Seeing that Mishaela was more confused than before she'd asked her sister that question, Logan explained, "We have been honored with a visit by Scura, the goddess of darkness. From what I gather, it appears as though your sister accidentally awakened her when she touched the garnet."

"That's correct." The goddess nodded.

"Wow. A goddess. In the flesh!" Arrigan gushed. "Er, using 'flesh' kind of liberally there, but it doesn't make this any less amazing! This is amazing! I figured I'd eventually get to meet one hanging out with you and the Resistance, Logan, but no idea it was going to be so soon! This is... wow. I'm at a loss for words."

"Are you really?" Maceida asked him, with a laugh. "That sounded like plenty of them."

She had a point– and when Arrigan realized this, he turned slightly pink. "Well, yeah, I guess so."

"How did you know that was going to happen?" Mishaela asked Chiara as that was transpiring.

"I didn't." Chiara frowned in confusion. "That's the part I'm hoping gets explained to us."

"Wait a minute. I live here, and I see children touching this thing all the time," Lisandra pointed out. "And Mishaela just poked it a few minutes ago too. How come none of them woke you up, but Chiara did?"

The level of lighting in the area shifted as Scura shifted her position; whether for comfort, or to appear more amicable to the youths in front of her, was difficult to tell. "You have many questions. This has always been common in young humans, but is refreshing to see live on, all the same. First– as it is the most simple explanation to give– as for the matter of why Chiara awakened me but no one else did: there are two reasons for this. A goddess does not always reside within the gemstone relative to her element, something I am certain you may all already be aware of. With the City of Garnet being the most populous gemstone city, and this garnet being impressively deep in color, it gets particularly noisy sometimes with the amount of people admiring and touching it. So, I am not often here. However, I felt the pull to return here when Chiara's hand touched the garnet. This, I believe, is related to the power you were all once lent."

"Wait, so do we still have that?" Jasiela asked eagerly.

"Dude, there's no way we still have that," Jaiden replied. "I know. I've tried."

Logan raised his hand then, to direct the attention to himself. "I do believe this begs the question of why you sought us out this time, Madame Goddess. We know things are very turbulent in our world right now, but is it so bad that it requires this type of intervention?"

There was a pause before the goddess spoke again. "Oh, my apologies for the foreboding silence. It is merely that– how to deliver the message without invoking that inherent human tendency to panic when given bad news?"

"Is it really that bad?" Arrigan asked, already feeling that sense of panic welling from deep within himself.

"It is..." Scura began, before stopping and restructuring her sentence. "Have you, by chance, been noticing the occasional fissures appearing in this world? They have been most numerous in Compositora."

At this, Logan and Arrigan exchanged a look. "Fissures?" Arrigan repeated. "We've been seeing a lot of those, actually. And they're a problem, right?"

"They are." She nodded. "And they will unfortunately continue to be, until you are able to stop them from occurring. I do believe, though, that I am not the best fit for telling you the reason why they have been appearing as of late. There are others who are aware, and they coincide with your original motive for ever coming here."

"So, visiting our grandparents!" Lisandra said, pointing a finger in the general direction of their house.

"Indeed. But before you depart, I would leave you with this."

Yet another shift in lighting, but this one seemed more out of mood setting than a position change.

"It is a concept that I am aware you're all familiar with at this point. Never forget that everything you do has its consequences; and that there will always be people who will never be able to understand your actions, no matter what. They will be blinded by the way they have been affected. This, however, does not absolve you of further consequences."

"You mean the current situation in Compositora, right?" Gavin asked.

"This may be applicable to that predicament, yes. But it is something that, we the goddesses believe, will be applicable to many future occurrences as well. It would be wise to keep it in mind."

"Of course," Spencer-Lynn was the first to agree. "Thank you for sharing your knowledge with us."

Scura gave a short nod, before yawning again. "I believe in you, children. In the meantime, I think I am due for another nap."

The Fabric of the Universe

F arther away from the city center, the houses began to become less tall and more wide, with more space between them. The area was also more green, housing more native plant life even with the cobblestone roads creating a network of pathways to navigate. Logan led the way down a specific, quiet street before pointing at one particularly large, ivory-colored slab house with a light brown thatched roof. "There it is," he said. "Our destination."

"That's such a huge house!" Jasiela noted. "Your grandparents must be important people."

Logan shrugged. "Well, that and they had nine children. Also, they've always been the type to house other people to help them get back on their feet. They currently live alone, but that's not usually the case at all."

As the group walked up the path to the front door, the trees that lined the path blew in the wind, and the insects that lived within them chirped, at a volume that was comfortable. Under different circumstances, this would have been a soothing experience– but given everything that had transpired up until now, it was difficult to imagine it as such. Logan knocked on the door, and waited for a response. At first he worried that no one was home; but then he had to realize that, as knowledgeable and powerful as his grandparents were, they were grandparents, which meant that their ability to instantly answer a door would not be as prominent as his own.

When the door did finally open, it made everyone stand at attention. The man who was at the door– his short hair more white than black at this point, a slight slouch making him appear just under average height, and just a bit of muscular tone to his build– seemed to command respect just from his aura; but at the same time, he exuded just as much kindness and welcoming. Not unlike... Logan and Phoenix, actually, which made it very easy to believe he was related to them.

The lines near his brown eyes creased as he smiled, recognizing two of his grandchildren. "Lisandra, you've convinced your cousin... and some of your friends to come and visit, have you?"

"Hi, Grandpa. I wish I could say this is a pleasure visit, but we're here on serious business!" Lisandra replied. "Can we come in? Please?"

"We wouldn't be intruding like this unless it was really important, I assure you," Logan added.

The old man nodded, a smirk on his face. "Of course. I can feel that there is much for us to discuss with you, as well. Come in, and make yourselves at home. Feli! Brew your largest kettle of tea, we have guests!"

***

Somehow, the mysticism in the Oliveira home could easily be felt by walking through it. Part of this, undoubtedly, had to do with the decor. Some aspects of the home were normal; the hardwood floors, the royal blue walls, the neatly organized dishes in the china cabinet. However– whether it be the candles in their holders scattered down the corridors, or the paintings on the walls that shimmered a certain way when the light hit them, or even the intermittent figurines carved from stone– there were multiple adornments that seemed to be more magical than met the eye. Even so, it was also impossible to ignore how cozy the place felt, as well. Being here made it obvious why Logan and Phoenix– and Lisandra too– held their grandparents in such high regard.

Now in the kitchen, the group happened upon a woman with her gray strands of hair obvious, amidst the flowing black tresses atop her head; pulled back into a low ponytail with a lovely dusty rose-colored scrunchie, which complemented her simple sky blue, short-sleeved dress. Her head turned the moment she heard the footsteps approaching, and she smiled just as warmly as her husband had when he'd answered the door. The lines at the sides of her eyes and mouth creased– indeed, in a grandmotherly way.

"You didn't tell me that our guests were of the most important type, Augusto," she said then, removing the chrome kettle from the stove just as it began to whistle. "I can tell based on the manner in which you have entered this house: you have obviously come to discuss something of great importance. I do not intend to undermine that– but, it is such a beautiful day. Why don't we hash things out in the garden? The flowers are just lovely right about now."

"Flowers? In February?" Jaiden asked.

The nearest access door to the garden was in the kitchen; just a short walk away, the scenery was that of green leaves, blooms, and the smell of nature. It was as if everyone had walked into a botanical garden, rather than someone's side yard. Farther out, around where a few benches, chairs, and tables came into play, there was indeed a bed of tulips in brilliant pink and white hues.

"Huh." Madeline bent on one knee to observe the tulips at a closer angle. "They're not dead."

"You seem to be surprised to see this garden." Ofelia was standing right behind her, which was odd because she certainly wasn't there before.

"Whoa! Hey, lady, you can't be sneaking up on me like that, do you know how hard it was to override my fight sense?!" Madeline complained.

Based on the lack of a reaction from Ofelia, it was like she hadn't even heard that.

"So..." Jaiden said as everyone began to sit on the benches and chairs in the sitting area of the garden. "Our friends here are very confident in your ability to help us with our current predicament.

And it's not that I'm not myself, but I don't think anyone has explained why exactly that is. If we have the time, I'd love to know."

After a brief silence, Augusto was the one to respond. "I have always believed that it is imperative to make time for knowledge. I will tell you, but be aware that this is an answer that requires historical context.

"In the days where our world was still quite young... how to put it? Because of the manner in which our world was created, there were always various methods of our people recording our history– but because all of our cultures are so vast and varied, there took some time before we realized it would do well to have some type of centralized intel about... everything, really. And so, a small group of people from different cities were tasked with researching this world and all of its intricacies, and recording what they found– as well as recording important contemporary information, for the generations to come. One of these people was my grandfather, Duarte Oliveira.

"It is quite the task, to learn about all of the world's intricacies, because of all of our different languages and customs, and of course the goddesses and the presence of magic. Even with there being a group of people, there was no conceivable way they would have ever been able to compile all the necessary information regarding our world at one time. And so it goes: when one person's life has met its end, one of the following generation will continue their research. Ofelia and I are of a particularly noteworthy intersection of this tradition; my father passed while I was fairly young, so the torch was passed to me at an early age. As well, she is part of the bloodline that conducts research in the City of Heliodor."

"So, although my sister continues to prepare to further the research our father will leave her in time, I grew up learning many things about the world in our part of it," Ofelia finished.

"Wow, so it's like you guys getting married was a real meeting of the minds," Jasiela noted. "I can see why these two put so much confidence in you."

"Now, will one of you be so kind as to catch us up on why you've come to visit?" Ofelia continued. "I believe that Lisandra called it 'serious business,' and I know that a young woman of her standing would never lie about the severity of an issue like that."

Lisandra nodded. "I sure wouldn't! As for what's going on... honestly, it would probably be easier to tell you at this point what *isn't* going on. We came to you for advice 'cause we're in way over our heads and could use some sage advice to get a hold on things. Where should we start, guys?"

Everyone took a moment then to decide how to form everything into a coherent story.

"Well, it's..." Logan started. "There's this interesting group of people in Compositora that despise the Resistance for reasons that none of us have any control over. Their leader was able to capture Thunder and Hunter and has since taken them who-knows-where, which is why you don't see them with us. So now, in addition to trying to think of ways to get them back, we also have been trying to get to the bottom of those weird things that are like tears in the fabric of the universe. We encountered one of the goddesses in the square on our way here, and she suggested you may know something about that?"

This did indeed appear to pique Augusto's interest. "It is such an honor to be graced with a goddess' presence. I hope you are all aware of that."

"On our best behavior, I assure you!" Madeline placed a hand to her chest.

"Could you describe how your experiences with the fissures have gone?" Augusto asked then.

"Yeah, sure, but they aren't always the same," Logan replied. "For example, on one of the days I was heading home with Arrigan here, it took the form of a cluster of spherical, glowing clusters with rings around them. It didn't affect me much aside from a brief moment of feeling unwell, and he didn't even notice it. The most recent time I saw one was a bit similar to this, but the spheres were in a couple of lines as opposed to a cluster. That one was a lot stronger. It literally knocked me off my feet."

"I also saw this happen in Trelana once, but it was like... something on the ground," added Arrigan. "Similar to some kind of oil spill? The only reason we're all so confident that that isn't what it was, is because of how badly afflicted some of the people in the vicinity were by its presence before it disappeared. My mother had to stay in bed for the rest of the day."

"Hold on just a tick. Something I don't quite understand is, if it's different every time, how do you know that they're all related?" asked Gavin.

"It's not different *every* time, but we've been classing them all to-gether because of their similarities," explained Logan. "Despite the visual differences, these are all brief occurrences that make our world temporarily unstable in the area, and that people nearby report af-fecting their health, their sensibilities– their ability to stay alert and level-headed. There are also some reports of this being accompanied by things showing up in unusual places; think evergreens showing up in the desert, or snow in the tropics."

At this, Augusto raised an eyebrow. "I have an additional ques-tion. Has there been anything discernible regarding the timing of these occurrences? Has something notable happened around the same time?"

The garden became silent once again. "Sure, that'll take some time to think about though," Logan replied. "But now that I *am* thinking about it– Arrigan. Wasn't one of those times around the same time that we had to fight against some of those anti-Resistance types that had gotten a bit too rowdy?"

"I think you may be right," Arrigan added. "And that report of the most recent time in Compositora... the timing may actually coincide with when we saw our captain and our strategist get taken hostage."

"You sound like you may know what this means, Grandpa," Lisandra finished.

"I do believe so." Augusto nodded, taking a sip of tea from his cup, before carefully placing it back on its saucer. "I am told that all of you are familiar with the goddesses' ability to lend an individual some of their power."

"Well, all except one," Spencer-Lynn corrected. "But she catches on pretty quickly, so continue?"

"The goddesses trusted us with the ability to wield some of their power for a few reasons, which meant we ended up learning about the way it worked pretty fast," Brecken replied. "What I remember, possibly the most, is being told that the way a human would wield their magic is different than the way a goddess would. I wonder if that has anything to do with it?"

"Oh! Yeah, yeah!" Madeline pointed a finger. "I remember that! The goddesses were able to create this entire world with the magic they wield, but the palace that the Dictator creature whatever created, was in shambles less than a year after he disappeared."

With this reminder, everyone began to reflect on seeing the palace in such dire condition.

"I'm going over all of my studies in my head..." Logan started. "There's levels to that, aren't there? That the disparity between a human's power and a goddess' power isn't just about potency; it is also within the particular ways that magic can be applied. There are things a goddess can do with her magic that a human could not conceptualize. Correct?"

He was given a nod from his grandmother. "You've studied hard, Logan."

Logan's response was to bashfully smile. "Well... yeah."

"We've been worried, for the past month or two. All of these fissures, the shifts in the atmosphere... they are all indicative of the veil that separates our worlds being torn apart. You see, this veil is... the closest thing I could liken it to is the atmosphere on the other planet, but even that is not quite the same. In order to obscure this world from that one, the veil has to cover this entire world at all times, which means that it is intrinsically a part of it. To tear into the veil is to tear into our world itself."

"Oh, that doesn't sound good," Chiara said softly.

"What would even start that happening in the first place, though?" asked Spencer-Lynn.

"True to the current conversation, the first thing that comes to mind is a person using magic that is not natural for them to have," Ofelia said then. "When you all were entrusted with borrowing power from the goddesses, they lent it to you willingly, and you accepted it with very little– if any– reservation. But if, for example, one were to take power from them, without consent..."

Confusion permeated the air. "Is that possible?" Mishaela asked. "To take power from a literal goddess without them wanting that to happen? That sounds like it shouldn't even be possible."

"If it were... I could only think of one way this could come to pass, and it would be a technicality," Augusto replied. "When a goddess lends her power, and the recipient accepts it– the recipient could, in theory, pull much more from the goddess than she intended to give. This can happen in small quantities sometimes, with none too disastrous consequences, but... if a human got ahold of powers that they were not intended to have, and proceeded to use them in a manner that a human normally never could..."

The wind blew particularly briskly, then.

"I'm gonna assume that's not something that would be very good?" Maceida asked.

"Well, it's…" Logan paused. "It's not good in the way that– it's not good regardless of the means. Meaning, even if you were using those powers for something universally good, it would still negatively affect the world because they both don't have the goddess' blessing to use that power, nor the capacity to use that magnitude of power correctly. The best analogy I can use to explain it is it's like giving a child a flamethrower; even if they're knowledgeable enough to point it in the correct direction, it will affect the surroundings in ways they can't control because they were never supposed to have that thing in the first place."

No one present could dispute that a child with a flamethrower would be a horrible combination.

"So, if Flavian is the child in that analogy," Arrigan said. "How do we take that flamethrower away from him?"

"That's the part I'm not completely clear on," Logan replied. "It would be great if our elders could impart some wisdom about that."

Both of the elder Oliveiras exchanged a look of worry. "The easiest way would be for the person to simply return the power to the goddess they stole it from, but that may have repercussions if the goddess is feeling particularly spiteful that day," explained Ofelia. "There would also be the possibility of someone– you all, I would assume– subduing them enough that the goddesses would simply be able to take their magic back. In both cases, however, it is important to note that this needs to be done as soon as possible. The longer someone possesses foreign magic, the more it bonds with their soul; and, thus, the more difficult it is to remove it from them."

"Which, I'm assuming, is also why we weren't given magic in a substantial amount for very long," concluded Jasiela.

"Correct." Logan nodded. "I feel as though I'm going to regret asking this, but something tells me I should: are there more difficult ways to get that power back to where it should be? You know, just in case any circumstances come about that prevent us from doing things the easy way."

"There is..." Augusto paused. "There is the fact that all of the magic one possesses returns to the world after their death."

The wind blew briskly once more, before it returned to normal, gently tickling the petals of the flowers nearby.

"By the way, why is it that these flowers can grow at this time of year?" Mishaela asked, gazing at the scenery. "Not just the flowers, but the vines, the... all of it. It's considerably cooler here than it was in Compositora, so it's wouldn't be warm enough to cultivate them, would it?"

"Indeed. These flowerbeds grew way too quickly, over the course of a week," explained Ofelia. "They would not usually be here. We've been putting some effort into researching this as well–"

Suddenly the ground began to rumble, causing everyone who wasn't already seated to scramble for stable footing or seating. A crackling sound followed, becoming more sharp and deafening, until the group was faced with a jagged, galactic fissure some feet on the ground– but only for a few seconds, before a bright light flashed. It faded quickly, and they were left with a tall tree– its bark coarse and dark, and its boughs weighed down by numerous pastel purple petals, which would occasionally fall to the ground, fluttering in the breeze.

"I'm guessing by the silence that that's not something that usually happens here?" Jasiela asked.

"I've never even *seen* a tree like this!" Lisandra replied, standing up and hurrying toward it– keeping a safe distance, but stopping close enough to be able to observe. "It looks so cool! And it even kinda fits in with the garden."

Arrigan was the next to stand. "Wait a minute."

He stood under the tree, placing a hand on the bark, before picking up some of the petals that had fallen. Holding them close to his eyes, he then looked back at everyone else. "This might sound a little crazy."

"Compared to everything else that's sounded completely sane so far?" Jaiden asked.

A nod, conceding that. "I don't know how it could possibly happen, but this tree, I– I'm almost certain that there's a photograph of my parents somewhere in our house, with one of these trees in the background; I think it's their wedding photograph, but th-that wouldn't... my parents got married in my mom's homeland, which is a tiny island that's so far from here."

"Yeah, Rima Dahlia, right?" Logan recalled. "So then– this tree, native to that area– just happened to show up here? Via one of those weird fissure things that have been causing trouble this whole time? I guess it could be a version of the way things have been showing up in unusual places, but so far, there's never been something as big as a whole tree being moved in this way."

"Does that mean things are getting worse?" Maceida asked.

"It certainly doesn't mean they're getting better," was Logan's reply.

The longer she stared at the tree, the more thoughts formed in Brecken's mind about everything that had been discussed so far– and before long, she raised her hand to call attention to herself. "I have a question. If the fissures are progressively getting worse, and the cause of the fissures is the veil being torn into every time Flavian uses magic, and the danger to the world itself is kinda only a factor because of that damage to that veil… respectfully, aside from our world not being able to see yours, is there any reason you actually need it to exist?"

Everyone native to the magic world stared at Brecken as if she'd said something incredibly offensive.

"I mean, if there's any other purpose it serves, you're gonna have to tell us, because we don't know," Jaiden explained. "Because, from our point of view, what Brecken said makes a lot of sense."

"Another purpose… I… I don't think that it does, actually." Arrigan was the first person to speak.

Before he could say anything else, Logan had grabbed his arm, which startled him. "It doesn't, but that veil is the creation of the goddesses; we must care for it and protect it as we do with everything else in this world! What kind of madness would it be if we got rid of it?! It makes no sense! It would be sacrilege–" Logan then turned to his grandparents. "Would it be sacrilege?"

However, Lisandra was the first person to have the answer. "It's a bit of a gray area, mostly because the veil isn't mentioned a lot in the goddesses' teachings apart from explaining what it does. For the record, I don't like the idea of destroying it either, but you've gotta admit: when your choices are that and potentially having the world itself torn apart, which would result in a whole lot of– if not complete– death, then..."

Logan was silent then. Even with how devoted he was to the goddesses, he knew Lisandra had a point.

With the following silence, Ofelia said, "By the way."

"Yes?" Logan was the first to respond.

"You mentioned your captain being taken captive. Even with the very few times I've met the man, this doesn't seem like him at all, to be caught off guard that way. There appears to be a piece to this puzzle that you all have yet to share– which would also explain why you are all here, instead of looking for him."

"We don't know where to start!" Lisandra replied. "It caught us off guard too!"

Arrigan explained, "Lisandra, Maceida, and I were in the square when we saw that Thunder– and Hunter, the Resistance's head strategist– were taken captive. Although, I guess an important detail is that none of us saw them get caught, and we didn't see them getting taken away, either; we only heard the sound of the cage they were in closing, but we know that they *are* captive, because we saw them captured, and neither came home last night."

"Since we didn't see their departure, we really have no way to know where they could've been taken," added Maceida. "It would've been different if we could've trailed behind them somehow, but according to the guys in the Resistance that investigated last night, there was no trail to follow."

"I see." Augusto nodded. "Which points to the usage of magic, certainly."

"Is there any way we'll ever be able to find them?" asked Mishaela, in a tone unsure of if she wanted to hear the answer.

To reassure her, Ofelia smiled warmly. "There is always a way, child."

Next, it was as if a collective sigh of relief was had throughout the garden. "But... what is the way, then?" asked Madeline. "Right now it just sounds like we got outsmarted in every possible way. And if I'm being honest, it kinda sucks."

"How do we square up against people who can use magic and stuff when we're just normal people?" added Jasiela. "They could end us, especially since we don't have help from the goddesses like we did last time."

"I see. Yes, those are daunting stakes. But you have forgotten one thing: that there are people on your side, as well, who can wield magic."

It was rather easy to forget, with everything happening, that even with Thunder and Hunter out of commission, there were still Arrigan and the Oliveiras; and each had their own unique magic, which could be used together to accomplish many things.

"Have you all been taught about the oracles of this world?" Augusto asked then.

Confused looks were traded throughout the crowd. "No, this sounds new to me at least," replied Brecken. "I would love to learn, though."

An affirmative nod, before the exposition began. "In this world, there are, occasionally, people born with the ability to hear the goddesses– if they allow themselves to be heard, of course. This sense of heightened hearing means that these people are highly in tune with magic and the ways in which it works; not necessarily from a scholarly standpoint, but more so that they're simply able to feel magic differently than those of regular birth. Its flow, its presence, and any sharp changes to it. In the past, oracles were tasked with the more mystic aspects of society: creating medicine, guiding scholars, as well as being involved with entertainment like fortune telling and light shows. But as our society grows less dependent on magic and develops more elaborate technology, the oracles of today are few and far in between; and the ones that still practice their abilities find it difficult to do so."

"But, they still can, right?" Madeline asked. "Whoo-hoo, this is sweet! Now we just need to find one of those oracles. You guys wouldn't happen to know where the nearest one is, right?"

This time, Logan smiled. "No need to start a search!" he replied. "We're fortunate enough to have someone of that flavor along with us already. Are you still able to hear the voices of the goddesses, Lisandra?"

Everyone turned to Lisandra; she looked up, startled. "Uh, yeah, I guess... if they yell."

Arrigan stared, aghast. "*You're* an oracle?!"

"You learn something new every day." Lisandra laughed nervously.

The awkward silence lasted longer than anyone present would have liked.

"Anyhow, regarding this tree: it is something that has never happened here before," Augusto said as he, too, gazed up at the tree. "Although I always love visits from my grandchildren, I have to ask that you give myself and my wife some time to study this occurrence."

"Sure." Logan nodded. "Thank you for everything, Grandpa and Grandma. We should probably be getting back and discussing things with Phoenix– uh, Taylor– anyway. Maybe we can think of something after we've consulted all the books at our disposal. I'll tell her you said hello."

"Of course. Safe travels, all of you."

When everyone left, Ofelia turned to her husband and asked, "Is Taylor still using her middle name? I don't understand why she does that."

"I do believe she said so last time she visited," Augusto nodded. "I don't understand it either, but you must admit that there is something poetic about our granddaughter, who has directly aided in Compositora's rebirth, being called Phoenix. I cannot say if *she's* had this thought, but it's a name that suits her much better than Taylor at this point, don't you think?"

"Such a nice observation. We'll have to tell her so, once everything has calmed down."

Finding Where To Start

Returning to Compositora instilled a sense of both purpose and haste within everyone; but at the time of arrival, they quickly realized that the pieces of information they had were still too fragmented to take any action with.

These things were true:

That Lisandra's power would be vital to finding where Thunder and Hunter were being held, and retrieving them safely, and

That the strange fissures that would randomly appear in different parts of the world were indicative of the veil that hid this world from earth tearing, which in turn was affecting the existence of the world itself– which was caused by magic being used improperly.

But what was the group to do about these things, at the present time? What *could* they do?

"Don't you guys worry about me," Lisandra tried to reassure everyone when they'd all settled in at home. "I've got everything under control. Part of the education I've been receiving since before I could talk has been about how to awaken my power in a safe, controlled way. If you need me, I'll be at the market; I need to grab a few materials for ritualistic purposes."

"Not alone, you're not," Phoenix replied. "Remember, things are extremely hostile right now for people who are affiliated with the Resistance, and we can't take the chance of you being attacked again. If we lose you, we're dead in the water."

Lisandra smiled and pointed a finger. "Got it, field trip. I'll round up a crew, then."

"While Lisandra is doing whatever it is she needs to do, where does that leave us?" Gavin asked. "We're here to help, right? There's got to be something we can do."

"Well..." Phoenix hesitated. "This stage will be a little harder for us to help with because it's such a specialized thing. The tears of the veil are so spontaneous that we can't just go looking for them, and not all of us were around when Thunder and Hunter were taken hostage. I guess we could go over the notes that some of the guys were able to get about the square, and compare them to what the three in the square saw... or two, since Lisandra will be gone for a little while. Hopefully, something will be born from that."

"Okay. And what about those of us that aren't really the scholarly type?" asked Jaiden. "What can we do to busy ourselves?"

At this point, it was easy to tell that Phoenix was running out of ideas. "You can escort Lisandra to the square. I don't know, okay?

This is a very short amount of time to prepare an itinerary based on very scarce and fragmented information, so excuse me if I sound a little rude– I'm just... adjusting to the situation. Badly."

She sighed then, plopping onto the floor of the living room.

"We haven't learnt, have we?" Spencer-Lynn asked, sitting beside her. "I'm sorry, Phoenix; this really is a lot of responsibility to put onto a single person."

"What do you mean by 'we haven't learned?'" Phoenix asked.

"I distinctly remember that things almost immediately began to fall apart last time we didn't have Thunder to look to for guidance," she replied. "Logan mentioned this yesterday, before we all went to bed. The solution, though I can't say with certainty, is certainly not to place all the responsibility on one person again. If there's anything we should know by now, it's to approach things in a more... what's the word here? We need a more democratic approach."

Phoenix nodded. "But how?"

"By doing the thing she said: being democratic!" Madeline replied. "We know a bunch of things we can do to start making this make sense. We should take on those tasks based on what comes easily to us. The Pagliardi sisters are both really good at studying, for example, so they're probably the best people to help Logan go through all that magical knowledge about fissures and weird trees appearing and all that. It would make sense for Arrigan and Maceida to look over those notes from the other day, but probably an even better idea to have someone with them who has a clear head. Brecken is pretty observant, so she might notice details that those two wouldn't."

"And you and I accompany Lisandra because we're good at kicking arse if need be?" Spencer-Lynn asked.

"You know it!" Madeline agreed, offering a hand to help her up. "We'll be back. Try not to stress yourself out too much, all right, Phoenix? We'll get through this thing. I just know it!"

***

Chiara, Mishaela, and Gavin accompanied Logan back to the Resistance's headquarters; the library there was still probably the best compendium of magical knowledge in this town, so it made sense to consult with it again. On the way, the houses and decorative fixtures began to become gradually more sparse; it was as if this part of the town was still unincorporated.

Gavin was the first to question this. "Is there a reason civilization appears to dwindle in this area?"

"Hm?" Logan looked back at him. "Oh! There is, and it is quite a simple answer. The rebuilding effort has only recently gone out this far. In time, I'm sure this area will not look too much unlike the one we currently live in; but we must remember that for all the innovation here, industry has only existed in this city for about eight months."

"That does make sense," Gavin agreed. "It is quite remarkable, when you think about it, how much has been done for this place in so little time. It's truly magical."

Logan nodded at this. "A lot of work and research has gone into ensuring that everything is built– or in some cases, rebuilt– with materials that strike an optimal balance between object and magic; I think the rapid degradation of the former palace really hammered that in for a lot of people. The Compositora that is currently being built is one that we want to be able to be home for generations to come, so longevity is imperative."

"I really like the brick pavement, personally," Mishaela said then, looking down at just that. "Yes, they're bricks. But I've noticed that, when light hits them at the correct angle, you can see all of the shimmers indicative of magic. It's so pretty."

"Well, this *is* the origin point of the magic world," Logan reminded her. "If our reputation is going to precede us in such a way, we might as well have a little fun with it. Insert a little whimsy into everyday life, right?"

When they arrived at the headquarters building, Logan immediately noticed that the front door wasn't locked, and was slightly cracked. This immediately put him on high alert and– gesturing to his younger charges to move back just a little, he swiftly opened the door and swung inside the main area.

Following was a startled yell, as– on the other side– Handel struggled to stay on top of the stool he was currently standing on.

"Oh! My apologies indeed, Handel," Logan said, clearly embarrassed. "What are you doing here? It is not in good form to have the front door open like that."

"I know, but lately the door has been squeaky," he explained. "I figured it should get fixed now, before something bad happens. What brings you here? I'm sure you'd rather be somewhere enjoying the lovely weather today, so something must have gone wrong."

Logan waved this off. "Nothing you need to be concerned about, as of yet. But I have arrived with a few friends; we'll be perusing the library here for an undetermined amount of time."

Handel nodded. "Sure. One of the guys actually just did the weekly dusting a couple of days ago, so everything should be fairly easy to look through. Do you have an estimate of how long you may be here? If you'll be staying through dinnertime, I can let Ella know to make a little extra food for you all."

"Would you? That would be excellent. I didn't even think of food," Logan admitted. "You guys run a pretty efficient ship here these days."

"It's easier to do that when the numbers are smaller," Handel pointed out.

With a nod, Logan stepped back outside to signal that everything was okay, and that his three charges were free to come in. Other than the occasional hello that Logan would give to fellow Resistance members when they'd pass each other, they made their way down to the library fairly quietly.

This large space was the same as it always had been: shelves upon shelves of books, candlelit chandeliers, and stained glass windows. As Handel had mentioned, the place was recently cleaned, which meant it was easier to find their way around than if it had been as dusty as it could get sometimes. When everyone had made it completely down the stairs, Logan pointed to a table. "Could you all take a seat there? There's something down here I need to grab that'll help us with our research."

The three teenagers shrugged before pulling out their chairs and sitting. "I wonder what he's looking for?" Mishaela asked.

"It's difficult to tell, with how uncertain we always are about what exists here and what doesn't," replied Gavin. "It would be very cool if we used one of those projector devices, though. I was completely enthralled by them last time."

"Here we are!" The sound of squeaking wheels preceded Logan's appearance from around the corner, as he carefully pushed what appeared to be a mounted chalkboard to the table. "This will be useful for note taking; it is a board we can all see and contribute to, so we won't have to constantly cross-reference each other. That can get clunky if we're all writing separately."

"For sure," agreed Gavin. "All right, so what are we doing here then? Have we got a plan?"

Logan hesitated. "Not so much a plan, but I think I do know where to start, in terms of what kinds of books we should be looking in to find the information we need. Books about this world and how magic affects it, of course, but we should probably steer older when it comes to the time of publication. The reason I say this is because we're dealing with a phenomenon many people have never seen before. The last time that was the case, we found more information in the more historical part of the library."

For the next few minutes, all four of the group searched through the shelves of this library, grabbing books and sifting through them to decide if they were worth a more in-depth look through their contents. This lasted for about a half-hour, before they gradually made it back to the table to continue their research. Much time passed then, mostly quietly, before any notes were taken.

"Logan, before I write anything, I have a question." Chiara raised her hand timidly.

He smiled warmly. "Of course, Chiara. I will try to answer to the best of my ability."

"Okay." She flipped back a few pages in the book currently open in front of her. "In this book that I'm reading, the writer mentions a 'balance' pretty frequently, in a way that indicates it's something important to this world. I think I may recall someone else mentioning something like that at some point last time, too. But what is it? What's being balanced?"

"Ah." Logan nodded in response. "You are correct. As you all know, this world was created with magic. It needs magic to support its continued existence. But what you may not have known is that the quantities of magic necessary to do so are highly specific. It is imperative to keep an appropriate balance of every element abound, or else our world begins to be affected in various ways— all of which, over time, negatively affect our quality of life here. This is important enough that there is usually an individual tasked with ensuring this balance is not disturbed."

"The Keeper of the Balance, right?" Chiara asked.

"Exactly. They are— similarly to witches and some other beings in our world— human, but on a plane of existence that's different than, say, me and my sister and all of our friends. Though, now that this has been brought up..." Logan thought. "Our current Keeper has not been seen in quite a while. I wonder if this has anything to do with those fissures?"

The four pondered this for a moment.

"Does it– no. Would it make sense that way?" Gavin was the first to ask. "I mean, it sounds as though it would. Would it not be easier to wreak havoc upon the world if it's already not doing the greatest?"

Mishaela turned to Logan then. "When you said that nothing good comes of the elements being out of balance: how exactly can you tell? What starts happening?"

Logan took a breath before answering. "Well, that's a highly variable thing that's dependent on what's going on with the elements. For example, if there isn't enough water magic, we'll begin to experience drought-like conditions. If there is not enough light, our days will get shorter, and nights will become longer. But this works the other way around too; that if there is too much of an element, we'll be ruined by excess. Think of constant windstorms, or being driven out of our homes by invasive plant life."

"So..." the wheels were beginning to turn in all of their heads, however slowly. "When we went to visit your grandparents, Logan, something that was brought up was the incorrect usage of power; using power that a human isn't meant to have," Gavin said after a little while. "Would that be similar, sinve that's also a type of magic distribution? Do you happen to know how disastrous that could be, if left unchecked?"

"If he doesn't, I think I might." Mishaela picked up one of the books that she had placed aside when she had finished it. "The first book I skimmed over was about disasters and how they come to pass.

I think one of them mentioned the adverse effects of magic. I could be wrong, but I think I saw something about the worst things any one person could do."

"Yes, let's consult that for sure," Logan said, nodding. "We can compare it to what I know about the world's balance of magic."

As Mishaela and Gavin both looked through the book, Chiara raised her hand slowly. "I have another question. Something else that came up yesterday, that veil that's being torn into, and it affecting the world itself. Is there a way to separate them? That way, even if the veil continues to tear, it won't keep doing whatever it's doing to this world? It would give everybody more time to research how to keep that veil intact, too, without needing to worry about it affecting the world at large."

"Right about now, that's sounding like a great idea if it's an option," Gavin said then, looking up from the book he and Mishaela were reading through. "This book is detailing all manner of nasty things– if not for the human who stole the magic themself, then for the environment; the very survival of this world. It says here: 'if the misuse of magic that does not belong to humans persists for an extended period of time, it will drive the human to madness; and in that case, the state of the entire world is in danger. It can never be determined if the magic will overpower the human and have them die, or if the magic, continuing to be weld, will tear apart the world, to a state where all life ceases to exist.'"

"Are we going to die?!" Mishaela asked quickly.

Logan opened his mouth to protest this, but closed it. He did this a second time, standing, before finally being able to speak. "I really cannot say one way or the other."

All three faces turned to him with worry and fear plastered over them. Chiara looked as though she could start crying any second.

"I want to be optimistic, but I also don't want to give any of you false hope," Logan followed up, with a sigh. "And so, I cannot say. This isn't something I've ever experienced in all my nineteen years, so all of it is new to me as well. I don't want to die either, but... at this point, it would only be a disadvantage to completely discount the possibility."

"Where is your motivation, man?" Gavin asked him, abruptly standing up, and barely restraining the urge to reach across the table and grab him. "You aren't being yourself! You're usually so full of energy and happiness and that can-do attitude; have things gotten so dire that they weigh upon even you?!"

"I want to! To be like I usually am, that is, but this is so out of my wheelhouse that I– there's a part of me that feels helpless," Logan confessed. "My strengths are combat and history. I can't fight my way out of this, and history continues to make the picture more and more grim. What's a person to do in a situation like this, if not despair?"

"That doesn't mean you should just give up, though!" Mishaela pointed out. "You never have! None of us have! Even when it felt like the situation was impossible to surmount, we kept fighting– even if the fight wasn't physical, you know?"

Logan looked up at her. "Well, of course I haven't *given up*. Why do you think I'm here with you all now? What kind of man would I be if I left all my family and friends to die? But I am also only human, and therefore occasionally given to moments of little faith. Come, we'll all continue to work together to find a solution to our current predicament."

Everyone sat back down then, intent on finding an answer to the fissure problem that didn't end with anyone dying.

***

In the square, Lisandra was busy perusing the goods at a herbal stall as Jaiden, Madeline, and Spencer-Lynn busied themselves in her general area. It wasn't the most riveting thing to have been tasked with doing, but all three of them were waiting for someone to approach them in a hostile way, to give them a reason to lose their cool.

Lisandra, though, was having a hard time picking out the things she needed. "Excuse me," she waved her hand to get the stall owner's attention. "Hi. Got a question about these leaves over here. These are completely dried, right? And, if I were to bundle them up real nice and burn them, would the smoke still give off that nice citrusy scent– even if it's kind of like an afterthought?"

The clerk shook their head. "Not those. If you're looking for citrus scents, one of these over here will likely suit your needs better. If it interests you, I can suggest a few burning blends that contain the more citrusy leaves."

"Oh, would you?" Lisandra asked eagerly, her hands clasped together. "That would be just amazing!"

As they continued to speak, Jaiden turned to Spencer-Lynn, who was busy examining a can of some type of herbal medicine. "Not the most exciting thing to do for the day, huh?" she asked.

She looked up, only slightly startled. "I don't know. I'm learning a lot on this mission. Did you know there's some type of venomous fish here? It can evidently bite you whilst you're fishing for it."

Jaiden grimaced. "Yikes."

"Yeah, I only know this because of this medicine, here. It's supposed to mitigate the pain and scarring," Spencer-Lynn explained, before she placed the jar back on its counter. "I can concede that this errand is less exciting than I thought it would be, though. I wonder what everyone else is getting up to at this point in time."

"Don't worry, I'm sure Logan is keeping a seat beside him warm for you," Jaiden smirked.

Spencer-Lynn almost didn't hear that, but just as she was about to say something, Lisandra returned with her arms full. "Good news! The only thing I need now is an ash holder, which I'm pretty sure Phoenix already has at home. We can head back now; if she doesn't have one, I can always just make one from whatever's lying around."

"To the place of residence!" Madeline pointed back toward the residential district.

***

Recounting the day in the square meant that the memories weren't as fresh as they had been the day before– all parties could recognize now that it was a bad move to not immediately document these memories, but there was no point in chastising oneself over the mistakes of the past. For now, the group of three were hard at work taking down everything they could.

"I have another question. Right around when both of you agreed that something was wrong..." Brecken paused, trying to gather her words. "What exactly... I mean, I know you both mentioned having some sort of feeling. But was there something else that contributed, other than those feelings? For example, you know how when you get that kind of vibe that something bad is going to happen, but it takes another thing to set you in motion against it? That kind of thing."

This question gained a pensive silence from Arrigan and Maceida.

"In my case, it was like the confirmation I needed was Maceida agreeing with me, which I know isn't particularly helpful," Arrigan replied. "But now that I think about it– after we found Lisandra, only then did we hear that metallic clanging of the cage closing. Isn't it a bit strange how we didn't hear anything like that before then?"

"Yes, actually. I didn't see that cage beforehand, and considering how tall Hunter is and how much clearance the top of his head had, that's not something we would've missed when entering the square," agreed Maceida. "How did they do it, then? How did they manage to get a cage big enough to fit two fully grown people inside, into the middle of the square, without drawing attention to themselves?"

"Or- *or*. What if the appearance of the cage was what kicked off the disturbance?" Arrigan asked, pointing a finger. "Maybe it wasn't there before, but when it arrived, people– predictably– started getting really uneasy; and that created the shift in the crowd that we both picked up on."

Another pensive silence.

"Brecken, why did Hunter and Thunder ever go to the square in the first place, do you know?" Arrigan asked then.

"No, I don't. I'm sorry; I was in the bedroom with Chiara when they left; she was teaching me about chess to pass the time," Brecken replied. "But I do remember vaguely hearing Thunder speaking to someone before he left. Phoenix was gone when you guys got back, so it was more likely Logan."

"Have you got another idea about what may have happened?" Maceida asked.

Arrigan shook his head. "Not just yet. I just want to be sure that we're not being watched, but also, knowing what they were there for might give us more clues. It had to have been something that one of us couldn't do on our own, because it would be just silly for them to go themselves rather than ask us to pick something up or run an errand for them, right? So, hopefully, one of the Oliveiras can tell us."

Maceida affirmed softly, and took a breath before speaking fully. "I have a question. Arrigan, it's more likely a you question."

"Me? U-um, I guess. What is it?"

"I haven't gotten around to asking about it because I've been struggling to really process and perceive that I'm in a place that I never knew existed until a few days ago– and because of that, my attention span hasn't been the greatest. But..." she explained. "I've been able to grasp, from little bits of the conversation here and there, that the Resistance– or Thunder, at least– personally knows that man with white hair, the one who's responsible for herding he and Hunter like cattle. Am I right, or have I misunderstood?"

Brecken and Arrigan both let out a sigh that sounded like they'd been aged ten years.

"Unfortunately, I'm able to answer this," Brecken said then. "Flavian is a former member of the Resistance. The reason I'm able to tell you what happened is because I was present for what I believe is the reason he withdrew– and so was Spencer-Lynn, so she may have already mentioned that there was this really big, monumental battle in the town's square that resulted in casualties. One of the casualties was Flavian's partner, Etzel."

"Fiancé," Arrigan corrected. "They were engaged."

"Oh! I... wasn't aware. So that's why..." Brecken's expression sank even lower with this new information. "I cannot even begin to find words to describe the anguish with which he wailed when being presented with the news that the man he loved would no longer be at his side, but it was something I continued to think of long after it had happened."

"I'm told that after that happened, he didn't immediately leave the Resistance," Arrigan added. "But he did not have an active role in any of the plans that Brecken and the others set in place for their predicament, which– I think– was logical considering what had happened. I've never met him personally, he had resigned from the

Resistance by the time I moved here. But I remember Logan saying something about that event completely breaking him. How he had always been mild-mannered, but at least attempted to be friendly as well. After the battle in the square it was rare to hear him speak at all."

"So..." Maceida was processing all of this. "Then, his entire grievance with the Resistance is because he blames the entire organization for what happened?"

Arrigan nodded. "That appears to be what it is. When, um, when something happens that makes you realize that someone you looked up to is not infallible... sometimes, it can be a slippery slope. When viewing someone through a lens of critical scrutiny, it's really easy to twist everything they do into negativity. I think that's what got us where we are now."

"Right. Oh..." Maceida yawned just a bit, rubbing her eyes. "I can't imagine what must be going through that man's head right now, but I can imagine that right about now, it's not a place that's hospitable, nor rational. Should we be worried about how safe our friends are, as long as they're within his custody?"

"I wouldn't be able to say," Arrigan shrugged. "Remember, I've never actually met him. When Logan gets back, I'm sure he'll be able to add on to all of the things we've jotted down so far. In the meantime, we should continue to think about everything related to that day."

"Right." Maceida nodded. "Until then: Brecken, is there anything else you'd like to ask about the situation in the square?"

Imprisonment

When the sun rose, it always cast a golden glow over the side of the dungeon cell that Hunter slept on.

The window was barred, but it didn't have any glass panes, so it was easy to hear the sounds of birds chirping and feel the gentle morning breeze through the bars. If he could make himself forget about where he was and why he was there, this part of the day felt a lot easier. He was usually the only person up at this hour, which gave him time to reflect on his thoughts; reflect, and (hopefully) come that much closer to finding a way out of this place.

So far, he hadn't had much luck when it came to that. He and Thunder had scoured the cell relentlessly that first night, hoping to find any sort of secret passage or hole, but the search was fruitless; this place was as airtight as could be, which was impressive given its age. If the general damp, musty smell and the moss covering the stone walls didn't give away that this was an ancient place, the lack of current infrastructure certainly did. Whenever either man would be directed to the bathroom, it would take them much longer to make water flow than it did in any establishment in Compositora. Clearly, the sinks, showers, and toilets had not been used in a long time.

"Morning." Hunter was greeted with a dry wave from his superior– the same way it had been every morning here, but it still managed to startle him.

"Ah. Best of mornings, Thunder. Or should I say, as best as they can be?" Hunter punctuated his question with a sigh.

Thunder turned toward him. "You sound a lot more defeated than usual. Guess we've been here long enough for that already, huh."

Hunter didn't answer. Instead, he folded his hands in his lap and asked, "What do you think will become of us?"

True to his strategist nature, Hunter always asked the questions that others wouldn't think of asking– or asking aloud, rather, because Thunder certainly had wondered this a few times already. Of course he'd had to have at this point, but there had been something keeping him from asking it with his voice. Perhaps he was worried about making Hunter too anxious; or too proud to admit that he wasn't entirely sure.

He asked, "What do you mean?"

"I..." Hunter thought to himself for a moment or two. "Even with everything that's happened, I don't believe that Flavian is so much of a changed man that he'd kill us. He is not the same man that would timidly ask me to direct him to our books of folklore, of that I am certain; still, would it not have served him much more to have just killed us in the square, if that was his intent?"

"Oh, Hunter, always the sharp one."

Both men's heads turned to see their captor, dressed in a black pantsuit made of some floral brocade, his white hair falling over his shoulder in the same braid they remembered him with. It was almost a mockery, to see such shadows of a man that, before, both were quite fond of– knowing that that man no longer existed, and what stood in front of them now was only a shell of him; twisted, almost warped beyond recognition.

"You've come to visit us so early? You did not intend to jest when you said we were esteemed guests, I see." Hunter, although usually mild-mannered, did not flinch when he said this, and the sarcasm was delivered with nary a tremble in his voice. Impressive for any twenty-four-year-old, but especially one of his temperament; if the circumstances were any different, Thunder would have probably congratulated him.

"When there's a clear goal to be achieved, I'm not one to dally. You remember that, don't you?" Flavian asked, taking a look around the area before finding a small barrel and pulling it over to the cell, taking a seat and folding one leg over the other. He took a moment to swallow, moistening his throat, before asking: "...what are we doing here, boys?"

The question confused both Thunder and Hunter. "You mean, you don't know?" Thunder asked. "You're better than that."

Flavian tilted his head, before letting out a laugh that was only slightly amused. "Oh, no, no. I need you to analyze my question a bit deeper to understand what I mean. Of course I know what *I'm* doing. I am merely pointing out that it's been..." he paused, as if counting in his head, "almost a week now, and there have been no reports of your contemporaries attempting to bust you out of here before I could end you. That is not what I expected of you at all. Then again, I suppose that without you at the helm, there isn't anyone around to send young people to their deaths, is there?"

"You watch your mouth," Thunder pointed a finger.

"I don't believe that," Hunter said at the same time.

Flavian turned to the redhead. "Really? You think the rest of the Resistance is so cold?"

"I don't believe you'd kill anyone," Hunter clarified. "I don't believe you could look into the eyes of anyone you once called a comrade, a friend– Thunder and I included– and kill them. Even now, when you've changed so much, I do not believe for a second that you are capable of taking a life."

This made Flavian narrow his eyes, as everything that Hunter said sank in. "You're calling me weak, aren't you? You still think I'm that same little wimp from before? Well, you couldn't be more wrong! I learned, in record time, that if you're going to survive in this world, you need to be strong, and even more so than that; you need to be unforgiving. And now, thanks to a little help from a friend, I can make sure I'm both of those."

He stood, taking a few steps back before lifting both his arms, and summoning balls of lightning to both his hands. This lightning was immensely strong, so much so that the surrounding area rumbled as if there was an earthquake happening. The static from the bolts also made both men's hair frizz, and the fabrics of their clothes became electrically charged as well. It built in intensity– quickly, and relentlessly, to a point where it became painful– before it finally stopped, and the two were left with Flavian looking intensely satisfied.

"That amount of power…" Hunter was saying. "And of a specific element that you did not have control of before! Who's responsible for this?!"

"And why would I tell you? So you could try to gain the same power? Or warn your little friends about it?"

"Why?"

Both younger men turned to Thunder.

"Why are ya goin' to all this effort, son?" he continued. "I don't get it. I just… cannot understand what it is you want to accomplish, with everything you've done so far. None of it makes sense."

"Oh, doesn't it? Well, I'm not so stupid that I'd divulge my entire plan to you, but…"

Flavian turned on his heel, walking as close to the bars and Thunder's face as he could.

"You will never understand anything that I do until you've felt the hurt that I have. And so, it's my job to make sure that you do. I will not rest until, like me, you have nothing left."

Both men waited until the footsteps were so distant they could barely be heard.

"He is a shell of himself," Hunter muttered softly, before turning to Thunder. "Do we have any bright ideas on what to do next, captain?"

His response was to hum just a bit longer than what was usual for a response. Finally, he looked back at Hunter. "I don't know."

"You–" Hunter was so stupefied, for a moment, he found it difficult to form words. "You don't know?"

"I don't know." Thunder let out a sigh as he stretched, placing his hands behind his head. "You heard what the man said. Killin' me ain't his angle. So, we're faced with being in captivity. We do nothin' and that's where we stay, unless the kids are working on some grand plan right about now. We break out of here... how? And what would we do with Flavian? We both know that, even now, his beef is with me; he wouldn't go around hurtin' other people, so it wouldn't make sense to retaliate against him too much. After all, we don't wanna make all that stuff he's been sayin' about us be true, do we."

It was Hunter's turn to sigh. "A predicament, indeed."

"For now..." Thunder began. "For now, I think the best thing we can do here is bide our time. Logan and Phoenix are capable; they're probably trainin' up the kids to come find us somehow, and in the meantime we study this place to see if there's any pieces to the puzzle we can uncover that'll help us when it's time to liberate ourselves."

Hunter nodded. "I suppose that is all we can do, then. I will continue to try and think of ways to escape this cell, at the very least."

Thunder gazed over to where Hunter was now investigating the ivory bars of the cell. He would occasionally knock on them, most likely to determine if they were hollow, before busying himself with something else. Hunter was pretty capable, himself; he had a talent for being extremely detailed in just about everything he did, which was part of what made him a good strategist. Even now, having been trapped in a cage and now locked in some kind of dungeon, he hadn't lost his composure.

They'd get out of here soon, he just knew it.

With What We Now Know

The following days revealed much less than everyone was hoping for.

Even with them all taking their search for knowledge to the streets of Compositora, it was difficult to find information that they didn't already know. For all of her efforts, Lisandra was still struggling to harness her power in a substantial way. It was beginning to be difficult to not lose hope.

"What else can we even do?" Jaiden asked, seated at the dining room table with Logan and Spencer-Lynn. "It's like we've turned this town upside down, and yet we've made zero progress at all. There's got to be some kinda way those guys slipped up, or something?"

Logan shrugged. "Not so far. They've been infuriatingly good at keeping their operations concise."

A collective sigh sounded around the table.

"Wait. Logan," Spencer-Lynn turned to him, "I had a thought just now. What's the probability of the person who took Thunder and Hunter captive moving them out of the Compositora area?"

"Considering we haven't seen them since– and not for lack of searching– pretty likely," Logan replied. "Which only makes things even messier, because we have no way of knowing which city they went to, if that's the case. Ugh. I hate it here."

Spencer-Lynn nodded. "I asked because, if all the strange miscreants have gone and disappeared from this town, would it not make it easier to get into that area where the huge cage was? Remember, no one was able to get close last time because there were people guarding it."

"You're right," Logan pointed a finger. "After breakfast, I'll hash it out with Phoenix to decide which of us should go. So that is something, but we could probably also do with some more plans in case this ends up not bearing any fruit. Currently, there are only two towns you can get to from here via train. Based on the reported size of that cage, it would be too large and heavy to take on a ferry from the City of Garnet, so that at least makes the search radius that much smaller."

"Right, and there's mountains past the other city, right?" asked Jaiden. "Can't imagine anyone being able to get something that big and heavy over that type of terrain."

Logan nodded. "Which means our radius effectively becomes this city, and the cities on either side of it, train-wise. I'll go see if I can use the telephone down the block to get in touch with my family; they'll be happy to share any knowledge they have of strange happenings or people in the City of Garnet. When Arrigan wakes up, I'll ask him if he'd be willing to call his parents. I'll be right back; you two know the deal if my sister asks where I am, right?"

"Tell her where you are, that you'll be right back, and to downplay the urgency of the situation?" Jaiden asked.

With a smile and a click of his tongue, Logan left the room.

"Now to find something to get into while they're all gonna be busy," Jaiden said then, standing. "You staying put, Spencer-Lynn?"

"Ah, not likely, not for long anyway. Once Maceida gets up, she'll be pretty intent on discovering more of this place. She's pretty mystified about everything here, which I suppose is about right. Still, though, I don't think I've seen her eyes sparkle like they have here, ever, especially not since she got home. I think that, in a weird roundabout way, her being pulled here has been good for her."

Jaiden hummed. "Maybe that was the motivation, then."

"Motivation?" Spencer-Lynn repeated.

"Yeah. You know how the goddesses of this world have some awareness of our own, right? You were automatically gonna be brought back because you've been here before, I think, but maybe they were able to see that your sister needed this break from her daily life or something," Jaiden explained. "We all need one sometime, right?"

Spencer-Lynn nodded without a word, her thoughts of how dire things were for Maceida back home becoming top of mind. "Yeah. Sometimes."

"Well–" Jaiden stood up, with a grunt and a stretch. "I'll get out of your hair for now. Gotta get back to my room. Mishaela gets really overdramatic if she wakes up and things aren't like she expected them to be."

"See you later." Spencer-Lynn waved, before turning back to her mostly eaten bowl of oatmeal. Logan had assembled the bowl for her, so she wasn't sure what exactly was in it– she'd have to ask him what he'd added when he got back, because the combination had been delicious. She was confident there was brown sugar and some type of berry, at least.

Not much longer after she'd finished off the oatmeal, Maceida sat down in the chair that Logan had been sitting in. "Morning. What's on for breakfast today?"

"I think we're all on our own, today," Spencer-Lynn replied. "There's plenty of eggs and bread in the kitchen, there's corn flakes. Logan made me a bowl of oatmeal before he left, so I just finished that."

Maceida sat at the table, pensively, before turning to her sister. "You and Logan are pretty close, huh."

"It was one of those things where we got along instantly," she replied. "When I first ended up here, he was the one who explained everything to me, in a way that was digestible enough, considering. And from there, we trained together, baked for the Resistance together. I'm not certain of if you've caught on yet, but the Oliveira family is Portuguese, so we also have *two* languages in common."

"Ah, fun! I'm glad you've found an avenue to use your Portuguese; I know that's always been important to you. Well, there's no one here to make *me* a bowl of oatmeal, so I think I'll go scavenge. Keep my seat warm, aye?"

As she stood in front of the pantry, browsing through the foods stored there, Spencer-Lynn hesitantly turned her body in that direction. "Maceida, may I ask you something?"

"I'm more concerned over the fact that you felt you had to ask than whatever it is you're about to ask me." Her voice was slightly muffled due to being in the pantry. "All right then, what's got you so formal all of a sudden?"

"I didn't intend on being formal. It's just that the question involves an unfamiliar subject, so I get nervous whenever I think about it," explained Spencer-Lynn. "But I realize now that you're a good person to talk to about feelings, right?"

Maceida pulled her head out of the pantry quickly and turned to her sister. "No. Absolutely not. I am the *worst* person to talk to about feelings. How could you ever think otherwise? The whole reason we're able to talk to each other like this now, is because I can't sort out all the feelings that are inside my head."

"Yeah, but you're still really good at knowing what those feelings are, even if they're all tangled up within each other," Spencer-Lynn pointed out. "I can't even get that far. I'm not accustomed to this at all."

Hearing this, Maceida placed the box of cereal she was holding on the table, as she slowly sat back in her seat. "Wait a minute. Exactly what type of... *feelings* are we talking about, here?"

***

"It was such an interesting place."

Before this statement was uttered, it had been completely quiet in the spare bedroom; both Cambridge girls were gone, so it was just Brecken and Chiara, and both were very comfortable by now with complete silence between them in the same room. But then, Chiara had spoken. The surprise of it all almost made Brecken drop her croissant sandwich.

"What was an interesting place?" Brecken asked. She noticed then that Chiara was seated facing the wall, not a window or a photo, so it made it that much more difficult to understand what she meant.

Chiara turned, then, seemingly having forgotten that anyone was in the room with her. "Oh, I'm sorry, Brecken. I didn't mean to disturb you. I was thinking about the place that Logan, Phoenix, and Lisandra's family lives in. The City of Garnet, correct? It was about two hours away, if I recall, and yet it was as if we'd been transported to a different part of the world. Two hours is... I've been in the car with my parents and Mishaela for two hours before, and we hadn't even left the Chicago metro by then."

Brecken laughed, knowing this was probably brought on by the Midwest's penchant for never-ending construction. "I know, but even before you think about the fact that magic is involved here, maybe it's just high-speed rail. We don't have that in the US, so it's kind of unfathomable– or at least, not top of mind– but two hours would give a person a lot more distance on a high-speed train."

"It would, wouldn't it?" agreed Chiara, now considering the possibility of them having traveled a long distance at high speed. *Oh, if only I had paid more attention to what was outside the windows.*

"I do wish we were able to spend more time there," Brecken said then. "I understand why we couldn't, but it was such a charming city. The bustle of a very populated metropolitan area, plus all the mysticism that comes with being in a world of magic, and the slightest tinge of sea salt in the air, from the nearby, uh, I think it's an ocean–"

"You can tell when there's sea salt in the air?" Chiara asked.

"Pacific Northwest. Being in the Midwest, one of the first things I noticed was the air feeling different," Brecken explained. "I would have loved to see the marina."

The door cracked open slightly then, startling both girls; but both relaxing when Lisandra poked her head in. "Hey, sorry to interrupt without knocking; the door was already cracked, so I wasn't sure if anyone was in... anyway, have either of you seen Phoenix? I wanted to ask her about a book that I know she owns."

"I'm sorry, but I don't think I've seen her at all today," Brecken replied.

"I have, not long ago at all. She was in the front yard," Chiara added. "I saw her speak to Logan for a brief moment; I think I heard her say something about trying to get in contact with her parents, which is why I was thinking about the City of Garnet just now."

"You usually live there, don't you, Lisandra?" Brecken asked. "We were just talking about how lovely it seemed to be when we were there."

This made Lisandra come into the room, sitting on one of the pillows on the floor. "It is a great place to live! Well... I don't know if I'd say 'great.' Maybe just 'good.' It's just, when it comes to the gemstone cities, the City of Garnet is arguably the most formal one. It can feel a little stuffy, sometimes, because of that."

Both girls nodded, understanding. It would probably feel doubly that way for someone young and headstrong like Lisandra.

"Lisandra, I've heard you guys say 'the gemstone cities' more than once at this point," Brecken said then. "I think I remember Logan mentioning something about them being places that are particularly significant to the goddesses, or something..? I don't really recall. What I'm getting at, though, is asking if the reason everyone is so formal in the City of Garnet is because it's inherently a more sacred place."

"Oh! Nah, not really. It's just the way it is there; I think it has more to do with the first university ever being built there, so there's a lot of scholarly types, and they can be kind of snooty," Lisandra replied. "If you guys aren't busy, I can tell you what the other five gemstone cities are like."

This immediately got Chiara and Brecken to sit near her on cushions on the floor. "Please?" they both asked in unison.

"Sure!" Lisandra grinned. "Keep in mind that this is mostly based on what I learned in school, though, because I haven't been to any of these except one. So, it's funny you mentioned a city being inherently more sacred and pious, Brecken, because there actually is a city like that. That would be Lunagrad, where the most beautiful lunar stone resides in its city center. This is the city represented by wind, and people who are especially devoted to the goddesses mostly reside there. Since *this* place was a dumpster fire for ages, many of the former residents of Compositora relocated there. If you can stand people being especially particular about religious matters, this would probably be the best place to learn about the goddesses and everything they've done for our world– if we had time to go there, that is.

"When I said I'd been to one of these before, that's the City of Aquamarine. If you recall, you can get there from the ferries that dock in the City of Garnet, and since that's where I live, it's never been difficult to go there. It's a beautiful seaside city, and everyone there is so laid-back and chill about... everything, really. The drawback about that is, you run into issues sometimes if something serious happens while you're there. Still, it's my favorite vacation spot... not that I get to go on vacations often, with all my studying duties, but that's not really the point. Moving on.

"My grandparents mentioned the City of Heliodor, which is located close to the mountains. This city is represented by the element of light, but I'm told you wouldn't need anyone to tell you that if you visited. There are frequent thunderstorms there, so it's not uncommon to see a lot of partially burnt pine trees and buildings built with the best in lightning-diverting technology. It's also colder than a lot of other cities on average, so it's probably the least visited of all six cities.

"The City of Emerald– predictably, the city that represents the earth element– is just as predictably covered in greenery. It's located within the wetlands on the other side of the mountains, and has a relatively warm climate. I hear that the people there are very kind, and always willing to do what they can to make sure any visitors feel at home. I really want to visit there someday. Maybe I'll finally be able to when I'm an adult.

"Finally, there's Andesitia, the fiery city– named so because it's the city represented by fire, but also because it rests at the foot of a volcano. It hasn't erupted within my grandparents' lifetime, but it does make the surrounding areas very warm. The houses there are made of some kind of clay; they look really cool. I was reading a book once that said there's some produce that's specifically grown solely there because the volcanic atmosphere changes the growing conditions. I really want to go there too, someday. Can you even begin to imagine all the cool foods they must cook down there?"

"It does sound very lovely," agreed Brecken. "I wish we had time to explore your world, while we're here."

"Hell, I wish *I* had time to explore it," admitted Lisandra. "Maybe things will be different in the future, you know? Maybe someday, things will have changed so much that we could visit each other's worlds for fun, instead of just for duty."

"That would be nice," Chiara said softly.

Lisandra nodded. "Well, anyway, I'll get out of you guys' hair now. I really ought to track down my cousin. See you!"

***

Arriving at the front door with intent to leave, Maceida paused before slipping into her shoes. It had been more than a week at this point, but she still wasn't confident in her ability to navigate the city on her own yet. She really wanted to get some fresh air and maybe some of the local sweets, but it wasn't worth getting lost over. In addition to how much panic she'd bring upon herself, Spencer-Lynn would be worried sick.

"Maceida. Are you headed somewhere?" She was familiar enough with Arrigan's voice to know he was the person speaking to her before she turned around.

"Where, exactly?" She asked. "I think you've turned me around enough to know I'm abysmally bad at finding my way around."

"I don't know. Maybe you wanted to use the phone at the end of the block," Arrigan suggested. "No one has ever tried to call your world from it, so you could've been curious about if it was possible. I don't know."

Well, she was curious about it *now...*

"Anyway, if you're getting stir-crazy, I'm not busy. Do you want to head down to the marketplace? I have a craving for some food from some very specific stalls." Arrigan stepped in front of her to open the door. "I'll lead the way."

Today was cooler than usual, so much so that both young adults were grateful that they'd chosen to wear long sleeves today. After about five minutes of walking, Maceida suddenly realized why, and stopped in her tracks.

"The sun isn't out."

Arrigan turned to her. "Yeah, that happens sometimes," he explained. "It's usually sunny here, but occasionally we have an overcast day like this. The good thing is that, being in the desert and all, we don't have to worry about a spontaneous downpour– but it does still feel strange, sometimes, to not have the sun overhead."

"You won't be hearing any complaints from me," Maceida mumbled, as they continued on.

Arriving at the market, the crowds were thinner than usual–partly because of the cloudy day, partly because of the spectacle a few days ago now, and partly because of the time of day; it was about three p.m., so it was too late for the lunch rush, but not quite late enough for the last-minute dinner purchases. Currently, there was no line at the stand Arrigan wanted to go to most, so he put enough pep in his step to get over there before anyone else did.

Maceida had a mind to ask him what the rush was, but she happened to notice the chefs of the stall cooking before she could get the question out. "Oh, pierogies!" she said, pointing.

"It's already–" Arrigan paused. "You recognize these."

"I do! I had a classmate whose parents would make them for holidays, occasionally," Maceida explained. "I like the strawberry ones."

Arrigan thought some more. "That's right, Hunter told me about how cultures are somewhat shared between worlds. My mom makes really good strawberry pierogi– and that's the plural version of the word, by the way."

"Is it? I didn't know that. Huh." Maceida nodded. "I'll try my best to remember that."

Being handed his order, Arrigan gestured toward one of the sweets stands. "We can go there next."

Indeed, the aromas became more sweet as they drew closer to the stand making those delectable pastries. Today, there seemed to be a particular emphasis on cinnamon rolls, so they ordered a few of those.

"I'm sorry if we're, uh... what did you call it? Not close enough to each other yet for me to be asking about this, but I noticed that you speak with a different accent than everyone else," Arrigan said as they sat in the grass just outside of the square. There had been plenty of seating, but somehow he knew that both of them wouldn't want to be around the noise.

"Aye, so it is. I do suppose that, at this point, my accent would also be decidedly different from Spencer-Lynn's; about half my life has been away from home at this point," Maceida mused to herself.

"Oh, yeah. I keep forgetting that Spencer-Lynn is your sister," Arrigan replied. "It's mostly the fact that you two don't look alike, but it's– I know *why* this is, but it's also that Logan seems to know her much better than he knows you."

"Boy, does he," Maceida replied softly. Louder, she continued: "It's interesting that all of you here speak differently to each other, too, despite all living together. I remember you saying you've just moved here recently, but even the others are all so different."

"Yeah, a person's speech patterns will be highly variable here," Arrigan replied. "It's more dependent on one's community and family than where they live. It's interesting how, despite how different all of our backgrounds are, something like that is so fragmented. There's probably been studies done about that by people more intelligent and observant than I am, though."

"More observant than you? The person who noticed my accent being slightly different than my sister's? This I have to see." The smile on Maceida's face made it obvious she was teasing.

"Y-yeah..." Arrigan agreed, clearly flustered by having this pointed out. "But that's the way I've always been. I think it's because I've always been placed in a support role whenever I'd practice my magic, which requires a person to be observant in order to be effective. It does kind of fit my personality too, though, when I think about it, being a person who doesn't really like to be at the forefront of... anything, really."

"Hm? Why's that?" Maceida asked.

Arrigan blinked, surprised that anyone would ask; in his mind (and in most of his interactions with others), it was obvious. "Well, I mean, look at me. I'm this short, tiny guy who can't really do much in the way of face-to-face conflict, at least not directly, and I'm too timid to be any type of leader. It makes more sense for me to be in the background of things, doesn't it?"

"I suppose so. I can't relate, because obviously," Maceida gestured to herself. "Loud and tall girl, might as well be a theater kid. I kind of draw attention to myself even when I'm not trying. That creates its own problems sometimes. On some level, I envy your ability to not do that; but as a plus, that means we'll inevitably be a great team for whatever showdown is to come, right?"

"Yeah." Arrigan smiled. "I admire your ability to adjust so well."

Maceida shrugged. "Did I have a choice?"

She had a point. "True, but as far as I know, you did it without any emotional breakdowns. I couldn't even move here for school with that level of composure."

"Well, then, we'll get you to the point where you have it too!" Maceida grinned, standing up. "Whilst we're getting our plans together, we can work together to improve our weaknesses; I can teach you how to take up space, and you can help me with shutting up once in a while."

Arrigan laughed, standing and brushing his hands off on his pants. "Yeah. Let's do that. We'll be a team!"

Revelations

Somehow– and there was no way she could possibly articulate why– when Mishaela woke up the next day, she could feel that something was horribly wrong.

The house was still quiet when this feeling came over her; in the room she was in, Jaiden and Jasiela were still sleeping peacefully. She couldn't see Madeline from where her bed was, but assumed she was asleep as well. With the sudden sense of urgency that the feeling brought over her, Mishaela looked around her immediate surroundings until she noticed a small pebble on the nightstand beside her. Quickly, she picked it up and threw it across the room; apparently, at the perfect angle and velocity to hit Jaiden right in the face, with enough force to immediately wake her up.

"Ah! Damn it! What the–" she started, sitting up immediately.

"Sorry! I couldn't think of a better way to get your attention," Mishaela apologized quickly. "I can't put it into words, Jaiden, but something is... wrong, something about the atmosphere feels all wrong. Can you not feel it?"

Jaiden sighed, rubbing the last of the sleep out of her eyes. "How can you tell this early? Is anybody else even awake?"

It was Mishaela's turn to sigh. "You don't believe me."

"Now, hold up. I never said that." Jaiden turned to get out of the bed she was in. "The exact opposite, actually. Come on, you can tell me everything while we're investigating."

"Yeah– no, wait. There's a possibility we might end up leaving the house completely, so I want to leave Chiara a note so she won't worry about me," Mishaela replied, already scribbling a quick note explaining that she'd be roaming around with Jaiden and to not worry. With a nod, the two left the room, Jaiden being sure to close the door as lightly as possible.

As they walked past the other two basement rooms to head upstairs, Mishaela said, "I wish I had more to explain to you, but what I've said so far is pretty much it. I woke up, and it was like my stomach immediately dropped in the way that one's stomach does whenever they receive bad news, you know? Or get the feeling that they're about to receive bad news."

"And you have to admit, we've been getting plenty of that for the past few days, so it's not too unusual for you to be feeling that way," Jaiden added. "It might be a good idea to bounce those thoughts off of one of the Oliveiras. At any given time, at least one of them always seems to know what's going on."

Turning toward the living room, the stillness of the area alone felt odd; although this house was new to everyone, it still didn't quite feel right for it to be so quiet. The Resistance had always felt like a big family, and a lot of the reason for that was its captain; Thunder seemed to exude that sort of familial, fatherly presence that enabled everyone else to come together in a similar way. Without him, it was as if this house had been robbed of its very soul. It just didn't feel right to have him around.

Footsteps could be heard then, also coming toward the living room at a steadily increasing speed. Jaiden and Mishaela both could barely turn to see what the noise was before being faced with an uncharacteristically disheveled Arrigan, still in his pajamas as well.

"Sorry. I didn't sleep very well last night," he muttered. "Bad dreams. Horrible ones. Um, have either of you seen Logan today? I stopped by his room to talk to him about it, but he isn't there."

The two best friends exchanged a look. "Is that normal for him, to not be around at this time of morning?" Jaiden asked warily.

"I can't say it isn't." Arrigan shrugged. "Logan's probably the earliest riser in the house, so it certainly wouldn't be unusual to see him awake at this time. And then, he does what he does between school and Resistance work, so it would be equally as usual for him to not be in this house at all. But now that you've asked me that, I must admit, I'm starting to worry. Did something happen?"

"No, no! Please don't get all worried, Arrigan. It's just that..." Mishaela paused. "I woke up today with the feeling that something is very wrong. But if you say that Logan's absence is normal, wouldn't that be more of an indication that things are proceeding as normal, in that regard? I'm honestly more concerned with those bad dreams of yours."

The three began to walk down the hallway where the bedrooms on this floor were. "You don't have to worry about those; they've been a constant from before I met any of you," Arrigan explained. "I am... Logan calls me a 'chronic worrier.' If there's any pressing matters in my life that could easily go wrong, I'm probably going to have a restless night because of it. So not ideal, but not unusual either."

"So you probably haven't been getting a lot of sleep at all lately, huh?" Jaiden pointed out.

"Good sleep has been in short supply." Arrigan said this with only a small amount of resignation; fairly neutrally, as if this statement was as natural as the rays of light slowly pouring into the windows of this house.

It was easy to tell that both Jaiden and Mishaela didn't like the idea of Arrigan constantly having sleepless nights; but since there was nothing either of them could do about it at present, they let the matter drop as all three of them finally made their way to the living room. They were all expecting it to be empty, so it came as a surprise to see Gavin there, reading.

"What are you doing up so early, Gavin?" Jaiden asked, sitting beside him on the couch. "And what are you reading?"

"The day's newspaper, and I couldn't sleep," he replied. "I could ask the same of all of you. What are you doing at this time in the morning?"

"Well," Arrigan started, "it's not incredibly unusual for me to be up now, particularly whenever I have nightmares. I'm told Mishaela has this sinking feeling that something is going wrong–"

Arrigan was interrupted by the sounds of the front door's latches unlocking, one by one. The whole process probably took about ten seconds, but with all four of the people watching, they would all probably agree that it felt more like ten minutes.

At the end, though, Logan's head poked through the opening, and a mass sigh of relief echoed through the living room.

"Oh! You guys are up early!" Logan said as he closed the door behind himself, a towel draped around his shoulders. "Sorry if I startled you, or worried you in any way, but my mind was racing so fast, there was no way I was getting any sleep; so, I decided to go for a brief run along the river. If nothing else, the new path along the riverbank is good for that, hm? I think I'll get a shower and then prepare to start the day. Oh, but I think I'll need to remind my sister to get breakfast started first."

Breakfast did sound good. "Thanks, Logan," Mishaela said as he walked further into the house.

"Well, there's Logan, safe and sound," Jaiden said when he had gone. "I wonder what else could have gone wrong if everyone is–"

Jaiden's sentence was interrupted by a loud screech, clearly coming from inside the house, and also very clearly Logan. The volume of his scream meant that most of, if not all, of the people in the house came hurrying to where he was currently; Phoenix's bedroom.

Her *empty* bedroom.

"She could have just gone for a walk?" Brecken was suggesting as the last trio made it to the room.

"No, she wouldn't have gone this early," Logan replied. "If she had to, she would have left a note letting everyone know where she was, so we wouldn't worry. But aside from that, look around this room, and the state it was left in. It is indicative of there having been a struggle; mainly, the bed and the desk, here. I... I don't know whether I feel sadness or rage, but one thing has been made clear: by potentially putting my sister into harm's way, this has officially become personal."

The inflection currently in Logan's voice was foreign, as Lisandra peeked into the room, before being able to sense that something was off and coming in. "Hey, what was all that ruckus in here a few minutes ago?"

Logan looked up at her then. "Those bastards have declared war. They've taken my sister."

"They did wha–" Lisandra couldn't get her full sentence out before sudden images began to pour into her mind at rapid speed, bringing with them a cacophony of lights, increasing volume of sounds... it was too much for one person to stand, especially if that person was only sixteen, and the heightened activity soon caused her body to go limp, Logan catching her before she could hit the ground.

***

Needless to say, everyone else present was lost.

"I know some first aid if you need me to go retrieve anything," Gavin suggested. "Some ice? Medications? A... glass of water?"

Logan shook his head. "Maybe the water. It's just, I don't know if I have enough time to give a detailed explanation right now, but essentially: it is easy for an oracle to be overwhelmed like this when they use their power, especially if they're young and born in a time of relative peace, like Lisandra. Her unfamiliarity with the ability to receive messages or visions like this means that when it does happen, it's going to be a lot for her."

"That makes sense," Brecken said with a nod, prompting the others to agree and nod as well. Before anyone else could speak, the large gasp of breath that Lisandra took diverted all of their attention. Her body jerked alert for a second, her vision fuzzy, before she was able to sit up of her own accord, taking a moment to get reacquainted with her surroundings.

"Tell us everything you saw, in as much detail as you can provide," Logan said firmly, his hand tightly holding on to Lisandra's. "Nothing is too small, I assure you. We need to know everything we can if we're going to find our friends."

Lisandra was clearly still a bit disoriented, but she nodded, intent on showing that she was capable of helping. "Sure. Let me know when to start."

"Is anyone here really good at drawing?" Logan asked. "I can take over if no one else can."

Jasiela picked up the paper sitting on the table. "Don't worry about it; comfort your cousin. Let it rip, Lisandra."

She nodded again, and began to delegate what it was she had seen in her vision.

"The first thing I noticed was that the walls of whatever room the guys are in are made of stone, some kind of sandy-colored stone with some moss creeping up through the crevices. The ceilings were high enough that I couldn't see them, and the windows were really high up too, like this was some kind of basement. There wasn't much to decorate the area aside from a couple of beds and this one bookshelf with nothing on it, and the floor was made of the same kind of stone. This was obviously some type of dungeon, because there were ivory bars, made up like a jail cell, you know? At the time that I was able to see this happening, the sun was setting; I could tell this because there was this kind of golden glow on their faces.

"As for what I could hear, not much, but I don't mean that I was having trouble hearing again! Moreso that there wasn't a lot happening in the way of noise. There was this sound in the distance that I couldn't quite place... the closest thing I can compare it to is the whistling of a kettle when the water is adequately hot, but even that isn't the same. Even though this sound was distant, I could tell that up closer it would be much, much louder and have more, uh... more pressure behind it, is what I think it is? Also, something I think is important to keep in mind is that I don't think Thunder and Hunter know where they are, either. There's some evidence that they got knocked out before they were taken away, so they probably believe they're still here somewhere."

Logan nodded before turning to Jasiela. "What do we have for a visual, Jasiela?"

She turned the piece of paper toward everyone, showing a sketch of a stony room much like Lisandra had described. "Seems about standard for a jail cell in this type of society, I'd think."

"May I intervene for a moment?" Gavin asked then, raising his hand.

"If you've got input, be my guest," replied Logan, nodding.

"Thank you. One thing that immediately sticks out to me– although it is certainly not news at this point– is that what Lisandra has described is a type of architecture that is distinctly not of Compositora. We've been able to surmise for a while now that the place that our friends are being held is not here, but now we have a little extra information to try and locate them; is there any place in this world that is primarily built with this specific type of stone, or perhaps with ivory? Using ivory for cell bars is certainly a choice, by the way. I've never heard of that."

Gavin's tendency to notice architectural details was certainly coming in handy right about now, as everyone continued to ponder this.

"I don't think that really aligns with what we saw in the City of Garnet either," Brecken said after a while. "Most of the structures there appeared to be wooden and of a darker stone, if the houses are any indication."

"Yeah, that's about what you can expect throughout the entire city," Logan agreed. "Also, thinking about how moss tends to thrive in more moist environments means we could rule out certain locales just based on the volume of moss present in the room. Has Jasiela drawn it densely enough?"

"Uh..." Lisandra squinted at the piece of paper Jasiela was holding up toward her. "I think she may have actually drawn it *too* dense. There was enough to creep through the cracks between stones, but not too much apart from that."

Logan nodded. "Right, so that rules out the more wet parts of our world, and probably the colder parts too, because that amount of moss would be inconsistent with their climates."

The room fell silent once again as everyone began to think. What broke the silence this time, though, was the unmistakable sound of Arrigan gasping.

"Lisandra! You said something about a distant sound, right? Could you describe it again?" he asked frantically.

"Yeah, sure." Lisandra was surprised to see Arrigan this excited. "It was, uh... distant, but kind of similar to the whistling of a tea kettle. More of a hiss than a whistle, maybe? But like, with more pressure behind it, you know? And I'm sure it's a lot louder than what I heard if you were to be near whatever was making the sound."

Arrigan nodded. "I see. If you could again recall your vision: was there any sound that either accompanied or followed that was equally as loud, but more... thundering, rumbling?"

This required Lisandra to think. "Now that you ask, I think there was something at one point that was kinda like a rumble, yeah."

Immediately, Arrigan stood up from his seat on the couch. "Guys! I have to find a phone so I can call my dad! They're being held in my hometown, Trelana; that sound is a steam engine, and Trelana is the only city that both has steam engines, and meets the environmental capabilities to have that specific amount of moss growing between stones!"

Logan grinned. "Excellent detective work, friend! There's a phone right at the end of our block, if you want to make that call immediately. Here, you have to pay to use them," he handed Arrigan a coin. "As for everyone else, I can only imagine how excited we must all be to have a lead, but we have to approach this as carefully as possible. Let us begin to formulate a game plan."

***

There had never been a time in his life where Herman had done anything particularly scary, so Arrigan wasn't sure why he was so nervous when it came to the idea of calling his father. They hadn't spoken since he'd left home, through no fault of either man, so he was sure there would be no shortage of things to talk about. But there was always that nagging feeling in the back of his mind that his father would be discontent with him in some way if he ever reached out.

That feeling would have to take a back seat today, though.

As he waited for the line to connect, holding the receiver in his hand, Arrigan silently hoped that his father wasn't currently available, if only so that someone else could relay the message to him. Then again, how would he be able to sum up everything that had happened in a way that didn't make a person panic for the future? How would he do that with Herman? Maybe it would be best to withhold all the more alarming information until they, inevitably, saw each other in person.

"Hello? Trelana Police Department, Chief Navarrete speaking."

It was so strange to hear his father speaking in such a formal way. "Hey, um, I... Dad, it's Arrigan."

"Oh! It's been so long since I was able to speak to you, mijo! How have you been? How are Gavin and that group of kids he's always looking after? Your mom's gonna be so sad when she finds out she missed this call!"

"Dad, Dad, I'm... I'm not calling for pleasure, unfortunately. A lot has happened since I got here, and I... we all need your help."

Somehow, Arrigan could feel Herman's mood shift. "What happened, son?"

"It's much too complicated to get into over the phone, but it's not good, trust me."

"I can't think of any situation where I wouldn't," Herman replied. "All right, then. You called me for a reason. What is it you need from me?"

"The situation requires us to travel to Trelana, but we're not really sure how to do that. For reasons that are also too complicated to get into over the phone, we have a fairly large group, and I don't think Logan and I have the necessary budget to buy tickets for us all. I was wondering... kind of hoping... you'd lend us the money to cover the rest of the tickets. I'll pay it back as soon as I can, I promise."

"Arrigan. It's all right," Herman said gently. "Don't worry about it. You round up your friends, and I'll send out communication to have an official train car ready for you all within the hour."

"Really? Dad, you don't have to do that. I can– we can find another way," Arrigan replied. "I don't want you to think you need to keep doing favors like this for me. It makes me feel like I'm spoiled. At least tell me how I can repay you."

"No, no, I'll hear nothing of it," Herman insisted. "The only thing I want as repayment is, when you do finally get here, you tell me everything you know about what's happening and the reason you need to be here. If I'm gonna be helping you out like this, I would at least like to know what it is I'm helping with."

"Right. Yes. That's completely reasonable." Arrigan nodded. "Thanks, Dad. I'm really grateful."

Herman cleared his throat before replying, "Don't mention it. I'll let the guys know to have that train ready in about an hour. See you soon."

"Soon," Arrigan repeated before hanging up, disconnecting the call. He then placed a hand to his chest, relieved that his heart had finally stopped pounding.

Trelana

The wheels of the train chugged at high speed as it made its way down the tracks northeast. Under typical conditions, the commute from Compositora to Trelana took about 45 minutes, but with the clarity of the tracks and the speed at which they were currently traveling, they'd likely cut a lot of that time off. This was preferred among the party, though; time was of the essence, and the quicker they got to the next place, the quicker (and easier, hopefully) it would be to find a way to free their friends from captivity.

"What's the plan once we get to the city?" Jaiden asked. "Have we gotten that far?"

"Yes, actually." Arrigan nodded. "I think it would be a good idea to speak with both of my parents. I don't say this because I miss them– which I'll admit I do– but my dad knows all of Trelana's intricacies like the back of his hand. If there's some dubious location our friends are being held, if anyone would know where it is, it would be him. And my mom, she's much the same way when it comes to people. She's known for her kindness and ability to re-member people, so if things come down to a certain person, she'd know not only where to find them, but how to keep us on their good side."

Jaiden smiled. "That's awesome! Come through with the con-nections, Arrigan! And since they're your parents, you probably know where to find them, right?"

"Yeah." He nodded again. "We're more likely to be able to get ahold of my mom first, so I'll lead the way there first; once I've got her caught up with everything, we can make our way to my dad."

Meanwhile, in the cafe car of the train, Mishaela was preoccupied with bringing a cake over to the table that she was sitting at; the dish that the cake was on top of was a little heavy, so it required a fair level of concentration. As well, it seemed to be made of some crystalline material, so it may shatter if she ended up dropping it. That was not something she wanted to think about happening, especially since something that fancy had to be expensive, and the whole group was essentially being shepherded by two college students.

"Here we are, chocolate cake!" she said triumphantly as she placed the dish on the table– much to the delight of Chiara, Brecken, and Madeline. "There should be more than enough for the four of us, so feel free to make your slices as large as you like. There's probably even enough to take some with us."

Chiara was the one to carefully remove the top of the dish, just as carefully placing it to the side , away from the edge of the table. Clearly, she and her sister had to have had a similar thought process about the priciness of the dish. She then reached for the cake slicer, but paused when she realized she didn't see one. "Mishaela, how do we cut this cake?"

Mishaela opened her mouth slightly, before frowning and turning the cake some, even looking under the dish. "I knew I was forgetting something," she replied with a sigh.

At that time, Maceida passed the girls' table, holding a plate. "Oh, I see you took a look at the dessert offerings here; the good news is, it's highly likely that the cake of yours there is as delicious as it looks, if the lemon meringue pie is of any indication. This is amazing."

"Is it?" Madeline asked. "That's awesome! That makes me look forward to eventually finding a way to cut into this bad boy even more!"

"Hm." Maceida stared at the cake. "I think you'd have had to ask the staff to cut it, if you intend to eat it here; that must be why you weren't given a knife. When I bought my pie, I got two slices, but I recall the clerk asking if I wanted the pie *sliced*, as opposed to wanting *a slice*. You know? If that makes sense?"

The four girls looked defeated. "So I have to bring it all the way back to the cafe?" Mishaela asked, sounding very tired.

"At this point, it's probably more worth it to just bring it with us and eat it later," Madeline added. "Remember, this trip is supposed to only be like, 45 minutes. We spent 20 of those waiting for that cake, and we didn't immediately come here and get it, so we're probably in the late stages of this whole commute at this point."

"The way you tell time is always interesting, Madeline," Brecken replied.

Soon after, the train's intercom chimed with the bells of an announcement. "Attention, all passengers. This train will be arriving in the city of Trelana in approximately three minutes. Please gather your belongings and prepare to exit the train in a timely fashion. For more information regarding connecting trains and schedules..."

"Oh. She was right." Brecken looked up at where the announcement speaker was placed, in one of the corners of the train car. "I guess this is something that will have to wait until we settle down in the city, then. I'll go ask for a box."

***

Disembarking from the train, there was a very short walk through the station before ending up outside and being once again amazed by the scenery outside. Like the City of Garnet, Trelana was a sprawling city with lots of buildings and even more people to match. The difference was that, in contrast to the pale colors and Victorianesque buildings, Trelana's architecture was composed of more grays, browns, and bronzes; more metal and steam-powered apparatuses, and the closest things one could find to skyscrapers were here, standing at least ten floors above the cobblestone ground.

"This feels like what Chicago must have been like in the days of the 1920s or so," Chiara noted, gazing up at the taller buildings. "I suppose that's why I feel strangely comfortable here. It's almost like being home."

"Yeah, even the newsstands and carriages feel very in line with the old pictures I've seen," agreed Mishaela.

Overhearing the girls, Arrigan smiled. "Is that so? I'm glad you're able to find comfort in my hometown. Um, since I'm the only one of us familiar with this area, I guess you should all follow me. My mother works for Trelana's tourism department, so she's probably in their office at this time of day. That'll be in the downtown area, which is fortunately not far from here. It's this way."

Everyone began to follow Arrigan, walking down one brick-paved path after the other before eventually coming to a stop in an area with busy streets in a grid formation, a cacophony of people running about to fulfill their daily tasks, or seeing the sights; of which there were plenty. There were even more tall buildings– these, perhaps, the tallest– a small park to the east, an ornate fountain to the north, and some abstract art sculpture further on. It was at this point that Arrigan turned back to look at the group.

"It's a lot, isn't it?" he asked.

"But not overwhelming," replied Jasiela. "We're all from big cities back on Earth, so this is a level of activity that we're all used to."

Arrigan nodded. "Yeah. So, it's easy to get lost in this area; be sure to stay close by. The office my mom works out of is in that direction–" he pointed– "right across the street from the park, with the orange and yellow awning above the windows and doors on the first floor."

Passing the park, it wasn't too busy due to the chillier weather, but there was a family walking along the path; a group of children no older than twelve playing catch with a frisbee; a man and woman– siblings, judging by their resemblance– walking a dog. Although it was a lower traffic day, it was still possible to tell that this city was full of energy.

Arriving at the office building, several chimes above the door announced the arrival of visitors. The interior of the building, on this floor, was one large room with many desks facing each other, and a stairwell in the distance; at this time, the only person in the office was a small, blonde woman who wore black-rimmed, square glasses and a long-sleeved orange dress with red and pink carnations decorating it, and a tan blazer over it. She appeared to be busy, judging by the fact that the tinkling of the door chimes didn't cause her to look up from her current task.

"I'll be there in a minute to help you distribute the drinks, Anna," she said distantly, her hands occupied with a contraption that looked similar to a typewriter, and seemed to function similarly to one as well.

"Take your time," Arrigan said in reply.

"Thank you. It's just that this letter is very important, as I've been saying for the past... week." The woman looked up then, clearly confused, but both clarity and surprise washing over her face when she registered who had come into the building– and wasting no time in standing up from her desk, running over to give her son a hug. "Arrigan! Oh, what are you doing here so soon? You're supposed to be in school for another four months, isn't that right?"

He laughed. "Yes, but the situation has changed– well, that situation hasn't, I'm still in school. It's just that things are happening that take precedence over school. It's related to that day recently where you got sick, Mom. Everyone, this is my mother."

"The city of Trelana's tourism consultant, Kasia Navarrete– pleased to make your acquaintance," she added, in a manner much more youthful than someone with a nineteen-year-old son.

"Mom's work has to do with designing the city's advertisements– whether that be promoting the sights, or government-sponsored classes and events, or coordinating special events. That's why I was so confident that she'd be able to help us; if there's anyone who we'd need to get in contact with about a particular neighborhood or operation, she'd likely know who since her work takes her all around the city."

"Something has happened that takes precedence over school, you said?" Kasia asked, in a pensive pose. "What could that be? I know you wouldn't lie about something that dire. And who are all of these people?"

It hit Arrigan then, how badly he'd be blindsiding both his parents with all of this. For a fleeting moment, he almost regretted coming here– but soon recovered, telling himself that now was not the time to be overtaken by anxiety. "It's a long story, one that I already promised Dad I'd tell him when I see him, and we'll be headed that way next," he explained. "We stopped here because I knew it would be a good idea to have you in the room when we go through the detailed explanation."

"Ah, I see." Kasia nodded, before smiling. "What a coincidence; I was going to recommend you go and see him, anyhow. But I do still have work to take care of here before I can leave. Why don't you go on without me, and I'll catch up to you all later? After all, we both know your father will get emotional and want to catch up with you."

"Yeah. That he will," Arrigan chuckled. "All right, then. I can't ask more of you at the moment, since this *was* kind of sudden. See you in a few hours, then?"

***

"Next, we're heading to that tall, red brick building." Arrigan pointed to the target building, in the distance.

As the building drew close enough that its visage could be seen– the large flight of stairs, the distinctive lampposts at the base of the stairs, and the three automobiles parked in front of it– there was a pause in conversation as everyone took it in.

"This building..." Jasiela said hesitantly. "It... looks an awful lot like a police station."

"It is." Arrigan turned toward the group. "My father is chief of police here in Trelana."

"Aw, man! Is there any reason you kept that to yourself?" Madeline asked. "You could've mentioned that your dad's 12!"

"What? My dad's a grown man. What are you talking about?" The look on Arrigan's face conveyed he didn't know whether to be confused or amused. "You can trust my dad. And I'm not saying that just because he's my dad; that's pretty much everyone's assessment of him, and you'll see why soon."

The modernity of Trelana's police station was something that took everyone (except Arrigan) by surprise. This was the first building that had some sort of equivalent to central air; even though it wasn't very warm this time of year, it was still clearly running at a lower capacity because it could be felt when one walked through the doorway. In the main reception area, there were benches for visitors to wait, and at least four people either typing away on typewriters or filing things into folders. A few decades removed, this felt a lot like any executive office back on Earth.

As the group approached the main desk, one of the people working there clearly recognized at least one of the crew that had just entered. "Good afternoon, Arrigan! It's been a while since I've seen you. I... thought the chief mentioned you moving for a while to study."

"I did. I'm not back permanently; it's a long story," he explained. "I'm sorry, I don't have the time to get into the specifics. Speaking of the chief, is he around? Available? I kind of need to speak with him as soon as possible."

The desk clerk nodded, turning to take a look at a notebook. "Hmm... oh, you're in luck; it looks like his lunch break was due to end about a half-hour ago, so he should be back in his office right about now. If you give me just a moment, I can call up there to make sure."

"Could you? That would be amazing!" Arrigan nodded. "Thank you so much."

Picking up the phone, the clerk waited a few moments before saying, "Hello! Front desk. Is Chief Navarrete in his office right now? I have an important visitor for him here. Is that so? That sounds good, then. I'll let him know, thank you." They placed the phone back down and turned back to Arrigan. "You're in luck. I'm told he's just finishing up an important errand and should be available in less than five minutes. I'd wait a few here before heading up."

"That's great! Thank you," Arrigan said again before waving, and returning to his group of friends.

"We're in luck. Dad should be available soon, so we can just hold tight here for a little bit before heading to his office." Arrigan exhaled in relief, placing a hand on his hip. "That's such a relief."

"Arrigan, if it's okay for me to ask... is the relationship between you and your dad, you know, not the best?" Madeline asked. "I mean, I wouldn't be surprised seeing as he's a cop and all, but you've seemed tense every time he's come up in conversation, and you've been stiff as a board ever since we stepped foot into this building. Again, not something you have to get into if you don't wanna, but."

"Now that she mentions it, I don't think you've ever told me that either, but I *have* noticed your body language change whenever your father is the subject of conversation," agreed Logan. "Which has always been interesting to me, seeing how Thunder is so fond of the man."

Arrigan sat on the benches with everyone else as he began to consider how to answer this question. "It's... a little difficult to explain, but I don't mind trying. Dad is a great person; he loves people, and has never been anything but warm and loving to everyone, and that includes my mother and me. But he is a much more social creature than I am, which means we've approached life a lot differently, between the two of us, and it's led to misunderstandings, historically. There has never been a point in my life where I doubted he loves me, but he is of the mind that the way to have me get better at social experiences has been to force me into them, rather than have me get accustomed to them at my own pace. That and I just– I don't entirely disagree that that should have worked. There's a less than small part of me that always feels like I'm failing him somehow, and I just kind of live in fear that someday he's going to wake up and realize that for himself."

The area was silent then.

"Well, damn." Madeline was lost for words, which was rare.

"Despite this, you all have nothing to worry about when it comes to meeting him. As I said, he loves people, and I don't see any reason that he would feel any differently about all of you, especially considering your affiliation with both me and Thunder. Plus, Logan, I've already told him about you a few times in my letters to him and Mom."

This made Logan's face light up. "Oh? I'm flattered!"

"You sound surprised, but it made sense to tell them all about the people I'm living with, especially the one I spend so much time with," Arrigan explained.

The sound of the glass doors behind the front desk sliding open diverted everyone's attention, and they were faced with someone that truly could only be described as a mountain of a man; his head only slightly cleared the top of the doorframe, his brown hair cut in such a precise fade into the swoop at the top of his head that it didn't feel farfetched to assume a ruler was used while shaping it. At first glance, his broad shoulders, large arms, and full beard looked intimidating, maybe even a touch scary; but it didn't take much longer to realize that there were aspects of him that conveyed kindness so much louder. His warm and welcoming brown eyes; the equally warm, slightly brown tone of his skin; his arms, which looked like they gave only the best hugs. The energy had shifted when he had entered the room, but in a way that was neither positive nor negative; something similar to reverence, but not quite as formal.

Before the front desk clerk could say anything, Arrigan had stood. "Dad."

Everyone else behind him exchanged glances. "Guy clearly takes after his mother," Gavin said softly.

The man swiftly closed the gap between them, wasting no time in gathering Arrigan in a hug so tight that he ended up lifting him off the ground. "I know it's only been a few months, but I missed you so much! Everything feels so different without you around. You don't make a lot of noise at home, but the absence there is still so obvious. At least three times a week I eat lunch and wonder to myself, 'did Arrigan eat lunch today?' Which I know you do because you never miss a meal, but–"

"Dad, it's– I– I'd really like to feel the ground under my feet again, if that's okay."

"What? Oh. Yeah, of course. Sorry about... that." He let go, looking ever-so-slightly embarrassed. "I should introduce myself to your entourage here too, shouldn't I? Nice to meet you youngsters; I'm Herman, and on behalf of the force and everyone else who calls this city home, welcome to Trelana."

"Thank you; we simply wish it was under better circumstances," Logan replied. "As much as we'd have liked this to be a pleasure trip, we've got some urgent issues going on."

"Mom will be here when she's done with her tasks for the day," added Arrigan. "I didn't really explain anything to her either, so you'll both be getting the story when she gets here. It's a lot, so do you think we could use one of the conference rooms for it? If for nothing else, to accommodate the number of people here."

"Yeah. Okay. That's definitely possible. I, uh…" Herman looked around, before his eyes focused on a brown-skinned man with salt-and-pepper curly hair. "Karthik."

The man turned, raising his eyebrows. "What's happening, Chief?"

"Can you watch my office for the rest of the day? There shouldn't be much going on, but maybe take note of everything that does? I have to…" Herman held out both his arms toward Arrigan, "help my kid. My son."

"Sure." He nodded.

"Excellent. Follow me, everyone. I know exactly what we need."

***

Heading back through the glass doors behind the front desk, Herman led everyone down a flight of stairs. "Here in Trelana, it wouldn't be wrong to say that the police force is intrinsically tied to the governance of the city itself. We have a mayor here, but because most of the infrastructure here was initially set up by the force, we've kept a close association to mayoral duties. Many people here consider the mayor and chief of police on equal footing. I say all of this to say: there are a great many resources at our disposal here because of the way our government is set up. If it's information you need, you've come to the right place." He looked over his shoulder then, "*Is* it information that you need?"

"In so many words, yes." Logan was the one to answer.

"I'll try to hold my curiosity until my wife gets here, then," Herman replied, stopping at a door and pulling a key card from his pocket to scan. This opened a nearby door, which revealed another corridor. "Don't be intimidated by all the security measures; it's just that there are some very confidential things in the rooms beyond, so we have to be careful with them."

Continuing on, there would occasionally be a door to a meeting room along the corridor. There was one room that specifically appeared to be a laboratory before a split in the halls, but Herman continued on the other way.

"What's down the other hall?" Jaiden whispered to Arrigan.

He shrugged. "I don't know. I've never been down here."

"Don't say that, it's gonna make me even more curious," Jaiden sort of whined.

"Ah, here we are. This is the perfect room to sort this all out." With another scan of his key card, Herman opened the door to the room at the end of this hallway. "After all of you."

Entering the room, it was easy to see why it had been chosen. The overall area was very large, with a long, wide planning table with many chairs in its center. This table also appeared to have a similar projection mechanism as the one in the conference room at the Resistance's HQ building. Around the room there were lots of file cabinets, maps, and scattered random objects in clear boxes. This definitely appeared to be a room of important information.

"Feel free to have a seat while we wait," Herman gestured to the table. "If I know my wife, she should be here soon, so we shouldn't be waiting long for her."

"What is this place, Dad? I don't think you've ever brought me down here," Arrigan said as he took in the scenery.

"You are all now in the police building's planning room. In the old days, this was where the city's elite would gather to discuss plans for the future in regards to infrastructure and defense. There's less need for that these days, though, so it doesn't get used as often. That's why I never showed you this place, Arrigan. There's never been a need to come down here before."

He nodded then.

There was a faint beeping on the other end of the door then, before a uniformed officer arrived with Kasia in tow. "A very special guest for you, chief."

Herman grinned. "Thank you for escorting some of my most precious cargo."

With a wave to the officer that had escorted her, Kasia took the seat beside Herman and turned to the group of young adults gathered around the table. "Well, you've got me here now. Who wants to start telling us about what's going on?"

Everyone exchanged glances then, not sure of who should speak or where to start. "I suppose I can do that," Logan volunteered. "By the way, I just learned that even though I haven't introduced myself to either of you, you both actually already know who I am. Hi.

Logan Oliveira, member of the Resistance. You may be wondering why I'm the only one who's here with your son and all of our favorite friends here. Well, things haven't exactly been going swimmingly in Compositora, as of late. It is a complicated situation, but basically– our organization, the Resistance, has earned the ire of a group of individuals for... reasons, and the leader of this group has taken some of our organization captive, including our captain and my older sister. We were able to find out they're being held somewhere within this city, but we don't really know where to begin looking, which is why Arrigan suggested coming here and speaking with you about it all. I trust him, so I have no reservations in placing my trust in you both as well. I just ask that you help us with all your might. This is, after all... personal to me."

The room was silent, then. Logan hadn't shown much emotion about the situation up until now, but he was currently dealing with a certain amount of uncertainty surrounding the well-being of his only sibling, not even a year after she'd been seriously hurt. That kind of thing had to weigh heavily on anyone, even someone as perky and eager as Logan.

"I think I might know where to start." Herman's voice broke the silence as he stood, walking toward one of the walls of the room. Everyone's eyes followed him closely.

"Due to its proximity to the desert, Trelana gets very hot during the summer. It's said that in the days before buildings and cooling systems, our ancestors learned that it was much cooler underground, and made an elaborate network of tunnels under the city."

Herman turned on a light situated on the wall, revealing a map of said network. It was large, and intricate; one would not be incorrect to liken it to the tunnels of an anthill. The paths twisted, turned, and even overlapped at some points.

"When we learned how to make buildings cooler during the summer, we didn't need the tunnels anymore. It's said that, because of this, it wasn't long before they were taken over by miscreants, who used them for their own sinister dealings. That's why we have these." Herman pointed to a few large rectangles drawn between the walls of the tunnels. "Certain parts of the tunnels were expanded upon to create rooms for who knows what kind of operations. I'm willing to bet anything that one of these rooms is the place Lisandra saw in her vision."

Everyone took this in, then.

"There is a detail that will make this a little more complicated," Kasia added. "The tunnels have been closed for years now. Decades, even. When the police force was established, one of the first things they did was seal off all of the entrances permanently, to curb the amount of crime that happened down there. Although that *does* make me wonder how the man you're looking for got down there in the first place."

"Oh! Yeah. That's the part we didn't get around to telling you yet," Arrigan replied. "The problems don't start and end with our captain being captured. We, uh, might be going up against a guy who's kinda accidentally tearing the fabric of our world apart with his magic."

Herman and Kasia exchanged a look.

"It sounds worrying, but it's cool! It's okay! We can handle it. We're practically pros at this kind of thing by now," Jasiela explained.

"*We*?!" Arrigan asked softly.

Another look between the married couple. "Well," Herman finally said. "If you're going to take our only son into that type of situation, I only hope you've got a plan."

"We have…" Lisandra paused. "The makings of a plan. There are some gaps we need help filling in, which Arrigan's very confident you guys can do; that's a big part of the reason we came here."

"I guess we can start with this: back when the tunnels were accessible, where were the entrances?" asked Mishaela. "It would be easier to break open a previously established entrance than to just blow a hole into a wall, right?"

"Not necessarily. With how old those walls are, there are probably some sweet spots…" Herman trailed off as he searched through a few files. "To know for sure, we'd have to do some reconnaissance around town. But I'm also trying to locate the records because, eventually, it sounds like we're gonna have to get you kids in there too– and nobody says you have to use the same entrance they did. It might be more beneficial if you didn't."

"So about the gentleman potentially tearing apart the fabric of the world," Kasia started. "I don't suppose you have a plan for that, yet?"

"Sorta. The reason he's able to do that is because of some added boon from the goddesses, so we have to find a way to have him give that back," Lisandra explained. "And we all know that's easier said than done, but it's not impossible. Honestly, I'm hoping that we can knock enough sense into him that he realizes what he's doing and gives it back himself."

"You know, really thinking about it, that's the part of all of this that strikes me as a wee bit odd," Spencer-Lynn confessed. "Do you think that, even with the fissures and the like getting worse, he doesn't notice any of it?"

Everyone pondered this. "I think it's more that he may not have made the connection that he's the one causing it," Logan replied. "I want to believe that, even amidst whatever is going on in Flavian's mind, he isn't so deranged that he'd be motivated to end the world–but even so, I suppose we can't entirely discount that possibility, either."

"So, if that's what we're dealing with, what you're saying is," Madeline said, "this could get so serious that we'd need to consider killing him?"

Logan nodded stiffly. "We may need to consider that, yes. I don't like the idea, you don't like the idea, I don't think anyone does. But knowing that this extends far beyond the Resistance and Compositora, and affects our entire world..."

He didn't need to finish the sentence; everyone understood what was being implied.

"So the plan so far is to get into the tunnels, find our friends, and defeat this guy before he brings on armageddon, by any means necessary, basically," Lisandra summarized the discussion. "We're still gonna need to hammer out the fine details, but this works."

Scattered sounds of agreement circulated around the room.

Arrigan placed a hand under his chin. "So now that only leaves one loose end: in order to get into the tunnels, that resulting blast... it's going to be pretty loud and potent, isn't it? Even if Dad does something along the lines of issuing an official statement telling everyone to not worry, something like that is going to turn heads, you know, or cause a certain level of panic. What can we do to ensure that we don't cause a riot, or not have regular people getting in the way, while still opening up the tunnels?"

The room fell silent again.

"Dumb question, but are we absolutely sure there's not a way to quietly blow a hole into the tunnels? Like, with magic or something?" Madeline asked.

"Doubt it," replied Lisandra. "The noise will be less about the blast and more about the wall we barge in through crumbling, so there wouldn't be anything that could be done about that, you know? It's like, even if we made the spell as quiet as possible, we can't stop the wall from crumbling audibly."

Madeline nodded. "Right, right. Well, there goes my idea."

Small, fragmented discussions floated around the room until, as if being struck by inspiration, Maceida slammed her hands on the table loudly enough that it got everyone's attention. "Hey! When we were coming here from the train station, I saw this huge platform in the town's center, what is that?"

"Oh, the Wielka Scena. It's a stage," replied Kasia. "It's usually used for... well, in the past, multimedia performances or town announcements, but it has been some years since it's been in use."

"Right, of course– but does it have lights, a sound system, the whole nine? Would it be functional if one wanted to use it today?" Maceida asked.

After a pause, Herman was the one to answer. "I don't see why not. It's all controlled by that tower that's due west of here, which is government property, so someone maintains it along with the rest of the building. This I know because it's usually someone from the force hired out to do it. It has lights, sound, microphones... probably even pyrotechnics— everything you'd need to put on the flashiest show on the mainland, if you wanted to."

"Excellent. One last question." Maceida turned. "Jasiela, didn't you say that you occasionally sew and design clothing?"

Jasiela blinked in confusion. "Yeah, I've been at it for six years now– but what does this have to do with anything?"

Maceida's radiant smile was unparalleled. "I have an idea."

Watch The Bellflower

t exactly 5:00 p.m. lights switched on in Trelana's city center
plaza, attracting the attention of everyone in the area. Madeline sat in the tower that controlled the amphitheater's mechanics, with Jasiela, Chiara, Gavin, and Arrigan's parents with her, ready to control everything from her seat. Kasia was seated with her, because she would have to make sure everything continued to run smoothly when the younger party had to leave, but everyone else was standing.

"I cannot believe we're actually doing this," Jasiela whispered.

Madeline put a hand up to shush her, quickly, before flipping a switch. More lights came on then, illuminating the area, but carefully keeping things on the stage still dark– for now. As more people wandered closer to the stage to see what was happening, the air felt suffocatingly tense. It felt as though everyone in the tower was waiting on the next signal.

"This is about seventy-five percent of the town now. Madeline, Arrigan, you might want to get going," Herman said.

"Roger that!" Madeline stood and saluted, before heading down. Arrigan stood to follow, but then hesitated. "Dad…"

"Later, son." Herman smiled. "Be brave. I'm proud of you."

"Right. Later." He nodded, before hurrying to catch up with Madeline.

Herman smiled again, watching them leave, before turning toward the control panel. "Well, those lights and the size of that crowd means there's no turning back now. Jasiela, you're up."

She affirmed, sitting in the chair and adjusting the volume of the PA system. Once she was comfortable with her position, she inched closer to the microphone, ready to make the announcement.

"Ladies and gentlemen, for your viewing pleasure this evening, presenting: Sweet❀Etoile!"

~~~~~

"You want to do *what*?" Arrigan had asked Maceida, when she'd finished explaining her plan to everyone in the drawing room. "How could that *possibly* help?"

Gavin raised a finger. "Well, if you've ever attended any kind of live show, the music alone would be loud enough to drown out any other sounds in the immediate area; and, if the music's played live, the vibrations from the instruments would feel almost the same as the explosion underground, right?"

"They'd feel about the same, yeah," Herman nodded. "And that's before you even get pyrotechnics involved. Not to mention, it's been so long since there's been a show that it would be easy to get most of, if not all the town there, keep 'em distracted long enough so that us blasting the tunnels open doesn't raise too many eyebrows.
~~~~~

It's unorthodox, but it's not a bad idea at all. But before anything happens that makes me eat my words on that, do you mind walking us through your process, Maceida?"

"Sure." She nodded, confidently. "The idea is that we spread the word around the city that, for the first time in years, there'll be a concert held in the city center. It's been years since that happened, right? Which means it's going to cause a stir— as you said, enough to distract everyone from the tunnel blast. That means that the blast has to happen as the concert is being held, so we'll need to split up and then meet at a later time. We also need enough vibration to ensure nothing feels out of the ordinary, though, which is why I didn't volunteer to just put on a show myself with the strings. We need more voices, more sound. Idol concerts are some of the loudest I know!"

It was easy to tell that most of the room still needed to be sold on this.

"Let's say we go through with this idea. Where would we get the instruments?" Mishaela asked.

"Actually, I probably have the connections for that," Kasia raised her hand. "My line of work requires me to know a lot of people in the city. Because of this, I know many who play instruments; I'd just need to know which ones you need. That, in addition to... you said something about costumes. I have plenty of materials you all can use; I do some sewing work as well, so I could be an extra pair of hands once we've secured the band."

Maceida nodded. "That's where you come in, Jasiela."

"Me? I mean… sure, I know a little about idols, a couple of my friends back home are into that scene. I guess I could try and whip something up, but in this amount of time?"

"It doesn't have to be something amazing; just something that fits the aesthetic," Maceida replied. "Spence can help you."

Spencer-Lynn turned. "How did you know I was into idols? Have I ever told you that?"

"You didn't, but I mean, a bunch of cute feminine girls singing and dancing, plus you being able to read their untranslated interviews and whatnot, it seemed likely." Maceida shrugged. "Leave the dance and vocal instruction to me! The last unaccounted-for thing we'll need is a practice space, which I assume shouldn't be impossible to find, right?"

The room was silent again until Herman said, "I'd imagine you need to go back to Compositora for a while, but while you're in town here, you could use the area where the training courses for the force are held, whenever they're not in use. We just got done training a new class of cadets, so that leaves you with pretty much an open availability."

"That *almost* makes up for you being a cop," Madeline replied.

"It sounds like you have things all planned out, so I guess I can't complain too much," Arrigan said then. "I just have one more question. When you explained the idea, Maceida, you framed things in a way that implied there's going to be more than you up on the stage. Who's all going?"

"Right, then. Well, Jasiela will be busy with costume design and sewing, so it wouldn't be right to ask her to do all that *and* memorize a song and dance routine. Likewise, Madeline will have to be on-site when we blow a hole into the tunnel walls, so she can't be on the stage at the same time. I couldn't possibly do that to Chiara, either."

Somewhere in one of the corners of the room, Chiara sighed in relief.

"So, then, could I possibly have all the remaining girls join me? Jaiden, you're welcome as well," Maceida placed a hand to her chest and smiled.

Jaiden smiled back at her. Maceida, who had known her for maybe two weeks, had already been more cognizant of her non-binary status than many of her own family members. "Thanks, Maceida. I think I will. Dancing is fun, and while I'm not the best singer, I do at least know how to stay in tune."

Gavin asked then, "What about those of us that are of the non-feminine variety? I'd suppose we just help out where we fit in?"

"For one thing, I'm gonna need help building this explosive," Madeline said to him, turning. "I have to gather some ingredients and containers and stuff. I'd feel a lot more confident in us getting this right if you and Arrigan are up for lending your hands to the cause."

"Wait a minute." Logan paused before pointing out, "I think this means that, from here, our group will need to split up. There are not any safe places in Compositora to test an explosive; and, even if there were, it would be best for you to test it here because you'll get to test it on the type of terrain you'll be blasting through; plus, there will need to be some additional studying of the tunnels, right?"

"He's a smart one," Herman agreed. "Right, well, anyone that needs to stay here is welcome at the Navarrete home. It's not fancy, but it'll suit your needs well enough."

"I guess that's that then," Madeline agreed. "See you guys soon?"

Jasiela was the first to give her a fist bump. "On the other side of the tunnels," she agreed with a chuckle.

From then on, the group split to take care of their preparations.

***

Things started picking up, then.

Madeline, Gavin, and Arrigan stayed in Trelana to study the areas that were most likely to provide a clear entrance into the underground tunnel network, as well as study the best combination of materials to create an explosive. This was something that was delegated to the police station's training grounds after the first day, as Herman was worried that the explosions in rapid succession would draw too much negative attention to his house. Even so, both of Arrigan's parents gladly took on helper roles in the investigation; while Herman was able to access records regarding when certain structures were built and what they were made of, and once she had been given the sheet music for the performance, Kasia worked hard at finding people who played the appropriate instruments and practicing with them.

"Madeline, Gavin, may I ask you two a question?" Kasia had visited the training field one day as she held the sheet music she'd been sent.

The three working on the explosive turned around quickly, as if they'd been startled. "You caught us at the right time; we were just about to set this off," Gavin replied. "We can make time. What's on your mind, Mrs. Navarrete?"

"I was reading over the sheet music I was given for the performance, and there are a lot, *a lot* of notes in the margins mentioning that the tempo and instruments can vary. There are a bunch of suggestions and color codings and... I'm honestly shocked she managed to get this done that quickly. Anyway, all of that to say: the notes are so plentiful that it's a lot to parse. I don't suppose either of you are familiar with this genre of music? Some familiarity with– what was it called again– idol music would be immensely helpful here, but I believe this is a genre that solely exists in your world."

Gavin let out a small sigh. "Yes, and only within a specific part of it, at that. I'm not too terribly familiar with the whole scene myself, but I do know that the arrangement is usually more pop-inspired? The kind of up-tempo, dance music, uses some drums and bass. Not unheard of to hear pianos and horns, right?" He turned to Madeline for an answer on this.

"Yeah, that tracks," she replied. "I don't have first hand experience with it either, but one of my sisters does. Anything that makes it more upbeat and happy is probably what the aim here is. Something that makes it easy to dance to, you know? Do you– you guys *do* dance here, right?"

This question, although asked sincerely, made Kasia and Arrigan both laugh. When Madeline really thought about it, it was a silly thing to ask, wasn't it? As if dancing wasn't as innate to the human condition as humming and singing.

"You mentioned there being horns, right?" Arrigan asked. "When we're done for the day, I can get my trumpet. Maybe hearing one of the instruments will help with visualizing the whole arrangement, maybe. I think we'll get a lot farther if we–"

"Arrigan, the valve!" Madeline pointed just as he let it go, causing the prototype explosive to detonate; the last thing any of the youths heard before smoke clouded the area was Kasia shouting something in Polish. When they could all see each other again, they were coated in dark gray soot from head to toe. Gavin coughed, covering his mouth with his elbow.

"Sorry," Arrigan said softly. "Maybe I should stay here instead, at least for today. Clearly, we've got a lot of work ahead of us."

Kasia nodded. "There's no rush. You all should continue to work on that, and I'll... go home and take a bath."

***

Meanwhile, in Compositora, practice for the performance was on. Maceida was able to use a song and dance composition that she had drafted up for her courses, but had ultimately discarded because she had felt like it had been missing something. Even with her recomposing it from memory, speeding up the tempo to make it more idol-like, and moving things around to account for the parts she couldn't remember, she still felt that way; but this was when Brecken had volunteered to help spice it up a little, and her knowledge of jazz helped bring the song to where it was on this day: at a point where the choreography could be practiced.

Practicing without a track to practice to made things difficult, but not impossible. It helped that everyone, at the very least, had the ability to stay within the rhythm of Maceida's count. As time went on, she would ask people to switch positions depending on how well they were comprehending the steps, or how the dynamics looked, but it was still clear that this would be difficult until Kasia was able to get back to them with an official backing track.

Difficult didn't mean impossible, though, as Thunder would probably say.

"Good morning, Maceida! How is everything progressing?" Logan asked, holding a tray of ice water as he made it to the courtyard where everyone was working on their dance routine. "I brought you all the most refreshing ice water. Even with the day not being as hot as it could be, I figured you would all need the hydration."

"Hey! Is that water for us?!" Jaiden asked in the distance, not wasting time in closing the gap when Logan nodded in response.

"I think we're making some good progress, considering," Maceida replied then, picking up one of the glasses herself. "Could we be doing better? Absolutely, but in my completely professional and not at all biased opinion, things aren't so bad that we need to consider a different plan. We can simply put the more challenged dancers in the back. It worked all the time for the dance cover group I used to be in."

Logan nodded. "Uh-huh. Well, glad to hear you have everything under control back here. I don't suppose there's anything you all need my help with, though? Since we're not fighting a horde of magical zombies or anything, I haven't had much of an active role in this plan. I'm on the verge of getting bored, even."

"Hmm..." Maceida studied him. "Actually, I think there may be. How tall are you, Logan?"

"How tall am I? Uh, like five foot eleven I think, last time I checked," he replied. "About the same as you, right? This is a really specific question, Maceida."

"So it is, but it turns out I've got the perfect thing for you to do."

While Jasiela was busy in the Resistance HQ sewing part of one of the stage costumes, she had to look up when a blur of black hair in her peripheral vision caught her attention. Turning to the window completely to be sure she'd seen this correctly, she sat the skirt aside and pondered for a moment before walking over to the window and opening it, leaning out of it enough that she could be seen.

"Logan, you are *not* learning the idol dance," she shouted out.

"Oh, but I am!" he replied, waving. "See, Maceida wanted to be able to tell how the whole thing will appear to the audience to get standing positions down, but she can't do that regularly because she herself is part of the performance. So since we're more or less the same size, I'm filling in for her so she can give the others feedback on their steps and placement!"

"It's effective," Maceida defended herself, feeling criticism coming on.

Jasiela merely shook her head. "If that's what works, then I can't complain. Plus, you're oddly good at those steps, Logan."

"Actually, that's likely because I've always liked dancing!" he replied. "But with the Resistance and all, I had to shift my physical hobbies to a more offensive form. It's always fun to learn a new dance! If your sewing is not incredibly pertinent at this very point in time, I think you should come watch; perhaps even join us!"

"No can do, my man. I've got to get back to work," Jasiela replied. "There's no way I'm gonna have you guys on that stage looking anything less than perfect, so I have to be as meticulous as possible. Which means, no fun allowed for the next few days."

Logan nodded in understanding. "Your dedication is much appreciated! Back to work for both of us, then!"

Jasiela laughed as she waved, before coming back inside and picking up the skirt in progress. It wasn't fighting with magic, but at least this plan let her use another kind of magic that always seemed underappreciated, in her life back home.

***

When Jasiela got to the point where she had a mostly done stage attire– with plenty of help from both Spencer-Lynn and Chiara– she called the latter to examine it as it sat on the one dressform that she'd been able to find in town on such short notice. "Well? What do you think?"

Chiara studied the intricacies of the costume: its ribbons, its trims, the lovely shades of green, white, and brown. "It does make me think of sweets," she replied. "Mint chocolate chip, especially."

"That's what I wanted to go for," Jasiela confirmed. "As soon as I saw the colors that Mrs. Navarrete had in her stash, it was the first idea I got, so I ran with it. This one is Jaiden's, by the way– I'm probably gonna make some tiny modifications here and there based on everyone's height and build, but this is the meat of the design, basically. I like it, but... as someone who's not into J-pop, even I can tell that there's something missing here– I just can't put my finger on what it is."

"Hmm." This made Chiara think too, but she was just as far removed from the J-pop scene, if not more. "Oh! Why don't you have Jaiden try it on? Maybe with them wearing it, it'll make what's missing more obvious."

Jasiela pointed a finger. "That is an excellent idea. I knew it was a good idea to have you working with me."

Soon after, the prospective idols were called into the room as Jaiden modeled the finished stage costume. There were various sounds of approval and awe as everyone took in the lovely colors and frills of the ensemble, but once the look had been digested, the room became silent as they all began to think.

"Oh! Well, I can think of one thing," Spencer-Lynn said. "The concert is going to be happening sometime around or after golden hour, right? So there will have to be lights on. Idol isshou usually have parts that are sparkly when they perform on stages like that, so the bright lights don't completely consume the performers– sequins, rhinestones, that kind of thing. If there's nothing that catches the light like that here, we can have a look in the marketplace."

"I have an idea too! Do you think that you could pick up some ribbon and craft flowers whilst you're out?" Maceida asked. "I have the perfect finishing touch in mind."

Jasiela was busy writing this all down. "Ribbons, craft flowers... and sparkly things. Got it, that's all doable. Any other ideas?"

Mishaela raised her hand. "One more. I know a little bit about idols, and I think the thing I probably remember the most is that there's generally the most variation when it comes to hairstyles and accessories. I'm sorry if you've done this already, but have you made any things like that to go with the attire?"

"Huh. No, I didn't even think of that." Jasiela began to write that down. "But it makes a lot of sense, now that you say it. This does give me a nice, nifty little shopping list of things to pick up, though. Who wants to come along with me? Chiara, you should come. You've already been a big help so far."

She turned, taken by surprise. "Me? Um, I... sure, that sounds fun."

"Count me in, so you guys don't get lost," volunteered Lisandra. "I'll show you to this one store that has the best beads."

***

Just two days before the concert was scheduled to go on, everyone in Compositora woke up to the shocking and very unfortunate news that Logan had been captured.

It was an especially unfortunate turn of events since Arrigan was back in Trelana, which meant the group in Compositora was now without a leader. After some discussion over breakfast, it was decided that they would return to Trelana a day earlier than anticipated–for multiple reasons, but mostly, to prevent any more abductions.

"I don't understand how he was so careless to get caught, though," Lisandra said as everyone rode the train back. "At this point, I'm wondering if it was intentional."

Several of the party turned to her, intrigued. "You think he may have allowed himself to get caught on purpose?" Jaiden asked. "Why would he do that?"

"I don't know. It doesn't seem like it'd be a very *good* idea, but on the other hand, we know a lot more about those cells and tunnels now than we did when everyone else got taken away," Lisandra pointed out. "Nobody can ever really know how my cousin's mind works, least of all me, so I guess it's equally possible that he just had a moment of being a dumbass and got caught organically. Still, I wouldn't be surprised if this was part of some elaborate plan he's cooked up."

"I just wish he would've told us, if it is," added Brecken. "We wouldn't be so worried."

"Well, you know how things like that are– the more people know, the harder it is to pull it off," Spencer-Lynn pointed out. "Still, what is he thinking? With the level of power that our opposition has, it's dangerous for him to do anything on his own. He should be well aware of that at this point."

"I guess we won't really know until it's go time," Jasiela replied. "I think we're getting close to the station. Did anyone ask where to meet the other half of our homies?"

"I did, so I'll lead the way," Lisandra replied. "We'll be meeting at the police station."

The walk to the station felt longer than it had before, but when it had finally been reached, everyone's attention was caught by a small pillar of smoke streaming up into the clouds somewhere behind the building. There was no indication that there was any kind of emergency happening– no one else around seemed to notice, there was no change to the appearance of the building, and there were no smells of anything burning or something otherwise chemical– but the gradual change of the color of the smoke from a light gray to a color more dark and brooding was attention-grabbing, if nothing else.

After wordlessly deciding to check out what was happening, the group was greeted with Madeline, Gavin, and Arrigan in the station's training area, all with varying levels of protective gear on; behind them was some sort of round container, where the smoke was coming from. It looked even more foreboding up close, but it also looked to be mostly contained, so nowhere near as worrying as it could look.

"Oh, hey guys! Welcome back!" Madeline waved.

"Good to see you again, Madeline," Jaiden replied. "And the guys, of course. Please bring us some good news about your end of this whole operation."

"Well, things are appearing to be going quite well," Gavin replied. "As you've no doubt noticed at this point, we've managed to get to a point where the explosion is controlled and odorless. There's still some work to be done regarding how much smoke it gives off, but this is something that we went in knowing it would be difficult to mediate."

"Yeah, the explosion itself went off a half hour ago and yet," Arrigan gestured to where the smoke was still pouring into the sky, at such a small volume now that it would probably be stopping any time now, but was still clearly visible.

"Fortunately, we've still got a day to get this down!" Madeline finished, clearly eager to do so. "And you guys? Amidst the horrible news about Logan, I realized I forgot to ask how that performance thing is going. Are you guys ready to light up the stage in a way that the people of this city have never seen?"

This caused a tense silence between the group. "I do believe that depends on how you would define 'ready,' but I'm at least fairly confident that no one will fall off the stage," Maceida replied. "Actually, one of the reasons we decided to come over early is so we could do a dress rehearsal on the stage this evening, hopefully. I think I speak for all of us when I say that it would make us a lot more confident."

"Yeah. Well, just give us a holler if you need any help!" Madeline said, before waving and turning back toward the scene of the last explosion. "We've gotta make sure this bad boy is as inconspicuous as possible!"

~~~~~

The music began then, a rousing drumroll that lasted a few seconds before the lights switched on and Maceida turned, delivering the first few lines of the song.

As the rest of the instruments came in and everyone on stage began the dance steps, Jasiela turned her focus to the contraption
~~~~~

that measured the sound levels of the concert, waiting for it to reach the optimal point for her to give the signal to Madeline and Arrigan. A few paces behind her seat, Gavin and Chiara watched the performance. Everyone was now in chorus position, which was undoubtedly the best-looking part of the routine because it was the simplest. Everyone moved and stepped in time together, as if they hadn't conceptualized the routine in a matter of days.

"This is good," Gavin whispered to Chiara. "All very well put together."

Chiara nodded. "If nothing else, I knew the music and dancing would turn out well. Maceida and Brecken are both pretty musically inclined, so they knew what they were doing."

"Yeah. It's worthy of all of the attention, surely."

"It's almost time, guys. Get ready." Jasiela glanced back at the two, before waiting for the exact moment she'd been anticipating to give the signal. She knew when it would be, because it was when Brecken would be walking back toward the third row of the group; there was a point where she'd pass Jaiden, and accounting for response time and lighting, it was the perfect time to signal lighting the explosive.

"Are we ready?" Gavin gave Chiara one of his most encouraging smiles.

She smiled back. "As I'll ever be."

At what she perceived to be the most appropriate time, Jasiela pressed the button that would signal a light to burst out of the bellflower on top of the tower. As soon as she pressed it, she leapt out of the chair she had been sitting in, and the three began to run out of the tower. "Come on, let's go!" she said, Gavin and Chiara not far behind.

With the light signal going off, it meant that it was time to light the flame that would trigger the explosive.

"There it is. We've just gotta pray that the timing is right," Madeline said. It was easy to tell that even she was nervous about the whole thing.

"Yeah. Hey, that's burning pretty fast..." Arrigan noted. "You don't think it'll go off too early, do you?"

Madeline's face went pale. "I sure hope not."

Neither had time to try and think of an alternative method— besides, if they distinguished this flame and lit it again, it would go off too late, which was arguably worse— so they had no choice but to believe in the timing.

Initially, it had been the plan to have the explosive detonate about a half second after the pyrotechnics on stage went off, so that any resulting disturbance felt like it was simply part of the show. However, with the fuse burning much quicker than expected, it detonated about a half second *earlier* than the pyrotechnics.

In a panic, Arrigan shut his eyes and cast a shield around himself and Madeline, to protect them both from the smoke. The protective magenta-tinged bubble meant that the sounds and odors of everything in the surrounding area were diluted, so there was no way to know what truly happened until they opened their eyes— and for a few moments, everything felt too real and scary to do that.

When they finally did open their eyes, they were both shocked to see that most of the smoke had already subsided, and they were left with a sizeable hole in the wall beside them.

"How did we do?" Madeline asked, her voice squeaking– so in shock she couldn't bring herself to move from where she currently stood.

"Let's see." Arrigan dispelled the shield before tentatively approaching the hole, making sure the area wasn't hazardous before examining the space. "Hm. Well, I'm pretty sure that Gavin and Maceida will have to crouch a little in order to fit, but it follows all the way through for sure. I think we did it, Madeline."

She gasped. "We did it?"

"We did it!" Arrigan grinned as the two hugged, overjoyed that all of their trial and error had paid off, even if it hadn't gone exactly as planned. "It worked! We're alive! Now all that's left is to wait for everyone else to arrive."

We Must All Do Our Part

N ow that the diversion was successful, and the tunnels were able to be accessed, now came one of the more difficult parts: navigating the underground tunnels of Trelana.

As they all trotted through their entry tunnel, Jasiela said, "I still can't believe that actually worked."

"Of course it worked! Nothing that meticulously planned could ever fail," Maceida replied. "I know we've only just recently met, but it'd be nice if you'd have a little more faith in me. As the saying goes, there's a method to my madness!"

The rush of the group came to a halt as the tunnel where they were ended in a T formation. At this intersection, they could turn either left or right, but from here, neither tunnel looked incredibly different from the other. It would be impossible to guess which one would get them somewhere useful, even if they had gone with the plan of having maps.

"Are we splitting up?" Mishaela asked.

"As if we had any choice," replied Arrigan. "If we comb through these tunnels one at a time, we'll all get old and gray by the time we search them all, and I don't think we have enough time for that."

"We do indeed not have time for that," Gavin confirmed. "As we continue through these tunnels, we'll have to continue branching off from one another. There's more corridors than there are us, so we will all be alone at some point. Like we discussed, right?"

Everyone affirmed.

"Right. So no getting scared. We're in the thick of it now." Jaiden nodded, before turning toward the path heading east. "Keep in touch as best as you can, everyone."

The group split in half then: Jaiden headed toward the east with Madeline, Brecken, Gavin, and Spencer-Lynn. The rest of the party– Arrigan, Maceida, Lisandra, Chiara, Mishaela, and Jasiela — took the west corridor. When the paths diverged again, the groups split in half again, and so they continued on yet again, until another split.

After an offshoot path in which Brecken had fervently convinced Spencer-Lynn that she was fine going off on her own, the two diverged into opposite directions from the main path.

***

It had been so long that the tunnels had been dark and grim, that seeing the waning sun down one of the paths made Spencer-Lynn a little more excited than usual. She picked up her pace, but immediately stopped when she heard what sounded like a man's voice down the hallway. Inching close to where the hallways diverged, she forced the thundering of her heart out of her mind as she tried to listen to what was going on.

"There. Now, can we trust you to stay in one place while we get dinner ready?" the man's voice was saying. "Causing all this trouble; you should be grateful that we're feeding you."

"Grateful? For being placed in a cage like some twelfth wonder of the human world, or some other– please leave me to my solitude before I... say things I *really* do not mean."

From the shadows, Spencer-Lynn covered her mouth to hide her laugh. She'd know Logan's voice anywhere, but not just his voice– his overall way of speaking, as well.

After that, she was able to hear the man's footsteps, walking... toward her? Well, this wasn't good. There was nowhere to hide here, as far as she knew. Her hands frantically traced the wall she stood parallel to, hoping for some passage that she hadn't noticed before, as the steps drew closer and closer. Right when she knew the man was probably almost right beside her, she settled for holding her breath and trying to squeeze herself between where the wall and its pillar met, hoping he wouldn't turn down this path.

Luck was on her side today when he turned to go down the opposite corridor.

With a sigh of relief, Spencer-Lynn decided to catch her breath before heading down the hallway the man had come from as quickly as possible, until she found it: a cell, with Logan inside of it, as expected.

"Logan!" She remembered to keep her voice low, but even so, it was easy to both hear and feel the happiness in her voice.

He ran over to where she was standing, grinning, holding the same bars she was so that his hands would ever-so-slightly touch hers. "Spencer-Lynn! I'm so glad to see you, querida! You... you... are dressed like a... what exactly are you wearing?"

"What?" Spencer-Lynn looked down at herself, only just now being reminded that she was still wearing her clothes from the idol performance. Logan hadn't been around when everyone was fine-tuning the design, either, so he wouldn't have known what it looked like until today even if he hadn't been caught. "Oh! It's our idol isshou. I had to wear this as part of the plan to get yousins out of here, remember?"

"I see." Logan nodded, looking over her attire again. "I know this is hardly the time, but... it's nice."

Spencer-Lynn blinked, clearly surprised, before nodding, turning to try and hide her blush. "W-well, then... speaking of getting you out of here."

"Right. Actually, I've already managed to break out of two of these goddess-forsaken prisons, so I cannot imagine this one will be much different," Logan replied. "But I was just transferred here before you arrived, so I haven't had any chance to survey the area yet. Give me just a moment to do that."

Logan took a moment to look around the cell he was currently trapped in, before lingering on the area where the bed was placed against the wall. Narrowing his eyes– knowing for sure that something stuck out in this area, but not entirely sure what– he suddenly realized the issue, and hurried over, hopping on the bed so that he could flip the switch he'd seen. Soon enough, there was the sound of a latch unhooking.

"Was it really that easy?" Spencer-Lynn asked, incredulously.

Logan nodded, hopping off the bed. "At this point, yes. To be fair to whoever built these things, it probably wasn't as easy back in the heyday of these tunnels. I think the switches I've been finding were put in as a precaution in case someone accidentally locked themselves in here, but the type of degradation that comes with time has probably made them a lot easier to find. Would you be so kind as to help me pull this gate open? Pull to the right. Er, your right."

"The right, okay." Spencer-Lynn nodded, and both pulled the door; after a few seconds, it began to move, and Logan eased out of the cell.

"Perfect. With the both of us, I'm a lot more confident in my ability to not be overtaken again," Logan grinned. "If you'd like to hear some good news, we shouldn't be caught off guard; there's a room not far from here that I'm pretty sure has weaponry. The bad news is that, outside of that, I do not know the layout of this place as well as I'd like, but shall we work through that together?"

"That was the plan all along," Spencer-Lynn agreed, as they set off in the opposite direction that the man from before had gone.

As they progressed down the corridors that were barely visible– which only got darker as time went on– Logan abruptly stopped, an idea occurring to him. "Hold on. I just thought of an easier way to do this."

"Logan." Spencer-Lynn sighed. "Why are you like this?"

"Hey, to be fair, I've never done this before, so it wouldn't be top of mind. Could you stand lookout for me really quick? Shouldn't be more than two minutes at the most."

Spencer-Lynn nodded. "But be swift."

Logan took a deep breath, before clasping his hands together tightly, and trying his best to steady his posture; keeping his state of mind calm, so that he could concentrate on summoning the magic inside of him. After some time, he opened his eyes– and was over-joyed to see the faint light emanating from his outstretched arms. "Oh, it worked!"

This got Spencer-Lynn's attention. "Are you *glowing*?" she asked.

Logan nodded. "Yeah. It's something I only recently learned was possible, but the downside is..."

The light began to fade, quickly.

"I think it may have been mentioned before that everyone's ap-titude for magic is different, and mine is not remarkable. So, I'll only be able to do that for short spurts of time. After all, I need to conserve most of my energy for when we inevitably need to kick ass."

"This just makes me suspect even more that you went and got yourself captured on purpose," Spencer-Lynn said as the two resumed walking.

"Ah." Logan chuckled nervously. "Was it that easy to figure out?"

"Don't you dare chuckle at me!" Spencer-Lynn stopped this time, poking a finger at Logan's chest. "Do you not understand how quickly things could have fallen apart without you around? Did it ever sink in that you were the last of the locals we had, and that we could have just as easily still have been looking for the train station to get here? What in the world is your problem? Do you have any idea how much you worried me?!"

Logan blinked. "I just thought... you all didn't need me because the plan didn't directly involve me, and that I'd be more useful as a man on the inside, fighting. I'm terribly sorry for having hurt you so. It was never my intent."

Only then did it sink in, for Spencer-Lynn, that she had said "how much you worried *me*," rather than "how much you worried *us*," which caused her to feel more than a little embarrassed that she'd let that slip. "Aye, well... I suppose your side of it makes sense too, now that you mention it. But damn it all, man, would it have killed you to have told someone?"

"I think my sister may have had a point, when she used to say that I'm too impulsive," Logan admitted. "I see that now, and possibly more than ever. Come on, let's find the boys and my sister– and then I can work on making it up to you, querida."

"Making it up to me?"

"Ever making you worry, of course." With a handsome smile, Logan began to trot down the hallway again.

***

If the plan hadn't called for everyone to split up due to the number of paths in the tunnels, there would have probably been more thought put into why it was a bad idea to have Chiara go off on her own. As the tunnels grew darker and longer, and more silent, the only sound she could hear being the beating of her own heart, she could only become more and more anxious. It wasn't the darkness, inherently; even before the goddess of darkness in this world decided to dote on her for whatever reason, she had found darkness comforting in a way, and the silence as well. But the combination of these things with being in an unfamiliar place, a hostile place, meant that she had no way of knowing what could be lurking right around the corner, or even in front of her. She had the disadvantage. And who was to say if the disadvantage would be fatal, under these circumstances?

Having used the walls to feel her way through up to this point, Chiara suddenly noticed a faint source of light bloom in the distance. It was too far away to be able to tell what it was, but with the sun going down, she could either head toward the light or continue to fumble around like she had been. One of these was decidedly not ideal, and so she began to cautiously inch toward the light.

One step after the other, she continued to follow the light in hopes that it would reveal something about her surroundings. It didn't seem to be getting brighter even with her getting closer, she noticed after some time. Was it moving? What could be moving down here, without making noise?

Before she could think of possible answers to that, Chiara stopped walking to ponder if it was wise to continue following whatever the source of light was. This was a world of magic, after all, which meant she didn't have complete knowledge of what could be lurking in these halls. She hadn't yet experienced any hostile creatures in her time here apart from the holzomen last time, but that didn't mean they didn't exist. What if the light was attached to something larger, something more intimidating and hungry than–

Chiara was unable to complete that thought when something bumped into her from behind.

"What the–" the other person said, summoning light to the area. This was, clearly, not one of her friends, Chiara realized as her heart sank.

"An intruder?! How did you get in here?!" the person asked, their voice shrill and piercing.

Unable to speak or move due to the paralyzing fear she now felt, Chiara merely stood silently.

"Answer me!" they continued, raising an arm, brandishing a machete. "Or else I'll cut out your tongue so that you *can't* speak!"

Just as they began to swing the machete, the person grunted as if struck; and, indeed, they fell to the ground, limp. The machete clattered to the floor, as well. Behind where they had stood was a much friendlier face: Maceida, smiling as if she hadn't just knocked someone unconscious.

"Kid ought to know to not yell within the catacombs," she said, carefully stepping over their body. "Everything echoes. It's like putting a target on your forehead– are you all right?"

Still trembling just a little, Chiara nodded.

"Perfect. Do you want to help me check and see if they've got anything useful on them before the light wears off?" Maceida asked, already bending down to start the search. "Let's see... no, no. That's just pocket lint. This looks like it could be a key, but it could also be junk; let's keep that, just in case. Oh! Is this a map? I'm not certain how much good it'll do us, but might as well take it–"

"Th-thank you, Maceida," Chiara was finally able to choke out.

"What?" She looked up. "Oh, no, that's not– it's what anyone would have done when they overheard a friend being threatened, right? Now, try not to dwell too much on it, aye? Come help me try to make sense of this map instead."

Both girls did so then, taking note that some of the cells were colored in, and that there was a line drawn through some of the corridors. "I think the colored-in cells are the ones that are currently occupied, but what does the line mean?" Maceida said, almost to herself– but of course, loud enough that Chiara could hear. "And where are we?"

"I think that–" Chiara began to squint as the light dimmed. "Seeing that the line passes where a couple of the cells are, do you think this could have been this specific guard's route? That would place us somewhere within this path."

"I think you might be right!" Maceida nodded. "But how do we find out where we are on it? Especially in the dark?"

Chiara thought. "Which direction did you come from? I came from that way," she pointed back the way she had come, which was distinguishable because it was the only path at the intersection that was dirt-paven. "If you were behind this guard when you hit them, you had to have come from back there. So there's two paths left... and I saw a light source that way, straight ahead of me, but I didn't know if it was smart to follow it."

Maceida looked at the map again. "I think we should follow it."

"Really? But what if it's some scary creature?"

"I don't think it will be. I doubt these guys have those kinds of resources, but even so, a light means someone or something's walking around that doesn't have to worry about being seen, right? If we at least follow it, it gives us a better chance of leading us to something interesting."

That did make a lot of sense. "Okay. I think you're right. Should I follow you?"

"You should stay out in front. I'll lose track of you if you're behind, and I don't think we should leave you alone again," Maceida replied, making sure to pick up the machete the guard had been carrying. After all, better to face this place armed.

The two girls walked then, continuing the way that Chiara had been going. As the light from the unconscious guard extinguished, it took a few moments– but sure enough, the wandering light from before became visible again. However, after a few seconds of following it, a larger, brighter light shone from around a corner. Wordlessly, both girls began to hurry toward it.

Finding that it had led them to a cell, Chiara didn't stop running, and barreled into the guard in front of the cell at full force, knocking them down– and unconscious, when their head hit the stone floor.

From the cell, she heard Phoenix laugh. "Chiara! That was very unlike you."

"I... got a little excited when I saw you," she admitted shyly. "This guard wasn't much bigger than me, so I thought I could fight them."

"And that one wasn't carrying a weapon, which was certainly a choice," added Maceida, just now catching up. "Hi, Phoenix. Need an escape route?"

Phoenix could only laugh again. "I would greatly appreciate that, thank you; but good luck figuring out what that escape route is. I've been trying to think of one for days now, but haven't been able to come up with anything. I can't seem to find any secret switches or tunnels in here."

Maceida walked up to the bars, giving them a knock before pausing to think. After a few tense seconds, she walked over to the far side of the cell and pulled at the bars. "Oh."

Chiara and Phoenix watched, bewildered, as Maceida slipped out of her shoes before beginning to pull the bars the opposite way. "Had to... not be wearing... heels for this. The damn... thing... isn't even locked, it's just heavy," she explained amidst her grunts of effort to move the bars.

"Well, should we help?" Phoenix asked, clearly concerned. "You're going to throw your back out if you–"

With one more very loud grunt of effort, the bars slid back halfway, and Phoenix immediately stood and ran out of the cell.

"Back's already shot due to the giant tits, but thanks for your concern," Maceida replied, putting her shoes back on. "Oh, yeah- your brother managed to get his arse locked up too, at some point, so we should eventually also be looking for him. But before we do that, let's just get out of this area, aye? What do you say?"

"I couldn't agree more," Phoenix agreed. "Chiara?"

"Let's go find the rest of our friends!" she replied, as the three set off.

***

"Did you hear something, just now?" Hunter asked, standing.

"Yeah. Sounded like a person yellin' or something?" Thunder confirmed. "And something moved."

"Right." Hunter nodded. "It didn't sound very far from here. If I didn't know any better, I'd say that was the sound of someone who managed to open their cell all on their own."

Thunder pondered this. "Now, what kinda madman would do something like that?"

Both men turned then, abruptly, to the sound of a scuffle down the hall from wherever they were. It seemed to go on for a few minutes at the very least, but at the end of it- marked by a particularly notable scream- both then heard the sound of rapidly approaching footsteps. Almost as if someone was running–

"Thunder, Hunter!" They were then faced with Arrigan right outside of their cell.

"Arrigan?!" both asked.

"I can't stay, I'm not a good fighter. But I got the–" and that was as much as he was able to get out before he took off running again.

Confused, both exchanged a look before seeing a guard run in the same direction that Arrigan had gone. The footsteps continued for a little while longer before only one set remained, and Arrigan returned, badly winded.

"I'm sorry. I had to shake that guy before I could come back and release you two–" he gasped for air before pulling out a key and unlocking the bars. "If I was a better fighter, it wouldn't have been this hard, or taken this long."

"There is no need for you to chastise yourself so," Hunter said, placing a supportive hand on Arrigan's shoulder as he exited the cell. "Merely the act of arriving here, and procuring this key, and releasing us– it is more than either of us were able to manage in all the days we've been here. You must give yourself some credit for your bravery."

He was right, of course, but he made it sound so simple. Even in the thick of an enemy fortress, Arrigan found it difficult to shoo away his self-confidence issues.

"Now that solves one problem," Thunder said as he looked around the boxes on the far side of the room. "I know there's gotta be some weapons 'round here. If we're gonna face off against Flavian, we're gonna need to be armed."

"Face off? So then, you already know what he's been doing to the veil?" Arrigan asked.

"Would be kinda hard to not realize, with how unstable everything's been here the past few days," Thunder replied. "Damn it.

Nothing in any of these. Guess we got no choice but to make tracks, boys. Hunter, I know you've been cookin' something up in your head these past few days. Let's hear it."

Hunter smiled bashfully. "If you are insinuating that I may have memorized the path to and from the kitchen, where there are likely to be sharp knives, if nothing else... I suppose I may have no choice but to agree with that."

Thunder grinned. "Boy's always sharp! Lead the way."

As the three began to leave, they were quartered off by the surprise arrival of Jaiden and Lisandra. "Whoa! Hold on, these are friendlies!" the former exclaimed, pulling Lisandra's arm gently so she could stop.

"That we are," Thunder nodded, tipping his hat. "I don't think I've ever been so happy to see y'all girls."

Before Jaiden could react, Hunter gently placed a hand on Thunder's arm and said, "Thunder, Jaiden exists outside of the gender binary and, therefore, should not be referred to as a girl."

When Thunder turned to Jaiden with an eyebrow raised, she explained, "It kept coming up at bad times, when there was always something way more important going on."

"Well, I still wish ya would've said something. I'd never want you to feel like I wasn't accepting you as you are, or anything."

"You do know we would've immediately adjusted if you'd brought this up before, right?" Lisandra asked, also a bit taken by surprise. "I mean, if no one else here would, the Resistance would. They've had non-binary members before... plus whatever the hell Logan's got going on."

Jaiden laughed at that. "Thanks, guys."

"But even so, you're both dressed very girly, so I hope that doesn't get in the way of y'all being ready for whatever this fight's gonna bring," Thunder continued.

"I'm always ready," Jaiden affirmed. "Lisandra?"

"Are you kidding me? I've been waiting to get in on some action for practically the past sixteen years," she replied.

"There you are!"

The guard that had been chasing Arrigan had apparently had the bright idea to turn back and head toward the cell again, where he noticed that there were many more people than before standing in the area. Accepting that he was outnumbered, he took a step back, then another, before turning and beginning to run away.

"Get back here! I got this covered, guys!" Lisandra said, running after the man as she began to untie the ribbon from around her waist.

"Huh. So that's why she had that there." Jaiden placed a hand under her chin. "So, where to, guys?"

The remaining four made their way to the kitchen, led by Hunter. This was a trek that was agonizingly slow because of the darkness of the area, but eventually, they did make it to the large room, unmistakably a kitchen, judging by the faint smells of dinner and presence of light. Just when Hunter crossed the threshold to the room, however, he was met with a metallic clang as he was hit in the face with a skillet.

"Oh! Oh, Hunter, I'm terribly sorry!" Gavin apologized, the skillet still in his hands. "It was just— I heard footsteps approaching, I could tell it was a group coming. I didn't want to be overwhelmed by them, so I thought I should be stealthy to gain the upper hand."

Hunter nodded, checking his face to be sure he wasn't bleeding. When he confirmed that he wasn't, he looked over at Gavin. "It's a good strategy. Perhaps attempt to look before you swing, though?"

"Of course. Again, I couldn't possibly be more sorry."

"Think nothing of it. Now, will you assist in aiding us in our quest to arm ourselves?"

Everyone began to look around the room then, for items that could also double as weapons. There were plenty of knives, but less creative opportunities. After a while, Jaiden decided that the shovel in the corner was good enough on its own. This task was more difficult for the two gunmen, both trying to decide if it was worth it to use a less familiar weapon, or wait until they were able to track down some guns.

"Well, now, it seems that I've walked in on a touching family reunion."

All five heads whipped to where their white-haired antagonist was now standing, a few feet from where they were currently.

"It's you!" Arrigan said, pointing.

Taking a few steps closer, Flavian removed his hood, the loose strands of his white hair fluffing in an almost picturesque way. "You all are bold, if nothing else. I'll give you that. On some level, I even admire it– but that is where my admiration ends. I don't understand: what is it, exactly, that you fight for?"

"You herded us into cages like cattle; surely, you didn't think that would come without retaliation?" Hunter asked. "You may have been capable of catching me off guard once, but I refuse to let that happen again!"

"Yeah, and when you mess with one of us, you mess with us all," added Lisandra, having caught up with the group at this point. "You wanna square up? We can square up!"

Flavian stared at her. "Even knowing the power I possess, you would challenge me to a fight? I suppose I have no choice then, if you want to die that badly."

Raising both of his arms, he summoned several streams of lightning, so light that they would occasionally block out the ability to see, and which caused the floors to ripple and become unlevel, certain parts sinking much lower and causing the party to scramble for their footing. With more than half the party without weapons, they were at a clear disadvantage, but there was no getting away; they had to fight on.

"What do we do, what do we do?" Arrigan asked nervously as he steadied himself. "We didn't plan for this!"

"Well, you ain't always gonna have a plan!" Thunder replied as he picked up a heavy plate off the ground, tossing it enough that it reached Flavian's general area, but he was able to easily duck under it.

"You'll have to do better than that if you want to win this battle, old man!" he gloated.

"Will you get your head outta your ass for two seconds, boy– I don't wanna have to fight you at all!" Thunder pointed out.

"You've left me with no choice!" Flavian yelled, tossing an onslaught of icicles at Thunder and Arrigan. "Do you think I wanted any of this to happen? For years, the Resistance was the only family I had; do you think I wanted things to be this way?!"

He threw his hands onto the ground, causing it to tremor once more.

"Then why do any of this, you absolute walnut?!" Lisandra asked, struggling to stay on her feet.

"Why?"

Before anyone could react, Flavian had thrown a lightning bolt at Lisandra- it hit her, but thankfully, the fact that her light magic was as strong as it was mitigated some of the damage. She was nevertheless left trembling. "Hurts, doesn't it? More than anything you've ever experienced in your short life, right?! Imagine a pain more intense and wholly encompassing than this, and then maybe you'll understand what I've endured at the hands of the man you all follow so blindly! You don't get to–"

Flavian was cut off as Hunter punched him directly in the face. "What is your problem? That is a *child*! You would harm her directly? What kind of man could you call yourself after doing such a thing?"

"I don't care what you call me, or what you think of me," Flavian replied, wiping his mouth. "All I care about is that you all suffer."

As the fight progressed, water began to pool around everyone's feet, not unlike that fateful battle in the square, the battle that seemed so far away now, but that had changed everything. As the water began to rise, the unlevel ground only made it more difficult to maintain balance and attack for everyone, but not impossible. And so, they fought on, knowing they had no choice but to do so.

The sounds of the clash– whether it was the sloshing of the water underfoot, or the battle itself with its crashing and clanging and wielding of magic, no one could tell– gradually brought attention to the area in which the battle was occurring. This initially meant reinforcements for Flavian, but after a while, the arrival of Jasiela and Brecken was a sight for sore eyes.

"This is where the water is coming from!" Brecken said, in a way that indicated she was surprised, before a wooden pillar fell between she and Jasiela, causing them both to yelp as they hurried out of its path. Knowing that the situation must have been dire if there was a battle like this occurring, the two hurried to explore the cabinets at the edge of the room in hopes of finding anything useful to aid their friends.

As more people joined the battle, and it continued on, similarly to the historic one in the square, it became more difficult for the smaller members of the party to maintain their footing. This, combined with a large number of the Resistance's side not having magic or weapons, meant that they had to be resourceful with how they defended themselves. This was a kitchen, so in addition to the coveted knives, there was plenty to use as a weapon; the skillet that Gavin had found, for one, or some of the rope that was usually used to dry herbs. Even certain ingredients, used intuitively, proved useful; such as the citrus fruits to stun someone, or hot water to mimic a steam spell.

"Why are you all so damn persistent?!" Flavian complained. "Don't you all understand that things will never get better as long as we keep leaving things in the hands of one organization? All humans are flawed! Why are you content with being complicit?"

"You don't understand!" Phoenix replied. "What you've set into motion is more than just yourself and us, you know! You're wielding magic that isn't yours, and it's affecting the entire world in the process!"

"Haven't you seen those weird fissure-y things and felt the way the world grows more unstable?" added Lisandra. "That's you! That's always been you!"

Flavian blinked at this. "What? ...No. No, it's not! You're lying!"

"You'd have noticed it if you took one second to notice the world around you changing," Thunder pointed out. "But you haven't, have you? You've been so consumed with your grief that nothing else mattered to you."

The water continued to flow.

"And no one is blaming you for that! Grief is messy, and takes a lot of time and effort to get through," Logan picked up. "But we are in a very bad way, as of now, and we cannot change that you are the origin of that bad way. And as long as you continue to use that magic that you were never meant to have, it will keep having an effect on our world– until, eventually, it is torn apart."

"You're lying!" Flavian lashed out, attempting to hit Logan with a punch, but faltering just enough that the younger man was able to parry the blow, but not effortlessly; the action clearly left him winded. "You're just trying to get me to be complicit again, but I don't have to listen to you! Why should I?"

He charged up a large fire spell, but the time it took to conjure such a thing meant that Arrigan had time to create a wall around it, preventing it from harming anyone. "Because this is your home as well as any of ours. Your actions don't exist within a vacuum, Flavian."

"If you keep tearing holes into the veil, it'll tear apart the world too, and nobody would survive that," added Mishaela. "Not even us, from another world. Not even you."

Flavian held the stare that Thunder was currently giving him. "Is that what you want?" he asked, making sure to put every ounce of emotion he had into the question. "Do you want to die so badly that you'd take every single person in this world down with you?"

The two men continued to stare at each other.

Suddenly, the water level in the area began to lower. Everyone looked around, startled.

"I asked for the strength to get through the days, but when I was so graciously offered just that, I became greedy. The warmth upon receiving a goddess' magic is like no other. It is sustenance after a period of starvation. It is a warm hug from someone you love, or being able to eat your favorite candy nonstop. I had never felt such a thing, and so, I became greedy. I just kept taking and taking, even when the goddess asked me to stop. I couldn't. I needed more.

"The veil is intrinsically linked to Terre Fermecat itself. It is an ancient thing, made of magic that no mortal could ever replicate. Because of that, no mortal can repair it, either. If it's in that bad of a way, the only way to stop it from destroying our world is... if it no longer existed."

Flavian's gaze was trained onto the floor. "And so…"

The silence was tense.

"And so this really *is* the way it has to be, huh?"

He smiled then, but there was no joy to be found in his expression.

"I see, now. In the process of trying to figure out how to live without the man I loved more than myself, I've become someone else entirely. A monster… one so selfish that, in bringing the world down with himself, would deny anyone else the chance to live their life with the one they love most… the thing I never got to do with Etzel."

He placed both hands on his chest.

"Thunder… I'll be sure to tell him you're sorry."

And with that, he closed his eyes tightly, and screaming in anguish from the pain required to do so, summoned a large magic spell combining all of the elements– one contained enough that it shouldn't make the tunnels collapse inside themselves, but potent enough that, it was certain– he wouldn't survive it.

***

It happened so fast that no one could stop him, but as Flavian fell to the ground, a stream of light beamed from his lifeless body, shooting out through the ceiling, and straight toward the heavens. Many other colors soon joined it, causing a light tremor in the area.

"Whoa, what's happening?" Brecken asked.

"The magic is returning to the goddesses," Logan explained. "With this, the balance between the elements will be restored. Now comes the part that I really didn't want to do, but... everyone, center your magic around the remnants of the last spell Flavian cast, even those of you with no magic; there may still be some left from when you borrowed power. This should be enough to destroy what remains of the veil."

"Are we sure we should be going through with this?" Arrigan asked.

Logan sighed. "Unfortunately, yes."

As everyone began to offer their power to the spell, the lights continued to flow up to the sky.

"Shall we get you strapping youngsters back to the surface, then?" Hunter asked, noticing that Thunder continued to stare at his former report. He knew that he'd likely want to wait until he could be moved, for a proper burial. "This ordeal has been thrilling, to be sure, but I do quite miss the feeling of sunlight on my skin and fresh air. Let us make haste to the exit; all of this rumbling worries me."

"Hear, hear," agreed Phoenix. "Thunder, you coming?"

He looked up then. "Right behind ya, kids. I just gotta make sure I do right by this kid one final time."

Emotions Bloom

The ride back home to Compositora was anything but calm, after all that had transpired.

Emerging from the tunnels, the sun was just rising. Not too far away from the hole that had been blown into the wall to get into the area, the party soon noticed that Herman and Kasia had set up a campsite a few feet away from the entrance. When asked, they insisted it was so that no curious citizen would wander into the maze, but it was also quite obvious that they wanted to be sure Arrigan made it out of the ordeal okay.

It was easy to see that Arrigan found it difficult to leave his parents behind after all that had transpired, but– according to all three members of the Navarrete family, at least– he had a much easier time leaving than the first time he'd left Trelana. He insisted that continuing to go to school, and living with the Resistance was doing wonders for not only his studies, but his bravery, and prowess with his magic and fighting; his parents could only agree, and after some very tight and emotional hugs, sent him on his way.

Herman also made sure to give Thunder the biggest bear hug possible, and promised to treat him to dinner and a beer "the next time he was in town."

And now, the party was on a train, traveling at high speed, back to Compositora.

"Goddesses, my entire body is just sore," Phoenix complained, rubbing her back. "Those beds in those cells were *not* a way to live. I can't wait to be back in an actual bed."

"I only wish we could've found you guys sooner," Jaiden replied. "Believe me, we really tried."

"Still, you found us, and I can't complain about that," she replied. "I'm told that you all came up with the idea of... putting on a concert to get into the caves? I was curious about the matching outfits. That's certainly a Logan type of plan."

"It would be, but I cannot take credit for that stroke of brilliance this time," Logan said in response. "Please direct any and all accolades to our newbie here," he held an arm out toward Maceida.

"Well, I mean, I can't deny: it *was* kind of batshit," she added. "At times, I wasn't certain it was going to work. But I'm so glad it did! And everyone who was part of the show made such lovely idols. I would never object to taking the stage with any of you again, if the circumstances allowed."

"I simply wish I had been there to see the final product," Logan said.

"Hey, whose fault was it that you didn't?" Lisandra pointed out.

Everyone laughed as the train continued to chug down the tracks.

***

The next day, the Resistance held a memorial for Flavian.

He was put to rest beside his fiancé; really, there was no better place to put him. Since he hadn't been a particularly noteworthy member of the Resistance, the gathering was small, but this was preferable, in a way. Even within the organization, he had never been the type to attract a lot of attention. The small crowd would have likely been to his liking.

After everyone finished leaving flowers and other small gifts at his grave, Thunder stood at the tombstone. "Usually, this is the part where I say a few words on the behalf of the departed. And I still will do that, but today I've entrusted the majority of the memorial to a young man who's a lot better with words than I am. It's... it's become clear to me, now more than ever, that it's about time to trust more of y'all with some of the responsibilities that I've been shouldering for all these years. Many recent happenings have been pointing me to this conclusion, but I think the biggest push was seeing for myself how Flavian had been driven to madness– arguably, as the result of my own actions. He felt that he had lost everything when he lost the man he loved. I don't want anyone else to feel that way, and I can't help but feel that delegating some of my responsibilities will– if nothing else– instill a sense of purpose in those who receive those duties, so that you won't, as well as it meaning that you all will do just fine in the wake of my absence— my death, when that comes to pass. Hunter?"

The redhead nodded, taking Thunder's place at the head of the congregation. "Yes, of course. Thank you for entrusting me with such an important duty on this day, Thunder. My initial reaction, when you first approached me with the idea of having me speak here, was that I wasn't capable of doing such a thing. Me, someone who has up until fairly recently done little but buried himself within the confines of our libraries, shying away from human interaction, avoiding any chance at being seen. The more I continued down this train of thought, the more I realized why I was the one asked to speak: I am, as far as I'm aware, one of the few remaining members of the Resistance that could relate to Flavian. We'd speak, sometimes, more so when I first joined the organization. Both of us were timid young men who would welcome an untimely death if it meant we would not be perceived. We drifted apart naturally as time passed, but never failed to catch up when either of us had the time to, and he was always pleasant. To his dying day, there was still a part of me that considered him a friend.

"I will say, though, that there was a point where his self-confidence made a leap forward, and– if I may be so bold– I am almost positive that point was when he met his partner, Etzel. I... cannot speak too much about their relationship, as I wasn't privy to most of it, but I was aware enough of the happiness it brought them both that I... I could feel a fraction of the pain that Flavian felt that day in the square, when he'd lost the love of his life. And I knew, at that very moment, that the man I considered a friend would change. I simply did not understand how much he would. A part of me blames myself for this, for not taking a more active role in comforting him over the loss, and assuming that it was best to give him space instead of asking. That is my burden to bear. But I must ask myself; we all must ask ourselves if any other outcome than this would have ever come to pass. There are certain aspects to life that we will never understand, no matter how much we ruminate upon them. I do believe that one of these aspects of life is that some of us are simply not meant to outlive certain people in our lives. Death is always served with a side of sadness for the living, but the size of that serving is not always equal; Flavian knew this, I'm certain, and in his final moments, decided that to rectify his wrongs– and in the process, be reunited with his love– would be worth much more than the amount of grief his passing would deal onto us all. Despite this, even if I am the only one who feels so– I will never forget the timid white-haired man who kept me company, those days in the library."

There was scattered applause as Thunder took his place at the podium once more.

"Thank you, Hunter. I'll close with this: everyone, when it comes to the people who matter to you– whether that be friends, acquaintances, family, anyone who you would struggle to live without– let 'em know that. Life's too short to have people goin' around, thinking there's no one left in this world that cares about them. Tell somebody you love them."

∗∗∗

The destruction of the magical veil that hid the magic world from Earth meant that it was possible, for the first time, to vaguely see the planets from here; not a clear sighting due to distance, but more than was ever possible before. It was a beautiful sight, to see the new twinkling in a portion of the sky.

"I wonder what part of your world that is," Logan said to Spencer-Lynn as they both sat near the bank of the river, where he'd run in the morning sometimes. He had mentioned wanting her to see the newly paved running path, with its flowers bordering it in dusty hues of purple, pink, and blue.

"Hm?" Spencer-Lynn looked up at the sky. Twilight meant that the stars and lights were just beginning to become visible. "Oh, there's no way I could possibly tell from here, but if we can see the lights from so far away, it's got to be a big city. Bigger than where I'm from; somewhere like Tokyo or London, or New York or somewhere."

Logan nodded. "Right. Bigger cities usually mean more lights, after all. If only we had more time, I'd show you what nighttime is like back in my hometown."

"Oh, that's too bad that we don't, then. I should have liked that; the City of Garnet was such a quaint little place," Spencer-Lynn replied. "I'd love to see it at night someday. At this point, though, I'm almost wary of saying, 'you could show me next time.' I feel as though the universe might take that as a challenge, and the poor people of Compositora have been through *enough* at this point."

She punctuated her sentence with a laugh, and Logan almost immediately joined in, knowing in his heart that she was right. It had been less than two years, and so much had transpired in this corner of the world. What he wished for, more than anything, was that things would finally settle down so he could catch his breath for once, enjoy going to school. His kingdom for such a thing, truly.

"I think we're all a little weary of revolution at this point," he agreed, smiling. "It's been a means to a wonderful end, to be sure, but I don't think anyone in this city would object to things quieting down for at least a year. But you know... it would not be quite so bad to have something else transpire in this part of the world again, if it meant the two of us would work together to solve it."

This made Spencer-Lynn turn to him, surprised. "Really?"

"Truly." Logan nodded.

"Well, that's..." Spencer-Lynn stood, clearly a little embarrassed. "I suppose that's not entirely unreasonable. I mean, until this place is fully rebuilt, there's probably not a lot to do– so us showing up brings about some level of excitement, right? And we've established already that we work well as partners, so I mean. I get it," she shrugged.

Logan grunted in effort as he pushed himself off the ground to stand, so they could both start on their way back home. "While that is all very true, I am afraid I'm probably not being very clear in what exactly I mean. Not on purpose, it's just... I don't– I've never. Wow. Two languages I could use, and they're both failing me, when it comes to picking out the best words to say. That's embarrassing. I appreciate you bearing with me, Spencer-Lynn."

"It's not so much me bearing with you as it is you having piqued my curiosity," she admitted. "I think that I've come to believe one of your defining traits is being extremely good with words, so for you to currently have none is very intriguing. Seria mais facil em Português?"

"Não seria." Logan said this quickly. "It's not a lack of having the words so much as it is– listen, Spencer-Lynn. Somehow, I have not been very forthcoming about this, but–"

Logan reached for her arm, holding it securely, right below her birthmark.

"Although I do enjoy the times where we're fighting together, or working together on other things, you are... someone I like a lot. At this point, you are quite precious to me, and I find myself becoming sad that it is already time for us to part from one another again. If it were my choice, there would be a way for us to remain in each other's company during times of peace, so that we could continue to spend time together in an environment that isn't so dire, for once. It's something I find myself wishing for more often these days; that we could have the opportunity to simply exist beside one another, and I could have the chance to show you how much I care for and admire you."

Clearly, this was a lot for Spencer-Lynn to take in; she opened her mouth slightly before closing it a few times, struggling to find the words. Finally she settled on, "Well, unless I'm mistaken, I'm not gone just yet, and I think we're doing a pretty good job of existing beside one another at the moment. And it's... something I quite like, Logan; existing with you."

Even with the setting sun, it was easy to see the pink in Logan's cheeks. "I, uh, I'm really glad to hear that."

"Since we won't be setting off just yet, am I incorrect to assume we'll be existing beside one another for the rest of the evening?" Spencer-Lynn asked.

Logan smiled, "If that's what you want, it would be my pleasure."

As the two set off to return to the residential district, they did so holding hands, their fingers intertwined.

***

The following morning was unanimously decided to be the last day in Compositora for everyone visiting from Earth, as well as Lisandra, who was to return to the City of Garnet– where she technically never got permission to leave, but seeing how dire things had gotten, her parents were thankfully giving her grace over this... this time.

"I hadn't thought of this until now, but..." Chiara turned to Mishaela as both of them sat outside the house. "Things will be different this time, won't they, when we return home?"

"What do you mean?" Mishaela asked.

"The two worlds can see each other now, right? Even if it's not immediate, someone will eventually notice this world floating around in space. It almost makes me fearful of what might happen here in the future; that, with all the evil and corruption that exists in our world, it may find a way to make it here."

Mishaela thought about this for a moment. "Maybe. That thought sort of terrifies me too, but on the other hand, this world is equipped with a group of goddesses that look after it. I'm sure they could just blow any spacecraft out of the sky that has malicious intent."

Chiara placed her hands together right in front of her lips, as she nodded. "That is a good point."

"Yeah. So– easier said than done, I know– try not to worry about it too much," Mishaela said then. "Our friends are more than capable of taking care of themselves."

As they continued to talk with one another, Gavin and Jaiden approached, returning from the market, where they'd gone to get breakfast. It appeared to have been a fulfilling one, as they were busy with their own conversation about what they'd eaten and how delicious and filling it had been; both conversations stopped, however, when the pairs were within earshot of one another.

"Hey, Pagliardi sisters," Jaiden waved. "Ready for our triumphant return to sleepy suburbia?"

"You know, it never does get easier to say goodbye," added Gavin. "That being said, I think this is probably the longest we've ever been gone, so no one could be blamed for missing their own beds and families at this point."

Everyone present could agree with that; they all nodded and uttered various sentences of agreement.

"Hey, speaking of which. I need to go and tie up some loose ends, and these are the type of loose ends that I feel like would only benefit from you helping me with them, Chiara," Jaiden said, extending a hand toward her.

"Really? Me, specifically?" Chiara asked, surprised.

"Yeah. You know, sometimes you have things that just... need the input of a tiny Italian girl," Jaiden replied. "Come on, it shouldn't take long."

Chiara was still confused, but could sense that Jaiden had other reasons for not being more specific with why she was asking her help, so she stood, following her into the house; leaving Mishaela and Gavin outside. It was quiet for a moment before Gavin decided to take Chiara's former seat on the bench.

"If you don't mind, now that this seat is no longer taken," he said as he sat. "The two of us alone like this gives me a nostalgic feeling. It's quite strange, isn't it? Those days where you were teaching me to play chess feel so long ago; but at the same time, it's as if it were just yesterday. Wouldn't you agree?"

Actually, Mishaela would agree there. So much had happened since the very first time these two had been brought to Compositora, but despite that, she was still only about a year and a half older than the first time. "It does feel that way, doesn't it?" she asked. "Although, I think the perception of time gets a little messy when you consider that it hasn't flowed naturally here, 'naturally' of course meaning 'in the way that we're used to.' When you spend weeks in one world just to find out that only a few hours have passed back home, it does start getting really hard to perceive time at all."

Gavin nodded. "So very true. It can really mess a person's head."

"You know," Mishaela turned to Gavin then. Her palms were beginning to sweat at this point, but she didn't know when or if she'd ever see him in person again, so she had to get this off her chest now. If not now, then when? "Gavin. There is something I've been trying to push out of my mind for various reasons having to do with my life back home and how all of that has been configured– I won't go into all the details right now, but I had a very strange moment the last time you were here. And this wasn't– it was the very first time I had ever thought such things about you, and it was probably just because it was at a time when you let yourself be vulnerable and open about feeling fear– but ever since then, I do have occasional thoughts of you being... kind of cute, you know?"

Gavin was quiet for a moment, before looking up as if something had finally clicked for him. "Oh, you're bisexual!"

"I am." Mishaela nodded.

"I thought that, because of– when I visited last year, you and Lulu. That's the second time I've assumed the wrong sexuality for someone in a very short time," Gavin chuckled nervously. "I think I need to just let you all start telling me first."

"Oh, no, that's–" Mishaela replied. "It's easy to make that mistake on our end because she is a lesbian, but I'm not. Who– who was the other one, out of curiosity? Can you say?"

"Yeah, I don't think she'd mind; Spencer-Lynn, she mentioned it one day recently," Gavin replied. "But before we get too off-topic, I must address what you said. I'm very flattered, Mishaela, because you're a very lovely girl– but I think you've made your own mistake in judgment. Even though you are a very lovely girl yourself, I don't quite feel those feelings for you– or any woman."

Mishaela was lost for words. "Oh."

"It's something I've only recently realized about myself. I'm still going through the motions of trying to figure out what it means, in regards to a particular orientation. But, in some roundabout way, being here and experiencing the anguish of a man who became positively deranged because he lost his partner..." Gavin paused here, unsure of how to say the rest of this sentence. "I'm reluctant to admit that I could see a part of myself within that. That... I'm probably gay. Was– was it this hard for you to accept, when you realized you weren't straight?"

Despite everything, Mishaela laughed at this. "Hard to accept? My guy, I'm from a Catholic Italian family. I cried for a week when I realized I liked girls."

Both laughed then, but the laughter lacked a certain amount of joy.

"I wish I could give advice, but all I can really say is that you don't have to tell anyone that you don't want to," Mishaela said then. "In this vein, I'm really happy that you felt comfortable enough to share this with me. It means a lot to me, to know that you trust me so."

"Yeah, well." Gavin was clearly embarrassed by this. "Between you and Chiara, you've both shown me so much kindness, it feels natural to be more open around you both at this point. I love being around all of this group, but there's something about you two that feels like home."

"I can see that," she agreed. "Well, we should probably head inside and group up with everyone so we know the plans around going home."

"Going home is very important," agreed Gavin. "You're right. Let's go. I need to be certain that I've said my most sincere goodbyes to everyone before we have to set off."

***

"You know, now I understand why you think so highly of these friends of yours, from the other side," Arrigan said to Logan as they both ate breakfast in the kitchen. "While a lot of the investigation and combat was us, they've all been very resourceful during their time here; and have all been wonderful people besides."

Logan nodded, a smile on his face. "I knew you'd like having more people here closer to our age. I'm glad this could be a positive experience for you."

"Even with all of the parts where I was scared for my life, I have to admit: it's been fun," Arrigan admitted. "Actually, this whole adventure has made me realize a few things about myself, which has convinced me that I'll need your help with something in the future, Logan."

"Hm?" he asked, raising a brow as he sipped his water.

"I want to be stronger." Arrigan was staring at his mostly empty plate when he said this, but the resolve in his tone could not be missed. "It's become so much more obvious to me during this whole thing, especially when we were in the tunnels, that I'm... kind of weak. I don't say this to degrade myself, but to criticize myself from a place of growth, if that makes any sense. I keep thinking of how I had to run away from that guard and lose them before I could do anything, whereas everyone else I mentioned it to said they just knocked them out. I wasn't able to do that. I tried, but I couldn't. I wasn't strong enough; the guard I was facing was able to brush off my attacks like they were nothing. You're the Resistance's combat trainer, right? If anyone could help me, it'd be you!"

Logan smiled, and with another nod, sat his cup back on the table. "You're right. I would certainly be the best person here to approach, for that kind of thing. And, fortunately for you, I have become invested in your improvement as a person."

Arrigan smiled back. "Oh, how I appreciate the honor."

"We can talk about this more when we've gotten everyone else back home, but it would be a pleasure to begin training you, Arrigan. It is an idea I've been silently hoping you'd warm up to," Logan admitted. "I can only imagine what kind of nimble tricks you could learn, with your small frame."

The two were then interrupted by Phoenix, walking into the kitchen to pour herself a cup of tea. "Last call for anyone who wants to go to the train station with us to see Lisandra off," she said. "We're leaving in less than five minutes."

Meanwhile, in the living room, everyone was doing just that: giving out all the hugs and goodbyes so that Lisandra could return home, to her parents, and resume life as a not-so-usual high school student.

"You did great this time, kid," Thunder encouraged her. "But if we ever need your help again, maybe try to get that across in a way that doesn't stress your parents out for once?"

"I don't know if I can make that promise, but noted." It was difficult to tell if Lisandra was joking. "Always a pleasure to fight alongside you and the crew, old man! That being said– and as much as I wanna believe it was all a piece of cake– this mission has humbled me in a way that a person can only get through real-life experience. I promise to work super hard on fine-tuning my oracle powers, so that I won't struggle to hear and detect things like I have been!"

"That is all we could ever ask for," Hunter replied. "And, if I am not mistaken, the very thing you've been training toward for most of your life. Go forth, Lisandra, and be strong."

"It's the only thing I know how to do!" she replied in a very sunny way, waving. "Come on, Phoenix. If we miss this train, it's gonna be really hard to convince me to get on a later one– just saying."

"This kid," Phoenix sighed, but in a way that made it clear she'd miss having her cousin around. "I might be back this evening, but if I'm not, I decided to stay with my grandparents and I'll be back tomorrow."

"Safe travels, guys!" Madeline waved, causing everyone else to pick up on it and begin waving as well.

"Yeah." Thunder turned to everyone else. "Now as for gettin' the rest of y'all home. I'm not the most knowledgeable about portals and their creation, but lucky for us, we got Logan and Arrigan here. Those two will be able to whip us up a safe transport in no time."

Logan gave the group a salute. "Leave it to us!"

Mysterious New World

T he serenity of the Alfaro home was something of a rare occurrence, so Jasiela couldn't be too upset that she'd become conscious of her own body at such an early time. The sun had only barely begun to rise, so she knew that most of her family couldn't have been awake yet.

As she sat up, rubbing her eyes and swinging her legs to the side of the bed, preparing to step into her brown teddy bear house shoes, she heard a TV switch on in the distance– one which almost immediately erupted in a cacophony of noise.

Somehow, she already knew this was some type of omen.

When she finally got to the living room, everyone else in the house had already congregated around the TV, which was blaring the news. Jasiela's parents and grandfather were speaking in Spanish, but so rapidly that her half-awake brain struggled to grasp any of what they were saying. She turned to her younger siblings, knowing they'd answer her in English, and asked: "What's going on?"

"They're talking about the discovery of some new planet or something," her younger sister Nayeli responded, and Jasiela noticed then that she was the one holding the remote. "I just got here before you, so I don't know everything yet, but what I've gathered so far is: based on what little research we've been able to do, it looks like it's smaller than Earth, but has its own atmosphere and seems perfectly viable for human life."

"I bet there's aliens there!" their younger brother Fernando interjected then.

"There's no such thing as aliens, stupid," Nayeli replied.

Jasiela was quiet. She hadn't thought of it until now, but there would be major repercussions to being able to see the magic world from here, wouldn't there? Who was to say how long it would be before some multi-millionaire would try to fly their private spacecraft there and ruin everything? For the first time, she felt afraid for what may happen– in some ways, even more than she'd feared for her friends' fate the past two times she'd been in their world.

Her phone began vibrating profusely in her phone then; her group chat with her local friends had definitely seen the news, and they were all buzzing about it, speculating on climate, sustainability, the possibility of aliens, and overall, just how cool the whole thing was. Nonexistent one day, here the next; it had to be the most intriguing phenomenon that any of them had been alive for!

With a soft mumble, Jasiela excused herself, and hurried back to her room, as fast as her legs could carry her, hoping that no one in her family noticed her leave, or that she was gone. Without any regard for time zones, she called the group chat that had all of her magic world friends in it, hoping that at least one person would pick up.

Fortunately, or unfortunately, it seemed that everyone else had been of the same mind; they seemed to all pick up one after the other.

"Guys, this is a mess," Madeline was the first on the line to speak. "I know that there was no choice on the other end but to destroy that veil, but now everybody from our world will find out there's a world of magic that exists, and who knows what kind of exploitation the corrupt governments of this world will try to enact on them!"

"Do you think it'll be that bad?" Mishaela asked. "Chiara and I talked about that before we came home. Don't get me wrong, it has the potential to be a disaster, but we also shouldn't assume that the magic world will be helpless. If things become dire, they have magic on their side to assist them through it."

"Plus, when you really think about it..." Jaiden started. "I mean, what *can* they do? It's not like it's possible to just fly up there and take all the magic away. One of the things we just learned is that magic has to be given, or shared; it cannot be taken away. Even in Flavian's case, that started out as a giving situation, didn't it? And I think the goddesses are smart enough to not give power to the people of this world without some level of scrutiny. They're very discerning."

A hush fell over the call.

"You guys make a lot of good points, but I'm still worried," Brecken was the next to speak. "I guess... I guess there's just a part of me that feels responsible for this, you know?"

The call got silent again. This was the elephant in the room that no one wanted to address– or perhaps no one knew how to address. It wasn't like there had been any other options at the time, but even so, their actions were done with the knowledge that they would be permanently altering the lives of everyone that inhabited both worlds. It was something that had taken a back seat because of the urgency of the situation, but now...

"There's nothing we can do now, right?" Madeline asked. "So maybe right now we just... shouldn't worry about it. I mean, if things get seriously bad, I'm okay with assuming the goddesses will pull us in again to right our wrongs, right?"

"Oh, yeah, good point," agreed Jaiden. "And I don't know about the rest of you guys, but I wouldn't need much convincing to do that. I mean, this would finally give me a chance to stick it to the man, like I've always wanted to! Even if it's not under the conditions that I've always dreamed of, a win is a win, right?"

"Well, when you put it that way..." Gavin said, making everyone laugh.

"It's easier said than done, but I think I can manage not freaking out over the whole thing for a little while," Spencer-Lynn was the first to speak after the laughter had calmed down. "In the meantime, I think we should all try our best to be cool about the whole thing. The last thing any of us needs is anyone finding out we knew about this world all along. Well, except Madeline. I think she's the one person who has the advantage of being able to play this completely straight."

Madeline gasped. "Wait! You're right! This is awesome! But even so, I don't think I will. Our friends on the other side are a little too human to keep my interest for long."

***

It's all our fault... isn't it?

In the days that followed, everyone went about their days as normal, but this thought continued to echo in Brecken's mind. She didn't dare open her mouth, but she struggled with the sense of personal responsibility she felt for how uncertain things were now. What would happen to her friends in the magic world? They had magic to defend themselves, sure, but this world had so much brute force on its side. Guns. Tanks. Heavy artillery.

The thought of any of her friends being threatened with weapons made her stomach sink, and even more so with the added element of her having brought it upon them.

"Miss Islington? Is something more important to you than Manifest Destiny?"

Brecken looked up abruptly, having forgotten amidst her thoughts that she was currently sitting in her American History class. Honestly, there were a great many things more important to her than Manifest Destiny even when the safety of her friends *wasn't* in question, but that wasn't something she could say in the middle of class... even if most of her classmates would agree with her. Instead, she cast her gaze downward at her history book, which was not anywhere near the page she needed it to be. How would she recover from this?

At her side, Chiara struggled with deciding whether or not she would jump in to help her friend out of this predicament. She wanted to, but aside from her usual anxiety at causing a scene- of which was expounded upon when considering she'd be directly contradicting an authority figure- she knew that Brecken would probably just tell her that it wasn't worth them both getting in trouble. Before she could move, someone behind the girls yelled out, "Is that seriously a question? There's so much more important stuff!"

"Who would actually care about this stuff besides colonizers?" another voice asked.

The laughter that followed ensured that the class would not get back on topic for the remaining five minutes; and when it was time to adjourn, Brecken silently thanked her small stature for the ability to slink out of the room quickly and undetectably before her teacher could call her aside.

"I'd ask what's on your mind, but I have an idea of what it is." Chiara's voice beside Brecken startled her- it wasn't often that the smaller girl was the one to initiate conversation- as they walked down the corridors, the bright red lockers lining the white brick walls in a very typical high school way. This particular wing of the school was frequented mostly by seniors, which meant it was less rowdy than the more common halls, since they were always the smallest class. As they made their way back to the main building, where the cafeteria and most of the homerooms were located, there was a noticeable uptick in noise and a subsequent downturn of personal space. Such was life in a busy high school like this one.

"I don't think I'm going to be able to concentrate on much of anything at this time, Chiara," Brecken replied, as they approached their lockers. "Not that hearing about the horrors of how our country was founded isn't fascinating, but am I wrong for feeling like we've got bigger fish to fry? I mean, we could potentially be on the verge of the very same thing happening to our friends."

Chiara nodded, resting her head on the locker beside Brecken's. The girls had tried to get lockers beside one another, but their homeroom teacher had insisted on assigning them alphabetically, which meant that Chiara's was further down the hall. "You're not wrong for feeling that way. 'You should never think that your feelings are wrong,' is a rough translation of what my mother says to Mishaela and I when we start sentences like that. On some level, I'm there with you. But... even if the worst came to pass, what could we do while we're still here and expected to carry on like this is as new to us as it is to everyone else?"

Not knowing was the whole problem, but before Brecken could say that, it hit her– just how profound it was to have Chiara, of all people, saying this to her. How was she so calm?

She tried it. "How are you so calm?"

The question seemed to catch Chiara off guard. "I don't know. It is a welcome change, though."

"At least one of us has our thoughts straight today," Brecken said then, shutting her locker and putting its combination lock back on.

"Maybe it's best that we revisit this after school. For now, I'm getting kinda hungry."

***

Returning to Belfast meant that, among other things, Maceida had to get reacquainted with how much it rained in Northern Ireland.

Of course it rained sometimes in Montreal, but she had genuinely forgotten how it felt to have not seen the sun in almost two weeks. No wonder her depression didn't seem to be getting any better. How in the world had she managed to grow up here? As she walked down the street with her umbrella in hand, she tried to remember. Had she been happy as a child? What was it that had brought her happiness? Maybe if she remembered, she could try to recreate it as an adult.

Her phone vibrated in her pocket, so she stepped aside to check it. Her mother, asking where she was.

Maceida sighed, remembering the conversation she'd had with Spencer-Lynn where she'd asked if home was the best place for her to be. Their mother, in varying subtle ways, had made it clear that she was not going to be easy on her until she went back to Canada.

What's her problem with you, anyway? Spencer-Lynn had finally asked, the day after they'd returned home from the magic world. Honestly, Maceida was shocked it had taken her this long, but even so... she wasn't entirely ready to tell that story. Not to her, anyway. The unfortunate coincidence was that Spencer-Lynn was probably the only person in their family that would undoubtedly side with her even after learning the history between Maceida and their mother, but Maceida was unwilling to tell her what the history was because she felt so guilty about how it had come to pass, given that parts of it would require rehashing some particularly traumatic memories.

Her phone vibrated again. This time, Gavin had summoned everyone to the group chat with an article written about the "mysterious planet;" that the spacecraft sent to investigate it burned within seconds of entering its atmosphere, leading the scientists involved to believe that this planet was not inhabitable to humans.

Excellent work, Goddess of Fire.

Almost immediately after, someone initiated a voice call.

"What does this mean? Are we all safe now?" Brecken was the first person to speak.

"I don't completely know that we are," Madeline replied. "Within our solar system, there are multiple planets that we've known for years are uninhabitable, but that hasn't stopped scientists from trying to investigate them in other ways. We can't say for certain how our friends would deal with some weird robot falling out of the sky. And if they didn't destroy it immediately, the idea of it getting footage of people living in the magic world that look like and speak like us..."

"It'd be disastrous." Jasiela said what everyone was thinking.

"Okay, so we should try and warn them in some way, right?" Maceida asked, beginning to walk again. She would be able to parse this a lot better if she was at home, especially if she was within the company of her sister. "How do we do that?"

The line went silent.

"Perfect. Loving the energy in the chat we've got here."

"Do we need to?" Gavin asked then. "They handled it this time, right? Maybe we're all getting ourselves worked up for nothing."

"Yeah. Well, it's kinda hard not to. Space colonialism has become a hot topic in the news lately," Jaiden pointed out. "And we're all pretty protective of our friends on the other side. Let's just do what we agreed on last time: operate under the assumption that we'll get summoned back again if things get bad enough. Sound good?"

"Sounds reasonable enough," Jasiela was the first to agree, but in time, the others voiced their assent as well.

"In the meantime, we can all enjoy watching everyone freak out about this mysterious new world."

Epilogue

- -

S omehow, a year later, life had managed to remain calm.

As he'd taken to doing lately, Logan sat on the bench right outside Thunder's house, and gazed at the sky at the sunset; where he could just barely see the makings of Earth, orbiting in parallel with his own world. It was calming, sometimes, to see the lights twinkle in the distance. When he reminded himself that on the other side of the haze and sparkling lights were cities and communities not unlike his own, the thought never ceased to amaze him. To think that the people there had their own lives, thoughts, duties. They could be cooking dinner right now, or singing, or reading. Maybe even gazing up at the sky like he was.

He'd often wonder if Spencer-Lynn was looking back at him, somehow.

"Logan! Oh, there you are." Hunter walked over to where he was seated. "I was going to inquire if you were willing to head down to the general store, as a favor. I am in the middle of preparing dinner, and it appears that I've run short on milk. However, it appears that you are quite intent on sitting there for a while, so I won't bother you further. My apologies."

"It's fine, Hunter," Logan waved it off. "It's no bother at all. Also, don't worry about your milk. Arrigan said he'd pick some up on his way back, and he should be getting here any moment now."

Hunter sighed in relief. "Oh, how fortunate. And I am very glad that Arrigan has acquired the courage– or the wherewithal, whichever it may be– to navigate Compositora on his own now. The feeling of independence that comes with the ability to do so must feel liberating."

"I'll bet. But I think it's more like Thunder kept saying, he just needed to get used to the city here," Logan replied, before pointing down the street. "I think that's him coming now."

Indeed, before long, both men were faced with a head of brown hair nearing them, carrying two bags of groceries. "Oh. Hi, guys," Arrigan said when he was close enough to be heard. "I'd have waved, but," he gestured to the bags he was holding.

"Certainly. I can relieve you of those bags, Arrigan; I was in the middle of cooking and have the need for the milk, anyway," Hunter volunteered.

"Really? Thank you," he replied, handing both the bags over. "What's on the menu tonight?"

Hunter smirked at the question, taking a moment to think of the best way to respond. "I would like for that to remain a surprise at the moment. That being said: if you like cheese, and creamy consistencies, tonight's dish will be something you will undoubtedly enjoy."

"I do like cheese." Arrigan smiled.

"Then it is my hope that you will not be disappointed," Hunter replied, turning toward the house. "I must return to the kitchen, for the meal's preparation was already in progress before I ventured out here. The last thing any of us would want is our food being so cooked that it is inedible."

Arrigan waved before taking a seat beside Logan. "Whew. That walk feels so much longer when you're carrying bags."

Logan nodded. "Absolutely. It's excellent strength training, though."

"So it is." Arrigan nodded, before both young men turned their gaze to the sky once again. It was darker, now, so it was easier to see the stars and the sparkling lights of Earth in the distance. This was considered a beautiful sight by all who regularly gazed upon it, and there was no reason for either of them to think differently.

Although he hadn't changed physically, as Logan looked over at Arrigan, he could undoubtedly see how much his friend had changed in the past year, in other ways. He was still as mild-mannered as ever, but the training he'd been undergoing with Logan had served him well when it came to how he carried himself. He sat, one leg crossed over the other, his hands folded over his knee. It still felt unusual to see Arrigan's hands so still, knowing how fidgety he had been before, but he now projected the image of a young man who felt at least moderately comfortable in his own skin. Even if that wasn't true, he had at least learned the art of *looking* confident, and that was progress.

There was also the fact that he'd been able to carry such large bags on his own, which wouldn't have been possible back when he'd first arrived in Compositora. Even if his build wasn't changing, he was definitely getting his strength up. His father would be proud of him; not just for the strength portion, but for the dedication he'd put into bettering himself.

"Hey, Logan?" Arrigan asked, but almost immediately followed up with, "No, never mind. Forget I said anything."

"I think we both know I'm not going to do that," Logan chuckled. "Now, come on. We cannot disregard the gift of speech, one which was given to us so lovingly by the goddesses. What's on your mind?"

Arrigan was silent for a good moment, his eyes fixated on the zipper to his hoodie, before glancing at Logan, and then up at the sky. "Those lights, the ones from the other world that we're able to see from here."

"What about them?" Logan asked.

"Do you ever feel as though, somehow, in some way... they're getting closer?"

About the Author

Michelle Rivera is an Afro-Latina writer from Chicago, IL. Growing up as a middle child in a large family, she spent a lot of her time within the company of either books or video games. In time, those media would encourage her to begin writing her own stories at the age of eight, and she hasn't stopped since. Her inspirations include various JRPGs (Japanese role-playing games), fantasy novels, and the experience of growing up in the Midwest US as a queer person of color.

If not writing, she can be found drawing, crocheting, sewing, or playing video games.

Join Us Online!

Are you a fan of the Revosaga series? Would you like to join a space to talk about it and meet other fans? You can do so by joining Revolutionary! The Revosaga Server, on Discord!

To do so, use your smartphone to scan the QR code below. We're excited to see you there!

www.ingramcontent.com/pod-product-compliance
Lightning Source LLC
Chambersburg PA
CBHW021211310726
48971CB00006B/1524